# This Side of Shadows

JK & Carol Allen

*To my mom, Carol, and Chris. Thank you for supporting me through this journey and for being in my life.*

*~JK*


*To my family and friends for all their love and support. To my mom, she is an inspiration. To my dad, for the support I had. To Julia, for the encouragement, editing, and friendship.*

~Carol

# PREFACE

When we decided to write this book together, we worked off of prompts, deciding on the story premise while putting our own spins on it. So you may notice the threads that connect and are parallel in the pairs of stories, but each has our own spin and our own style. We appreciate your support and, with gratitude, hope you enjoy our tales of monsters, both human and other spooky things.

# TABLE OF CONTENTS

# Soul Collector

## JK Allen

The cold wind blew through the shattered door hanging on its frame.

"Damn," I snarl, digging for my phone. I'd only just gotten keys from the landlord today and had a car full of my belongings. I wanted to unload, but first I'd need a door.

"Is this Paul?" My voice is quiet as I stand in front of the splintered wood that creaks in my ear.

"This is." His voice is gruff. I'll have to sweeten him up some.

"This is Neve, I know I just got keys from you, but I just got here with all my stuff and there's no front door. It's splintered."

"What's that now? No door?"

"I mean there are bits of wood dangling from the frame, but that isn't a door. I don't even know if someone is inside. Maybe I should call the cops."

"No, you just get in your car and wait for me to get there." I hear some muffled swearing as he grabs a coat.

I zip my coat up to my chin and plop back into the front seat of my tired car. I am happy it had made the two hour trek to get back here. I start the car, hoping some semblance of heat would come through the vents. Then went on the fingerless gloves, and then the cigarette. I breathe in, I exhale, watching the full crystallization of the plume of smoke travel over my ear and out the window. How long would this take to deal with? How long can it take to put on a door?

I get lost in these thoughts until I hear rapping at the window. The piled up ash on the end of my cigarette crumbles and vanishes into the crappy carpet. It's Paul.

I roll down the window. "See, no door. Just some splinters. Still haven't gone in to see if it's safe. You want me to call 911?"

"No need for that nonsense. Door guy is on the way. I'll check it out right now myself. We don't need no cops." His voice is loud, full of bravado. He clears his throat and walks up two steps. He kicks at the top step and scrunches his shoulders down. He practically runs through the doorway, splinters falling off his shoulders as he rushes through. He pulls a flashlight out and walks into the kitchen, out of sight.

I light another cigarette with shaky hands. I only breathe in halfway. He is gone for an eternity. I think I hear noises from inside the house. Loud thuds and knocking noises. I don't know what makes the racket. There's no furniture in there yet. I take a long drag and look up. Is that a face in the attic? I definitely saw something slink back into the shadows. I take a longer pull and the cigarette is spent. I don't even notice I light another right after I tamp out the first.

Finally there's the clattering of legs going down stairs and Paul, the landlord, emerges unscathed. He gives me a thumbs up sign, and I exhale. The door guy shows up two minutes later. I finally stop smoking. I leave the pseudo-warmth of my car and sidle up to Paul.

"Thank you for being my knight tonight. I really didn't want to call 911."

He looks at me like I'm absurd. "It was nothing. Everything's perfectly safe, and the door will be finished in ten minutes."

Ten minutes is a long time to be around another human. They expect you to talk and be pleasant, but most of all to be normal. That's hard. I take a few steps away from him to relieve the building pressure I'm now feeling. I cough and my face flushes a deep red. I hope the cloak of fallen night will cover my embarrassment.

He glances at me, then stares at my car. "You moving all that in tonight?"

"No, I'll sleep on an airbed tonight and get to work in the morning." *Or next week. Whenever.*

"Hope the weather's better for you."

"Hopefully." I attempt an unaffected smile at him. It is affected. I stop smiling and dig out another cigarette.

I'm done smoking by the time the door man leaves with his signed slip of paper. Paul slinks off without a word, just a slight wave in my general direction. I gather my courage and my backpack full of necessities and the bag with the airbed and comforter.

I cross my fingers and rush to the house, the new key on my ring. I turn on the kitchen light and look around the empty room. Dingy yellow kitchen, mealy brown carpet in the living room, then upstairs. I go back to the door to double check it's locked and bolted. That's when I hear it. The long creak of a not often used floorboard giving way. A shiver of ice courses down my spine. I remember the face in the window. It had been just a second. A second too long.

I debate setting up my bed in the living room. It's two floors down from the ghostly face, but decide I need a room with doors. Bedroom it is. One floor closer, but it has a lock. I run up the steps, bags battering my legs. I practically dive into my bedroom, toss the bags aside, and lock the door. I breathe a sigh of relief.

Within fifteen minutes, my bed is built and ready. I grab my backpack, which houses my ashtray and my oil pastels. I like to draw something every night. I pull out my sketchbook and get started.

I am lost in my art. So lost I don't hear the footsteps pacing above me for a very long time. I become slowly aware of the sound, and the hairs on my neck stand up. He's not wandering around aimlessly, he walks a straight line directly above where I lie. I look down at my sketchbook and see it's the face from the attic. Gaunt with high cheekbones and a devious glare. The image is now seared into my brain. I push the sketchbook across the room.

I lie back on the air mattress feeling exhausted but on edge. There's no way I'm turning off the lights tonight, but I'm hoping to get some sleep. It'll be hard enough to unpack, let alone on no sleep. I need a good start. I need a good start so it doesn't all fall apart like it always does. Like I always am. I cover my eyes with the crook of my arm. I count my breathing and drift off.

I know something is wrong the minute I swim up to consciousness. It's too cold. I'm shivering violently and turn to the source of the cold. The window has been flung wide open. I jump up and turn to see the door hanging off its hinge. That's when I look up.

It smiles at me with its too wide mouth. A snakelike tongue darts out as it looks at me. Its eyes are solid black, sclera to pupil, black as ink. A scream chokes me, caught in my throat. It is crab walking on the ceiling and the impossibility of this moment freezes me.

"You'll do just fine," it growls before it loosens its grip and plunges toward me.

***

We pull up to our new house, an old blue two-story with ugly black shutters. But it's our first home, and it will get fixed up like new, and I'm so relieved the drive is over, I'm grateful to see it.

"Christopher, can you believe we're finally here?" Heather says with a smile.

"Twelve hours," I groan, but her smile is brilliant, and I can't help but return it.

"We're home," she says with emphasis.

I grip her hand briefly, then climb out of the car. "Twelve hours," I call out into the night.

"Shhhhh, it's ten o'clock at night. Don't shout."

"At least you got to sleep the whole way."

"Well, I'm so gorgeous because I get lots of beauty sleep." She begins grabbing bags from the backseat. "It's why you love me so much."

I walk up behind her and grab her hips. "I love you for so much more than just your pretty face." She turns her head and gives me a melted look, and I lean in for the kiss. Despite the drive, tonight is a good night.

"Now, let's unpack the car and call it a night. We can start unloading the trailer tomorrow," Heather says, sweeping an auburn curl behind her ear. It springs back where it was, and I laugh.

"I bought wine on the road," I say with a debonair grin.

"Ooooh." She laughs. "Now grab a box."

We unload the car in less time than I anticipate, and I'm grateful to unwind. We play some music on her phone, savor the red vino, enjoy each other's company, and fall asleep exhausted on an old air mattress from my college days.

I see her. A young woman with dark hair that hangs in curtains around her pale face. She's seated in our bedroom, even though the walls are white instead of wall-papered. She is pretty in an unconventional way. She bends, hair swaying forward, and slides a crayon across a sketchbook on the floor. The room is bare, save an air mattress and an ashtray. She drops the crayon to light a cigarette and stops to listen. Footsteps. The steady plod of someone above her. Her face registers panic.

And then I wake up. Sun is streaming into the room despite the blinds, and I groan. My head aches. I need water.

I slide out from under Heather's leg and make my way to the kitchen. Scrounging through a box, I find a glass and fill it with water. At least the tap water tastes fine. Heather's got one of those filter things anyway to put on the faucet. I down the glass and sigh.

It's 8 AM. Earlier than I usually eat breakfast, but I find a bowl and have some cereal while I wait for Heather to wake up. We have a lot to do today. A lot to do this month in fact. We bought this house for cheap, but it's a fixer-upper, and I'll be doing all of the fixing. I rankle at the thought.

We moved here because Heather found a job teaching photography at the local college. Me, I haven't had real work in a year. We get by, and I do carpentry work on the side, but it's not what I'd prefer. Heather says she doesn't mind, but my mother's words haunt me. 'A woman wants to be provided for, Christopher. That's why she finds a man.' I swallow hard and throw the bowl in the sink. At least I can work on my novel. It's little consolation.

We unload strategically. After all, I'll be ripping up the carpet in most rooms and painting. No point in bringing in all the furniture yet. But we need stuff to live comfortably off of. That means most of the bathroom stuff makes it in and gets unpacked. Then the kitchen. We have a lunch of sandwiches.

"I'm so glad we moved back," Heather says, and I roll my eyes.

"We are not from here. Only you."

"Yeah, but we got this house cheap. It's been on the market for years. I knew we'd get a good price."

"Why hasn't it been sold?"

She pauses, looking uncomfortable. "Oh, probably because it's so ugly. I mean have you seen this kitchen? Dingy yellow walls. Old linoleum." She makes a face.

Something doesn't feel right about her response, but I don't want to argue, so I let it slide.

"What room do you want to do first?"

I don't want to do any room. This kind of work is something I was forced to do with my dad to learn a "skill" and I hate it.

"The bedroom," I mutter. "I want my bed in there."

"Start with the walls," she says, taking my plate. As if I don't know what I'm doing.

"Sure thing."

"Please don't make that face," she says from the sink, then pouts.

"What face?"

"You look angry. If you really don't want to do all that work." She clasps her hands together. "We can hire someone. I know it's a lot to ask of you."

I soften. "It's not a lot. And I know how to do it all thanks to dear old dad. It'll be fine. I can work on my book when I need a break. Why waste the money?"

"If you're sure." She turns to the sink with a smile. I gave the right answer.

***

I notice something is wrong as soon as I peel away a corner of the ugly flower wallpaper in the bedroom. There's a line of black ink that scrawls across the white wall underneath like a spider's leg. I take the scraper and run it up the wall, removing a swath of flowers as I go. Words jump out at me.

*Soul co—*

*No es—*

Another swatch removed.

*Soul collector*

*No escape*

What the hell? I remove piece after piece. Over and over, the words appear in a frantic hand. My heart races. What on earth does this mean? That's when I hear a thud above me. An icy shiver courses through me. I get a flash from my dream. The young woman with the cigarette in this room. The look of panic on her face as the footsteps pound above her. I steel myself and head towards the attic.

Now it is devoid of sounds. An eerie silence fills the house like clouded smoke. I smell the bitter kiss of old cigarettes as I make my way up the steps.

I'm surprised to see no one is in the attic. I take a breath, but the sickly jolt of adrenaline that spiked my bloodstream still courses through me. Nothing up here but a box by the window. I make my way towards it with shaky steps.

Some old clothes lay rumpled in the bottom of the box along with some books. A cold sweat breaks out on my neck. Sitting on top is a black sketchbook and a box of oil pastels, the crayons I saw in my dream.

I pick up the sketchbook with trembling hands. I feel eyes on me and whip around, the hairs on my arms standing on end. I scurry out of the attic and back into the bedroom.

The wall of scrawled writing greets me, and I swallow hard, clutching the sketchbook to my chest. I sit down in the middle of the floor and open the black book.

Faces. Charcoal, pencil, crayons. They're mostly faces. Old, young, pretty, strange, just a litany of faces etched out in shades of black and grey. Faces like carved stone. She has a way of portraying them. Happy, depressed, angry, silly. I flip through the book with a smile, lost to my surroundings and my beating heart. That's when I see it. The last page she drew.

It is nothing like her previous work. It is rushed, frantic strokes that blur and meld into the lines of the most horrific face. Gaunt, with a mouth that's stretched wide. A devious glare stares out at me, making my stomach clench. My hands are in fists. I force one open to turn the page, to get past the madness. The rest of the pages are all blank. I look right. Soul collector. No escape.

Heather's mad when she sees the writing. I need to find out what it means, but all she cares about is she'll have to pick a new color scheme since cream walls won't cover the words. They are written in every possible space in all sizes. The ritual of writing like that has seized my mind. Sure it's nerve wracking, but as a writer I have caught the whiff of a story that must be ferreted out. All she's going on about is how nothing goes with dark grey.

"Then pick blue," I snap, gripping the sketchbook.

"Why do you even have this? It clearly belonged to a psychopath."

"And why didn't you, who lived here most of your entire life, not tell me that a psychopath lived here? What happened to her? Huh? What happened in this house?"

She blanches. "Nothing happened. Stop going on about it. If you want to use this for story fodder, fine. Be my guest. But don't come at me about the house when you got nothing done all day. You were supposed to have all the upstairs rooms painted by the time I got home."

"You don't want to know what it's all about? I'm supposed to just paint over it and act like nothing happened?" I hold out the book. "Like she doesn't exist? Just so you can have cream colored walls with coral curtains? Do you even hear yourself?"

"So what, you're going to investigate? Well, let's just not do any real work for weeks while you go on some crazy goose chase of a mentally deranged woman who's probably been institutionalized. Sounds like a great use of time."

"Maybe you should paint the walls then. Since you're so keen on them being done."

"And I'm supposed to do that when exactly? When I'm doing my job? Shall I just quit my teaching position? Is that what you want?"

"Or maybe I should move back to my home, Heather. The home I left to come out here with you."

"My job is here. I'm not going to apologize for that."

"My job isn't here. I don't have to be here."

"You don't have a job."

I flush bright red. I can feel the heat radiating off my face and my hands tighten into fists.

"I didn't mean that." She looks mortified that she let the truth slip. That bitch.

"The truth comes out," I say, full of spite. Man, do I want a cigarette right now. Just to deal with this bullshit.

"Why are we even fighting?" She's about to cry, but I can't forget what's been said. The honeymoon is over, and I'm stuck here, with her.

She crosses her arms. "Put down the sketchbook."

"What's it to you?"

"It's creeping me out."

I huff. "Well get over it. I'm using it for book research. Don't even think about fucking touching it, Heather."

"Do not keep it in the bedroom. It's bad enough I have to stare at that wall."

"Don't ever touch it," I repeat.

"Look, take a few days to work on your story, figure it out. Don't worry about the walls. I have to buy new paint, anyways."

She smiles at me like she's indulging me. She's so manipulative.

"I'm going to bed," I mutter darkly.

Her smile falters. "Good night."

I walk past her without acknowledging her. I leave the sketchbook in what's supposed to be my office. My solitary desk is hunched against the wall. I put the sketchbook in a drawer underneath some papers. I will start to unravel this mystery tomorrow.

***

Heather's gone before I wake up, and I'm thankful for the silence. I grab toast and OJ from the kitchen and make my way to my desk. Opening my laptop, I grab some loose leaf paper and a pen while my computer starts. I sit and start searching the news. The whole world's gone to shit. I drag my hand over my eyes and begin.

Neve Williamson the cover page of her sketchbook says. I Google her name and hold my breath as the results come in.

A few pictures, an old Placebook page. Then I see the articles.

*Young Woman's Death Leads to Investigation*
*More to Local Death than Police Suspected*
*A Mystery on Fuller Street*

I read the first one quickly, eagerly.

*Resident was found inside a house on the 1100 block of Fuller Street who had died of an apparent suicide, but copious amounts of blood found at the scene leads law enforcement to believe that several persons had also died there recently. Preliminary DNA results find blood from at least two unknown persons at the scene. No other bodies were found.*

My blood is chilled, and I shiver violently. What on earth happened here? A suicide was bad enough, and those happened sure, but two unknown victims had met an ill fate here. Someone's watching me. I snap my head back and see a shadow move away from the door. My heart slams into my chest, and I am frozen to the spot. It had moved too fast. Too fast for anything natural.

***

Things get worse when I start ripping up the carpet. There's blood everywhere. Dried and tacky on the wooden slats of the floor. I spend hours scrubbing it away, feeling the grit of it deep beneath my nails. It curdles my stomach. I expected it in one room after reading those articles, but I've found pools of blood in three rooms already. Heather won't even talk about it. I'm left to deal with the chaos and gore on my own.

I start having bad dreams of the attic. The creak of floorboards under a heavy tread. A thin, old man, his hair a white halo around his head. A gaunt face with a too-wide grin. I sleep only for two or three hours a night and take up smoking as I try to churn out a story about a troubled, young artist who started hearing things in her house. I spend hours flipping through her sketchbook, staring in wordless horror at the last page.

Heather goes off to work. I pretend to be asleep when she wakes up. I'm tired of her worried looks and deep sighs. She lied about this house. I can feel the wrongness of the place now like an off-key note in the middle of a melody, there's a presence in this house that's discomforting. I drink too much coffee and light cigarettes just after tamping out the first and don't even realize it. A deep chill settles into the house and into my bones.

I walk across the street to get the mail. When I turn back to the house, I see the face from the sketchbook staring at me from the attic window. I suck in air through my teeth and freeze. A long, thin tongue snakes out and rubs against its meager lips. Then it slinks back into the shadows.

It takes ten full minutes to build up the courage to investigate. It has to be in my head from lack of sleep and all those bad dreams.

"There's nothing inside." I mumble to myself as I slowly trudge in. The hairs on my neck stand straight up and goosebumps break out on my arm. I smell cigarettes and the copper tang of blood as I cross the kitchen towards the stairs. There isn't a noise in the whole house, like I've walked into a vacuum, and it's hard to breathe.

I open the door to the attic slow as molasses. It creaks open, the sound making my heart pound. It's too loud, too much noise after the deadly silence of a moment before.

There's nothing there. The tension in between my shoulders snaps and I inhale. I run a hand through my hair and walk towards the window. I see the mailbox and let out a laugh. Silly me. Then I see a corner of the insulation curled up. I pull, and an old scrapbook falls out with a clatter that makes me jump. On the cover it says Soul Collector in red ink.

Footsteps rattle behind me. I spin around, but don't see anything. I can feel eyes on me, and I'm sure I'm going to have a heart attack. Adrenaline races through me, making my heartbeat erratic. I grab the scrapbook and run as fast as I can out the door, down the stairs, all the way to the kitchen before I stop. I look at the scrapbook in my hand, wondering when and why I had picked it up. It's white, yellowed with age, thick with rough edges. I open the book to the first page.

*Missing. Margaret Ann Sessing, age 14.* An old black and white photo shows a girl with dark hair and glasses. The next page is an article clipping. *Local youth reported missing. Susan Marie Thatcher was last seen Friday afternoon.* I flip through more pages. They're all ads or newspaper clippings of missing youth that span twenty years. My heart pounds. Someone had clearly hidden this book. Maybe it was evidence. Evidence of a horror so great, I can't even comprehend it. So many missing boys and girls. What had happened to them?

I sit in the kitchen and smoke until Heather gets home.

"Do you have to smoke in the house?" she asks, wrinkling her nose.

"What aren't you telling me about this house?" I demand.

"It's childish. That's why I haven't told you. Just some dumb local legend some kids made up."

"Tell me."

She sighs. "They call this the murder house. It's said that a man used to live here, an older man who never married. He was a mean, rotten thing. Anyway, some kids started to go missing. First just one here or there, then dozens in a week's time. Then it would stop for a long time. They say they all went missing in this neighborhood, right around this house. And on the days those kids disappeared, the old man would play his records and dance in the living room like he enjoyed the fact those kids were missing. People started to say he was to blame, and the music was just covering up the sounds of those children screaming. The police never arrested him, of course. It was all just a stupid rumor."

"But it wasn't a rumor. He did kill them," I say, tapping the scrapbook.

"If you're going to be ridiculous, I'm leaving," she threatens, her red curls shaking.

"He's the soul collector," I whisper.

"I've had enough of this," she shouts and leaves to the sound of the door slamming. I make a sandwich before exhaustion hits. I barely make it to bed before I fall asleep.

I roll over onto my back and open my eyes. The too-wide grin greets me. His eyes are pure black. He hangs from the ceiling, his face right above mine. My palms are sweaty and my breath comes too fast. He lets go of his grip on the ceiling and rushes towards me. I scream and struggle to free myself from the sheets I'm tangled in. He lands on all fours around me, his face just inches from my own. He starts to cackle, and I scream again. Only this time it wakes me up.

I jump back as far as I can and hit my head on the wall. I ignore the pain, ripping the sheets off me. There's a loud banging noise and my eyes shoot upward. The attic. He's trying to escape. Bang. No, that was the sound of a drawer slamming shut in the kitchen. I let out my breath, relieved. It's just Heather. She must still be mad, but I know I can get us to make up tonight. I feel better after some real sleep, and I've missed my wife. It's time to make peace and figure this shit out together.

I sit up in bed and light a cigarette. "Heather?" I call out. Another drawer slams home. She's still mad. "Heather, honey, come up here and talk to me. Please."

Silence unravels, and I take a quick pull on my cigarette. My eyes fall to the wall. You can no longer see the words, I did my job covering it up in slate grey. I rub my eyes and look again. I thought I saw an s and the start of a no. This will need another coat of paint. I hear a creak in the kitchen and wonder what Heather is doing down there. My fingers shake slightly as I finish my cigarette. Soul collector is clear on the wall now as if I had marked it with a Sharpie.

I hear a knocking sound on the stairs. Something striking the rails as Heather makes her way towards me. I turn on the lamp next to the bed. Her steps are short and dragging. Each one punctuated with whatever she is knocking against the rails.

"Heather, are you okay?" My heart is pounding as she climbs another step.

I see her now. She lifts her head, and I see her eyes are pitch black. Her head lolls on her neck like it's broken, and she lifts her hand to her face. She's holding a butcher knife.

She smiles and her grin stretches across her face. "It's time to collect another soul," she says in a voice that doesn't belong to her. "There is no escape."

# A Ghost Story in the Time of Coronavirus

**Carol Allen**

*Content Warning: Domestic Violence*

*Of course Nana died, it is 2020, after all.* Hillary wanted to say this to her husband of thirteen years, but knew it was a little insensitive. *Just like saying that Nana was like seventy-five, so she wasn't going to be with us forever. But that is still young for an old person. He is lucky that he had his grandmother with him for this long. Both sets of my grandparents were gone ten years ago. I guess I don't have good genes or good luck. My husband is the one with the luck. He has never gotten a speeding or parking ticket, when I can never find a decent parking spot.*

"Oh, honey. I'm sorry to hear that." She rubbed her temples. "She looked so healthy last summer." Hillary turned to grab a bottle of Ibuprofen and took two pills for her headache. "Did she get the virus? I thought she lived by herself, how could she get infected?"

*She was supposed to be quarantining, like the rest of the world. Didn't you help her with ordering her groceries online? Like we helped your parents?* Hillary wanted to yell, but held back and set her empty glass on the kitchen counter. She crossed her arms, and her running commentary stayed in her head. *I mean, Jesus, this makes me happy that my parents didn't live long enough for this craziness. I don't know if they would have listened to me and stayed home. Would they have risked their lives? I don't know, I didn't get to know them before they died.* She shook her head, her in-laws were staying home for the most part, but they still met with their friends. *At least they are meeting outdoors, so small victories. But only because it was warm in Florida, it won't be warmer here for another month.*

Her husband, Alfie, rubbed his brown eyes. He had worked overnight at the hospital. She wasn't sure if he was trying to hide his tears or if he was too exhausted to cry. The local hospital had been lucky to not see an overwhelming amount of COVID-19 cases, but Alfie seemed to be putting in a lot of overtime to help out with the few patients there were. He yawned and stretched his bare arms out in front of him, then over his head. Hillary noticed his more defined biceps, a result of his new routine. Alfie was getting ready to lift weights in the garage as a way to deal with the stress from these pandemic times. She admired her husband's attitude and sense of service. The time she spent with his colleagues was always filled with how their intervention helped countless patients. It was always an interesting conversation.

"Even if I'm taking care of the other patients, it helps the lung doctors." He raised his hands up at her stern expression. "I know that you know they are called pulmonologists." Alfie looked at his phone and answered a text. "But if I'm helping out in the ER, they can focus on the patients in the ICU."

Alfie said that he was happy to help out and do his part after his shifts. Surprisingly, he was willing to go to the grocery store for their weekly supplies. "I can go during the essential worker hour. Why put yourself at risk?" Hillary thought he was so caring and protective of her. She was used to his new routine of showering immediately after he came home from the hospital. Alfie kept his work clothes separate from his off duty clothes, and he was taking his work laundry down to the washer to do himself. "We aren't sure how transmissible the virus is, so better to be safe," he warned and kept his shoes in the garage. Also, he told her to leave their packages in the garage for at least a day. "We don't want to let the possible viral contamination into the house."

Hillary could only nod sympathetically and check her phone. The shelter of her home was something she was grateful for, and she would be able to stay safe. There was a worry about her husband's exposure to the virus, and she constantly checked the news for the updated case numbers in the state. Then she would look up the number of cases in the county. *Was it here already or just the metro area? I don't know anyone who is sick, but it's just a matter of time.* She shook her head at how there were already tens of thousands cases statewide. It was the way she spent a lot of her time home alone. An endless cycle of going between the news of the virus, of quarantine, of protests, of politics, then looking at funny videos. Kids, pets, comedians, or anything was welcomed as comic relief.

Then she found herself watching true crime shows and documentaries. They were something that she was interested in after discovering murder mystery novels. A young Hillary was a bookworm who devoured Nancy Drew books, after reading <u>Harriet the Spy</u>. Then she graduated to Agatha Christie's many books, and Truman Capote's <u>In Cold Blood</u> showed her that crime is real. She started watching the evening news with her father and would read the newspaper after he was done. This sparked her interest in journalism, but after college and her marriage, she cut back on her time reporting on local news and crime. Alfie talked about wanting to have a family when they bought their house and wanted her to have less late nights at the office. When she was given a chance to do articles for the lifestyle and social sections of the newspaper, she took that promotion. Alfie seemed happy since she wasn't on call anymore. But it was unrealistic for him to not be on call for his job, and she didn't ask him to change. The months and years of trying to get pregnant went by, and they kept trying. Then she was offered the travel section and she loved it, until this year. This year she wanted to stay home.

All these years later, she was now homebound, and her husband was still on call. Their house was their home after they had done some remodeling. They made one of their spare bedrooms into an office for her to write in, and it was full of her beloved books. The other bedrooms were guest rooms, usually his parents would spend a few weeks with them in the summer. Her friends from college would talk about coming into town, but schedules were always in conflict. Now that everyone had the time off to visit, no one wanted to travel. Nor did she want anyone to come over. Those guest rooms would stay empty most of the time. They were never blessed with any babies.

Hillary opened her laptop and placed it on the coffee table in the living room. She gave up sitting in her home office a couple weeks ago. After almost two months of lockdown, she needed a change of scenery. The view out of that window wasn't inspiring, she could only see the side of her neighbor's house, and nothing interesting happened. She didn't want to be a nosy neighbor, and didn't want to be like Jimmy Stewart's character in "Rear Window." There was enough paranoia going around, that she didn't want to suspect her neighbor of killing his wife. It was always the spouse she had learned from watching many true crime shows. *Well, almost always the spouse. I could try to write my own murder mystery, but I don't have a plot. Just like I don't have any ideas for work. Writer's block is a bitch.*

She opened a Word document and typed, *Two characters, married, one will be the killer?* It was a way to waste time and felt better than saying she watched Netflix all day. She told her husband she was researching for her next articles. Which wasn't entirely a lie, she did have a few drafts of articles saved on her laptop. The newspaper was asking her to write an article about traveling, or planning for travel, during this time of uncertainty.

Perhaps she could give a positive spin on the low cost of plane tickets right now or for booking a 2021 vacation. But she wasn't sure if she could put any positivity to a worldwide pandemic. *I don't think anyone will go on a vacation safely until like 2022.* She typed the note, *First places to hit once borders open up.* She thought, *If they ever do.*

The work group text was another way for her to stay connected. Everyone was friendly, but it was hard to listen to the different sections of the news say how historic things were. It seemed like everyone else did not have any issues writing and publishing. The paper also hosted meetings over Zoom, and she saw everyone excited with their pending articles or ideas. "We are living through history," the editor would say. They were exploring ways to use Zoom for interviews, and how it could increase traffic to the website. She tried not to roll her eyes at the boss saying, "We have to document these times for the history books. We also have to keep the public informed." Hillary attended less of the meetings, as she struggled to contribute to a travel column. How could she contribute to these meetings when she could not travel or be social right now? When she was on a conference call, she watched the screen and noted how many times a co-worker would drink from their coffee cups. She had a theory that the more drinks sipped, the higher likelihood there was something other than coffee in the mug.

*Also, less likelihood of wearing pants. But I don't want to prove that theory, so far the boss has the most ticks. Maybe he was wearing sweatpants or gym shorts. It wouldn't be that much worse than the wrinkled khakis he lived in on a daily basis. I may not wear the business casual dress code, but I do try. I will change into jeans and a nice shirt on meeting days. It also helps to put on some makeup. Oh, the boss scores another point for another sip.*

Hillary wanted to be productive. So she typed a tentative title to that article, *"Cheap Tix,"* then opened another document and titled that *"2022: Two Years Later, Is It Now Safe to Travel?"* She threw her long blonde hair into a ponytail and opened another blank document. She typed, *Why am I trying to write about travel during a lockdown?* Then she pushed her laptop away and turned on the television. "I need to eat lunch anyway." The laptop stayed dark for the rest of the day, as she watched a few movies, then left it on a television series until it was time to start making dinner.

The day she found out Nana died, she had finished making spaghetti with meatballs for dinner when her husband walked through the door. He took off his navy scrub shirt and threw it in the laundry room. When Alfie returned into the kitchen shirtless and wearing gym shorts he had changed into when he was in the laundry room, he washed his hands, then dried them with the daisy kitchen towel and told her that Nana had died.

"No, it wasn't the virus. I think they said it was a heart attack." He hugged himself and said, "I think she skipped her doctor's appointment because she was afraid of the virus."

"Oh, no. I'm so sorry, honey." She walked over to him and hugged him, "If there's anything I can do. Just let me know." She kissed his forehead and rubbed his fuzzy, brown hair. He shaved it off a few weeks ago, and she wasn't sure if she liked the buzz cut look. But this is what they were calling quarantine haircuts. The alternative was to let it grow long, and she thought he was too old to have shaggy hair. She definitely thought he was not old enough nor soft enough to have a ponytail. He was more like a young recruit and working out at dawn like boot camp. His muscles were more defined with his almost daily jogs and time spent in the garage lifting weights. He hugged her close and kissed her neck, sending tingles down her spine.

She hoped he didn't notice the ten pounds—or more—she had gained during her stress eating. *I should stop buying Oreos this week, and maybe start doing some exercising. Yeah, I'll start tomorrow morning. Then I'll do some real writing! If I don't write an article, I can work on my book.* She felt his breath on her ear and was waiting for another kiss when his phone vibrated on the counter. Alfie pulled away from her.

"Actually, there is something you can do." He looked at his phone and read another message.

"Do you want me to call your parents?" Hillary pulled at her blonde hair and twirled it around her finger. She had decided to let her hair grow longer, it hadn't been this long since her wedding day. She wanted to have a beautiful chignon and curls with a veil on that special day. Afterwards, she went back to chin length bobs for the convenience. Funny how easy it was to get back to convenience after the honeymoon. Did she think they would still be in the same small town ten years after he graduated from med school?

No, she thought they would be in a city by now. It seemed like his parents were going on more vacations together and had more fun than she was having. Alfie said that it was the luxury of retirement, and that they would be there too, when they had the free time. Now she had the free time, and she was still alone. *Maybe I should curl my hair tomorrow, like I used to when we were dating. It has been a while since we had a date night.*

"No, my parents know," he put his phone down, always screen-side down—for privacy reasons he explained. "It's just hard because they are in Florida, and then with my shifts at the hospital…."

"What? What do you need me to do?" Hillary crossed her arms and felt her headache coming back.

He rubbed her shoulder. "It would help us all, if you could go to the house and help pack it up."

"What about my work?" She did need to write some articles for the paper and to work on her book. Then there was her social media content. She thought it was good to curate content to get more views. Even if it was lifestyle content, it was better than not writing. *It was better than just eating snacks and watching Netflix. Plus, it might help get my future book publicity or get more readers for my articles if I never write that book.* Hillary pouted.

"My parents want the house emptied, well, mostly emptied, to sell it," he said and put his hands on her shoulders. "It's just full of memories for them. They trust you. I trust you to know what to keep or give away. Plus, they can't drive up with all the lockdowns between Florida and here." He rolled his eyes and said, "then they are too old to be moving boxes."

"I don't know, maybe we shouldn't drive up there either." Hillary bit her lower lip. "Would it be safe to travel right now? Is it even allowed?"

"I think it will be fine. It's the same state. Plus, we know how to be safe." He kissed her pouting lips. "I should be able to get some time off, but it might not be for a couple weeks. Since you don't have to go into the office, it would be so helpful for you to be there and get the boxes packed. Then I won't have to take so much time off, especially with this pandemic going on." He gestured with arms as he turned away from her, then picked up his phone and returned a text. "I just asked for time off, and it looks like they will give it to me in three weeks." He looked at her with his big brown eyes. "Can I count on you?"

"Of course." Hillary smiled. "Does she have WiFi at her house?"

*He could be really infuriating, but Alfie was right.*

*He was always right,* Hillary thought as she drove to Nana's. She could work from anywhere now that she didn't have to go to the office. Her job was just tied to her computer. She could write new articles from her couch or at Nana's house up north, if not for writer's block. Or if she didn't have general anxiety from the pandemic. She rubbed her neck, then rolled her shoulders. "I should have made him give me a massage before I left." Hillary nodded her head. "But he will have to pay for my hard work when I get back." She was making good time driving on nearly empty roads. She still left town after rush hour, but it was surreal being only one of a few vehicles on the highway.

*Is this how the zombie apocalypse starts? An unknown virus and deserted roads and cities. How do you prepare for the end times? I think I stocked up with getting all the canned soup and meats I could in February. But you can only eat so many tuna fish sandwiches and tomato soup before you order a pizza. A lot of different delivery foods.* But having a fully stocked kitchen made her feel better. She just did not feel like cooking or baking. *I do not need to bake any kind of desserts.* Hillary had started to do some workouts after Alfie went to work in the morning. She wasn't ready to start jogging, but she walked on the treadmill and lifted some small weights. It wasn't much, but she did feel better. Maybe with working out and this road trip, she could break her creative block. Maybe she could document this trip for an article and talk about how people are coping. If she encountered any other people.

*Nana's story could be a way to make this more personal. How well did I know her? She had always been nice to me. Nana Murphy said she liked my writing and said she tried to read all my articles. She asked me to help her with subscribing online to my paper. I thought she was very caring towards Alfie. Nana would always ask me about him. How was he doing?—Good! Nana, he's always good—How was his job?—He's a great doctor. I always hear about how his patients love him—Did he work a lot?—Of course Nana, he's a doctor. He's always working—At least, she didn't constantly ask us when we were going to have kids. She would say, "When it's time, it's time." In fact, she said that she wouldn't have gotten married if she wasn't pregnant.*

"How did I miss that? A shotgun wedding, well, things were different back then. I wonder if there was someone she wanted to marry instead of Pop? She was a little weird when I got engaged and did ask if I was pregnant. She said that I didn't have to get married if Alfie wasn't treating me right."

This chance to be home and to be alone with her thoughts was a blessing. She believed that this time could be a sign she should pursue her book idea. Hillary had been secretly trying to write a novel for years, but didn't have the time to develop her idea. That would change with her being furloughed, starting in June. Since the newspaper had to downsize the office and focus online, there would be fewer employed staff. She did some freelance writing before quarantine, and she could still sell her work to the newspaper. There was no need to tell Alfie; she technically wasn't unemployed. But he was preoccupied with work and with Nana's house. He stopped asking her about her day or her writing, like he did early on in the quarantine. He seemed to always be on the phone with lawyers or his parents in the weeks since Nana died. They barely talked when he was home, unless it was about her going to Nana's house. Hillary was looking forward to getting out of the house and away from Alfie's scrutiny. She found herself hesitant to talk to him about her career opportunities. She wasn't sure if he would be supportive of her not writing her articles regularly to pursue other interests.

*Write a book or start a podcast, those are the only options. What else can you do when there is a new virus in the world?*

*Just stay home, wash your hands, don't touch your face, and wear a mask. Or you can go on a road trip and pack up the house of a dead relative.*

"Good thing it's summertime. It would have been nicer if Nana hadn't died," she said to herself. Hillary had a lot to say on the four hour drive north. "I would not want to make this drive in the winter. All this green really is beautiful. The world really does go on, even with a pandemic. It is nice to get outside too. Fresh air!" She rolled down her window a little and took the ramp to exit the highway. "Finally made it."

Northern Lower Michigan wasn't that far away from her home, but long enough to not visit Nana Murphy more. *She was actually eighty-five, sure that's old, but not that old. I thought she was younger than that because she was so active. I mean she was still cutting her grass with that riding lawn mower. She would have said, 'I'm on my own, of course, I'm going to cut my grass, Hilary. I did it even when Pop was alive. He was always too busy with his girlfriends.'*

Hillary sighed and said, "But we couldn't have driven up earlier this spring anyway. We were all quarantining. Plus, I don't think it stopped snowing until April, and we didn't know she would die in May." She sighed again, it was getting real. The empty house would be proof that Nana was gone. "There's so many questions to ask her too. Did Pop really have girlfriends? Alfie always said that Nana was just jealous and that Pop never was unfaithful. How did he word it? He said that Pop was just helpful to neighbors from everyone going through the depression and the wars together. Pop made it home from WW2 when some of his friends didn't. Nana was younger than him and didn't understand." Hillary didn't understand the ten year age difference between Pop and Nana, but she did understand death. "Plus, there were a lot of missing kids and everyone was keeping an eye out. Pop even went missing when he went hunting that fall." There had been a lot of loss in Hillary's life, and the grief didn't lessen. She wiped her eyes and looked for the road for the lawyer's office.

*Oh, I should take pictures of the town. Good thing I took that picture of my lunch outside that red and white diner. It was a perfect picture of a cola, hamburger, and fries. All Americana with a slice of pickle instead of apple pie. I am watching my carbs now.*

Hillary exhaled as she parked the car outside the lawyer's office. It was a repurposed house. "Cute white shutters. I should look into putting shutters on our house," she muttered as she grabbed the small bottle of hand sanitizer from the center console. The alcohol stung her nose as she disinfected her hands. Shaking her hands, she scanned the passenger seat, looking for the black cloth mask she had worn on the drive up. She didn't want to lose it, the other ones were in a suitcase in the way back of her red SUV, and she didn't want to dig around for a new one. She was relieved to see it on her black leather purse, and put it on. "Why am I so nervous? There's no reason to be nervous."

The lawyer was a petite blonde, wearing a sleeveless floral top with a light pink skirt and a pink fabric mask. She stood up when Hillary entered with her black sunglasses up in her own blonde hair that was in a messy bun for the drive. Hillary stepped forward wearing her favorite white canvas shoes and tried to smooth out her wrinkled navy cotton t-shirt and her khakis shorts. The lawyer stepped away from her desk and away from Hillary. She said, "Hi, I'm Laura George, and I was Mrs. Murphy's attorney. I presume you are Alfred Murphy's wife?"

"Yes, I'm Hillary. Hello," she said and waved from where she stood near the front door. "No handshakes in the time of coronavirus, right?"

Laura nodded and pointed a manicured finger to a manila envelope on her clean black desk. "That is for you. It has the house keys and all the pertinent paper-work. Her will, the deed to the house, and those kinds of papers that I had. Oh, and there's the sheriff's report and death certificate."

Hillary grabbed the envelope and asked, "Is a sher-iff report normal in a heart attack?"

"Only if there is a crime." She walked back to her desk as Hillary stepped back towards the door.

"Crime? What crime?" Hillary almost dropped her car keys when she put the envelope under her arm.

"Oh, you don't know. They didn't tell you?" The lawyer stepped in front of her desk and crossed her arms.

"No, no one told me or Alfie about a crime." Hillary felt hot despite the ceiling fans and the open windows. "It wasn't just a heart attack?"

"Please, sit down. I'm going to get you some wa-ter," the lawyer said before walking into a room in the back. She returned with bottled water. "Please, take a drink, you look pale."

"I'm okay." But Hillary did take a sip under her mask when Laura insisted. "I'm okay. Well, I am a little shocked." She sat down in the brown leather chair next to the door and fanned herself with the envelope.

Laura continued, "I don't know all the details." She was back at her desk and was looking at a file she pulled from the top drawer. "I do know that there was a burglary at the house that night. She must have heard the guy in the house, and it scared her into a heart attack." The lawyer paused before saying, "I just wished she had been able to call for help. She was such a nice lady. I am sorry for your loss."

Hillary wiped her forehead. "Wow. A burglary. Did they catch the guy?"

"No, unfortunately," she said, looking at Hillary with her blue eyes and a furrowed brow. "I told the sheriff that you would be at the house, preparing it for a sale. He promised that he would have someone patrol the property more often while you were there." She cleared her throat. "If it makes you feel better, there hasn't been any other break-ins in the weeks since Mrs. Murphy's passing. The sheriff thinks it was a one-time thing."

"I hope so." Hillary stood up. "I think I should get going. Thank you."

Laura set the file back into the drawer and sat down. "Are you sure you're feeling alright?"

"Yes, it's getting late." Hillary adjusted her purse. "And I need to get to the store."

"Of course." Laura stood up again and smiled. "Don't be too worried, the front door was replaced because it had been damaged that night. I heard the locksmith put on an extra deadbolt too."

"Thanks again." Hillary let the screen door slam shut behind her and walked back to her SUV.

She looked at her phone and didn't see any missed calls. Hillary decided to just drive to the house and not call her husband. *I don't know how to tell him there was a burglary. Does he know about the crime? Would he not tell me about it? No, he would have told me about it, if he knew. I will call him when I get to the house.* Hillary placed her phone in her purse and put her SUV into drive. "If it gives me the creepy crawlies, I'll just stay at a hotel tonight. Hell, I'll stay there all week if I need to. Maybe all month." She blew a raspberry. "Will it take that long? I guess it could be four weeks in this town." Hillary shrugged. "Good thing I don't have pets." Then she felt sad. "Maybe a dog would be good right now. For the company and for protection. I don't know if I want to be alone right now." She sat up straighter. "No," she said, shaking her head. That wasn't true, she traveled by herself plenty of times for her job. She liked to be alone. She loved her husband, but sometimes it was nice when he worked overnight or was gone weekends. She did wonder if he was having an affair, but not enough to really suspect one. *He wouldn't do that to me. He's a good guy. He wouldn't betray me.*

Alfie didn't like her doing his laundry, because he preferred the dry cleaners or to let the hospital launder his scrubs. She would still look at his shirt collars for lipstick after putting away her laundry. His side of the closet was full of suits, collared shirts, and dress pants, and she liked to stand in the closet and look at them. They were her constant companion even before the quarantine. Alfie seemed to be going through a little midlife crisis, and he started going to the gym regularly. But he wasn't alone. He said he was going to the gym with a group of guys from work. They would work out or play basketball together. He said, "It's a good way to blow off some steam. Honey, you know how stressful my job can be. You don't want me to bring that stress home, and I don't want to be an angry person around you." She didn't think he went to the gym now that they were shut down. Alfie talked about the rules of these times, so she knew what was allowed or not. But he did go jogging in the morning, when the weather was nice. He said he would go by the river or just run around the parking lot behind the hospital. She didn't complain, he looked great, at peace, and had a lot of energy. She told Alfie that she wanted to go to the gym with him when it was safe to go.

Alfie had just laughed and drank from his water bottle. "Sure, that would be great to do. How long will that last though? I think the longest hobby you've had is your stint with the violin. What was that, like two months? Oh, maybe it was the painting thing. You were doing that art stuff for a while." He pointed to one of her paintings hanging on the wall. "You sure did a lot of those landscapes."

During the first few months of the lockdown, Hillary found herself stress eating. Since she was worried about going to the grocery store, she ordered delivery from the local restaurants almost every day. Now she could go into the grocery store, but she continued to get take out for dinner. She told Alfie it was to support the small businesses, and he agreed. He also told her that he didn't mind that she's starting to gain some weight. He teased, "I married you for better or for worse." Alfie kissed her. "In thickness and in health." She hit him on his arm, and he said before he went to bed, "I like your soft belly."

"Good, because if you didn't, I know a couple other men who would," she said, laughing. She wasn't a jealous person, but she did get hit on as a married woman. *Some people do not even notice my wedding ring or notice me standing next to my husband in grocery stores. A lot of those damn cashiers are flirts.* So Hillary smelled her husband's clothing for another female's perfume, and searched his face for someone else's lipstick. *I'm sure I'm not the only woman who likes your hard body.*

She drove up the long driveway to Nana's little white two-story wooden house. The sheriff's car was hidden by some of the trees on the property until he flashed his headlights as she parked. Then the sheriff got out of his car and put on a brown hat that made a tall man look even taller. He kept his mirrored aviator sunglasses on until he was right in front of her. "I guess you're Mrs. Murphy, here to clean up the house?"

"Yes, sir," Hillary said, showing him the copper colored house key in her hand. "I just came over from the lawyer's office." She had left her sunglasses in the car and kept her mask on.

He pointed to her key and said, "That will open the back door and it will work on the new door, but I have the new key for the new deadbolt." The sheriff handed her a silver colored key. "The original front door was broken in the burglary, so you can see, we replaced it with a new door." He walked her up the porch of the white house with green trim. "We could only get the red door this quickly, I know it doesn't match. But Mr. Anders at the hardware store has a white door on order. He picked one that was just like what your grandmother had." He shook his head. "Such a shame, you know. She was a nice lady."

"Can you tell me what happened? I just heard that she had a heart attack. I don't understand." Hillary placed the keys into the locks and opened the door. She peeked in and asked, "I mean, is it even okay for me to clean and pack up the house? Is it still a crime scene?"

"No, we got all the evidence we need. It's fine." He stepped back to sit on one of the white wicker chairs on the porch. "But it looks like it was a burglary. Some of these houses are empty for most of the year, and I think it was a crime of opportunity. The person or persons involved didn't know that Mrs. Murphy was upstairs in her bed. I think she must have heard them, and it scared her into a heart attack. Then they might have been scared into rushing out of here once they came up to her room and saw her there, passed away."

"Do you know who did it?" She leaned against the doorframe and looked at all the pine trees in the front lawn of the house and surrounding the property. "There are a lot of hiding spots for the bad guys."

"We were able to get some fingerprints, so we're looking at that now. These things take time." He put his sunglasses back on and stood up. "Don't worry, I have my guys patrolling the area more. We also don't require a quarantine for newcomers in this town, but it would be nice if you stayed on the property." He handed her a card for the local grocery store. "Mrs. Murphy had a regular delivery set up since the beginning of this coronavirus stuff. I talked to them and they would be happy to continue it. Just give them a call tomorrow. And here is my card." He handed her his card and said, "Don't hesitate to call me if you need anything. Of course, I will keep you updated on your grandmother's case."

"Thank you, sheriff." She put the cards into her pocket and watched him walk back to his car and drive off.

Hillary took a deep breath and walked back to her SUV to grab her luggage. She locked the front door behind her and went into the kitchen, leaving her stuff in the living room. She had to make sure all the doors and windows were locked before she could get comfortable. "I might have to stay in a hotel tonight if I want to get any sleep."

The kitchen was fully stocked with food, but she still called for a pizza delivery. She checked that the back door and the windows were all locked. She just stared at the door to the basement as she ordered a ham and mushroom pizza, large of course, with a two liter bottle of Pepsi, and breadsticks. She thought about ordering a salad to feel healthier, but added onions to the pizza instead. Once she ended the call, she locked the basement door by using the little slide bolt and then pushed the wooden kitchen table up to it. "That should be safe enough." She headed up the stairs after checking the windows on the first floor. The windows were all locked upstairs, she saved Nana's bedroom for last. The room was dark with the curtains drawn, but it wasn't as messy as she expected. *They must have taken a lot of her stuff as evidence, they even took the mattress.* There was a pillow on the floor next to the bed frame, the flowered pattern made her think of her own grandparents. "I think all grandmothers like flowers." She left it leaning against the bed frame. Then she quickly checked those windows while saying a prayer. She closed the door afterwards and whispered, "Alfie might have to pack this room for his parents." She usually didn't feel superstitious or scared of ghosts, but she didn't want Nana to haunt her. Hillary ran downstairs and waited for the pizza delivery guy.

After eating a slice of pizza, she felt better. Hillary stretched out on the couch, and pulled out the cards the sheriff gave her. She saved the phone numbers for the sheriff and the grocery store on her phone, then called Alfie.

"Hi, hon, I made it to Nana's," she said, stifling a yawn and sitting up on the couch. "I didn't remember the house being this big."

"Yeah, I guess it's been a while since we were there. How was the drive?"

"It was fine, it was nice not having a lot of traffic. Maybe I can use this trip in an article for work. Something like 'Traveling in the Time of a Pandemic' or something." She reached for a green pillow that had fallen onto the floor and put it behind her back. "How was it at work? How was your day?"

"Oh, it was fine. Actually, it's kind of quiet." He took a breath. "We got to have a lunch break. The nurses were nice and got me a ham and Swiss sub."

"Oh, a sub? That was nice of them." She rolled her eyes. "Did you tell them a wrap was better, less carbs?"

"Hillary, don't." He was terse. "I don't like it when you get jealous."

"I know," she said with a sigh and put her feet up on the coffee table. "I didn't mean it like that. I think I'm just tired after all the driving. Then I didn't know what to expect when I got to the house."

"What did you think, that the house would be a wreck? I mean we were there a few years ago and you saw how she was." He laughed. "I mean she was kind of a neat freak. I could not even come into her house if I was covered in dirt or mud when I was a kid."

"I don't know." Hillary wasn't sure if she should tell him about the burglary over the phone. "But you're right. Nana was a neat freak, there really isn't much to clean. Not even any dust, so that's good." She smiled and hoped that he wouldn't ask too many questions.

"Was her bedroom bad?" Alfie asked quietly. "I think they cleaned up after they gathered all their evidence."

"Did you know about the burglary?" Hillary sat up straighter and looked out the front window. "Why didn't you tell me?" It was getting dark, so she couldn't see beyond the porch. She went over to the front door to make sure it was locked. Then she turned on the porch light. "I think I will keep the lights on 24/7, it's so dark out here. I don't know how she could live here alone. But I guess it wasn't spooky here, until she died." Hillary shivered. "I didn't remember how dark the woods were."

"No, Hillary, I didn't know about the burglary until the lawyer called me after you left the office. She forgot to tell you to not worry about the funeral home. They have their instructions after she is released from the coroner." He sighed. "I got to go, babe. I'll call you after my shift is done."

"Ok, love you. Bye." She held her breath and waited for him to say his part.

"Bye. Love you," he responded.

When her husband said those words, she still got butterflies. Hillary smiled and looked out the window before closing them for privacy. She surveyed the areas by the pine trees, then her SUV, and didn't see anything in the dark. She hugged herself and went back to the couch. "What would I do if he didn't love me anymore? I don't know." Hillary frowned and stretched out on the couch. She picked up the remote from the coffee table and another slice of pizza.

Nana Murphy's television was mounted on the wall in front of her and she turned it on. "Yay! Nana has cable!" She flipped through the menu and looked for a comedy. "Definitely, do not want any scary movies tonight." She was going to sleep on the couch tonight with the television on. "And probably the lights on. All of them."

She didn't sleep very well, because the couch wasn't as comfortable as it looked. The cushions were too stiff, and she preferred to sink into a cushion or mattress. She decided to turn off the lights in the living room and sat in Nana's chair. When she sat in the green recliner, she curled up under a fleece blanket and tried to focus on the movie. It took all her concentration to not listen for any strange sounds in the quiet house. Thankfully, there wasn't a lot of traffic to make her want to look at every vehicle passing by. "Or is that a bad thing? Maybe it would be better to have more people driving by the house?" Hillary shook her head. "The rules to being safe and not a victim of a crime are contradictory. It's just random. You are lucky or you're not." She pulled the fleece up to her chin and yawned. "Maybe I should pick another comedy for the next movie."

A snore woke her up and she felt weird not being home. "Was I dreaming?" She yawned and stretched. "I think I was having a bad dream." She looked around and saw Nana's living room lit up by the television. "Nope, not a dream. Nana is really dead, and I am really in her house. But I think I had a dream that I was upstairs. Was I in her room? I don't remember now." The view of the television from sitting in Nana's chair, was not straight on. So she returned to the couch and channel surfed. Hillary remembered that Nana would sit in the corner and read or do her knitting. Nana didn't really focus on the television, it was more like background noise. "Speaking of background noise…." She turned down the television and tried to sleep.

After a couple hours, she heard some creaks and noises that woke her up. There was a banging noise. "Was someone breaking in?" Those noises stopped when she sat up. Hillary wasn't scared until she thought she heard the sound of a doorknob rattling. "Okay, that's not the house settling." She turned on the lights in the living room and didn't see anything other than the furniture and her luggage. Then she went into the kitchen and listened for the sounds again, but heard only silence.

"Was that the back door?" Hillary looked out the kitchen windows and could only see the pine trees in the moonlight. The back door had a light over it, and she flipped it on. There was nothing and no one on the back steps. The patio furniture was under plastic tarp that would make rustling noises when the wind picked up. The screen door was closed from what she could see. "What was that noise?" She thought about calling the sheriff. "No, I don't want to be the girl who cried wolf. Just breathe. Just relax." She walked back into the living room and kept the lights on and her phone near her. "I'll just turn the television up louder."

The next day was hotter than the day before. She wore a tank top and gym shorts as she started packing up the items in the living room. First, she put photos and frames in boxes with photo albums and scrap-books. That was after she looked through some of the albums. One of the scrapbooks was full of newspaper clippings. When she was younger, she loved looking at her own family's pictures and hearing about her relatives. There were a few times when Nana showed her a few albums and pointed out Alfie's relatives. She remembered Nana telling her that family history was important to know.

*"Not that I want to scare you, but now that you're married to my Alfie, you should know about his blood." Nana pointed to a picture of three people. "This is me, my husband, and Alfie's dad." It was the last picture of the three of them, before Nana's husband passed away. "We never found him, but we think he had a heart attack when he went hunting." Nana didn't say any more but flipped through the album to show her one of Alfie's baby pictures. "He was always handsome. Babies are cute, but a lot of work." Nana held Hillary's hand. "Don't rush into having them until you are ready. I wish I had enjoyed my honeymoon more, it was such a short time for me."*

*Hillary nodded and said, "We are going to take it easy. We want to find the perfect house first, and it looks like he is going to get that job at the hospital he wanted."*

*"What's this scrapbook? It's just newspaper articles?" Hillary had asked Nana. "Wow, there were a lot of missing people."*

*Nana glanced at it. "I'm not sure about that, it might have been Pop's scrapbook or Alfie's. They both liked to read the paper. I thought it was odd for a little boy to like to read the paper, after I found out he wasn't just looking at the comics. But he was Pop's twin, and if Pop did something, then Alfie did it too."*

Hillary flipped through the scrapbook again and looked at the faces pictured. "So many young girls. Just so young and in their teens." She noticed the article about Pop, and then the newspaper clippings went to national news stories decades later. "So it looks like it is Alfie's book. What did Nana say about the missing girls? That they stopped after Pop died. So he either was the kidnapper or he stopped the kidnapper. But they never found his body or found two bodies. Then she would shrug." *But it was hard to tell if Nana was joking or not. She had a dry sense of humor.* After putting tape on the last box of picture frames, Hillary made her way to the fragile souvenirs Nana had acquired throughout her life. There were a few angels that she had collected and a lot of ceramic pigs. "She did love pigs for some reason." Hillary looked at a box full of them wrapped in old newspapers. She had left a crystal one out. "I think I will keep this one." Her mom liked crystal and it made her think of her mom's collection. "I think Aunt Mary got that when mama died."

After tackling the fragile items, she decided it was time to take a lunch break. She went into the kitchen and looked at the food the grocery store had delivered. There was bread, lunch meats, cheeses, and pickles, so she made herself two sandwiches and brought them out to the living room. She turned on the television and watched some true crime shows as she slowly ate her lunch. *It was a bright sunny day, there was no need to worry about a thief or murderer with locked doors and windows. No need to be afraid.* A few hours later, she was still watching how an adulterous man shot his pregnant wife. Hillary turned to another show, this time a funny sitcom. "Better get back to work. If I can get the downstairs done, then I will do some writing today. But maybe I shouldn't have watched the shows about murder. I think I need a palate cleanser." She had avoided going upstairs, but she thought she could get the other bedrooms done quickly. Also, she needed to clean that bathroom before she could take a much needed shower.

Two sitcoms turned into two more, then she put her dishes in the sink and finished off her glass of milk. She looked out the window and didn't see anything in the backyard. "Just trees, trees, and trees." She leaned closer to the window to search the perimeter of the property and exhaled when she didn't see anything. "Just some birds and white butterflies." She left the kitchen and went to the foot of the stairs.

Hillary took a deep breath and went upstairs. "I'm going to clean the bathroom first," she declared and went to work looking through the products Nana used. Her new lotions, soaps, and creams went into a box. Nana's makeup, brushes, and other personal items were put into the trash. After Hillary cleaned the sink, tub, and toilet, she worked on cleaning the floor and made her way into the hallway. She looked at Nana's closed door and exhaled. "I think I can do the guest rooms." She packed up the clothes and linens in the two guest rooms and the closets. Hillary kept the sheets on the bed in the room farthest from the master bedroom, she might sleep in that room tonight. "Maybe." She looked out of the window and looked at the driveway and her SUV. There was still nothing out of the ordinary on the property, and she felt safer.

After her shower, she felt refreshed but hungry. She was back in the living room and back on the couch. *Ha! Just like home.* She had the television on and was towel drying her hair and thinking about ordering another pizza. She didn't realize how late it was getting, it was already after eight so there weren't a lot of delivery options. She looked at the kitchen and didn't want to go near the basement door. Plus, she didn't feel like cooking anything. She finger combed her wavy hair and picked up her phone. She was going to see what other restaurants were in town.

*Screech… rattle, rattle. Bang!* came from the kitchen. "What the hell was that? Was someone trying to come in through the back door?" She froze, holding onto her phone, and tried to look into the dark kitchen. "You can't see anything from here, dummy. Come on, you have to go look." Slowly, she walked into the dark kitchen and saw that the back door was still closed. Hillary turned on the light to the back porch and saw nothing scurrying away looking out of the window.

She released her breath through pursed lips and took in a slow deep breath through her nose. "Calm down. See, there's nothing to be afraid of," she said. Then she turned around and screamed. She thought she heard footsteps. Hillary ran to the living room and looked at the stairs. There was no one there. The front door was still closed and locked. The living room was still empty and the television played a commercial for fried chicken. "I should make sure there's no one up there." She took a step toward the stairs when the doorbell rang.

"OMG! You gave me a heart attack." She opened the door for the sheriff after looking through the peephole.

"I'm sorry to disturb you, I just wanted to make sure everything was alright before I got off my shift tonight." He removed his hat. His blue eyes weren't covered by his sunglasses, and she could see how the job had aged him. His hair may not have been very thin yet, but he had bags under his eyes and few wrinkles on his forehead when he raised his eyebrows in concern for her.

"I'm okay, but I thought I heard some noises." She put her hand to her forehead. "I thought I heard someone go upstairs."

"And you are alone in the house?" He was looking up the stairs.

"Yes, I'm alone." She crossed her arms and let the sheriff come into the living room. She shut the door. "But I thought I heard someone go up the stairs."

He was looking around the living room and into the kitchen. "Do you want me to check it out?"

"Yes, I would feel better knowing there's no one else in here." She watched the sheriff check out the kitchen, then he looked into the half bathroom before climbing the stairs. Hillary listened to his footsteps as he went through all the rooms upstairs. He finished with the inspection, then returned to the living room.

"It is all clear." He grabbed his hat from the coffee table. "I didn't see anything up there. The windows are all locked too."

"Good, maybe it was something on the television." She turned it off and grabbed her purse. "I think I'm going to stay at a hotel tonight."

"I'll walk you to your vehicle," he said, opening the door.

"Thank you." She grabbed her suitcase and followed him outside. She let him help her with her luggage and looked around the house and the property. She didn't notice the windows on the lower level earlier, they would let someone climb into the basement if they were open. The closest window to her was obscured by a bush with a skateboard sticking out from under it. "Sheriff, did your men check out the basement when you were looking for the burglar?"

"Oh yes we did," he said, looking at the side of the house. "Yes, we did, but none of the windows were broken. So it doesn't look like that was the way they got into the house."

"Good, well, goodnight, sheriff." She climbed into her SUV and drove towards the gas station. "I'll gas up, then look for a hotel," she told herself.

The small motel that she passed on the way into town looked decent, and the rates were affordable. So she decided to stay for the week, then she would see how she felt. She laid down on the bed and hugged one of the pillows. She thought about calling her husband. "But I don't want to tell him I'm a chicken. Plus, he might not be happy with me spending money on a hotel room." She pushed her face into the white pillow and groaned. She turned onto her back. "I should have just stayed at home. I can't imagine the housing market is booming here." She sat up in the bed. "I haven't even done any work." Her cell phone vibrated on the nightstand next to the bed. She looked at the word "Hubby" on the screen. "I could ignore it. But would he keep calling because he's worried about me? I'm just not going to tell him what happened." She picked up the phone and cleared her throat before answering, "Hello."

"Hey, what's going on? Are you still packing up?" Alfie sounded breathless, "Did I call at a bad time?"

"No, I'm done for the night. I got a lot done, maybe I will be done by the end of the week." She took a deep breath, she was talking fast, and she didn't want him to hear she was nervous.

"Really? That's good."

*Did he sound surprised? If he didn't think I could handle the job, he shouldn't have asked me to do it. Stop it, Hillary, don't take your anger out on him.* She put him on speaker phone and started to braid her hair. "Yeah, it will give me time to just focus on work," she said, then exhaled. "I haven't been able to even look at my laptop since I got here. I was really hoping to be able to get a few articles done before the deadline hits."

"Well, it's only been a few days," he sounded caring, "You don't want to pressure yourself. You know it doesn't help you."

She rolled her eyes, then smiled. "I know. Actually, maybe I will try to do some work before bed. So I'm going to let you go. Okay? Yeah, I'll just talk to you later."

"Okay. Good night," he replied.

She just ended the call. "Was that rude?" She thought about how she would feel if he just hung up on her and typed:

*Sorry, I just had a good idea for an article and have to write it down right now.*

She shook her head and deleted it to type:

*Sorry! Have an idea that I need to write or will forget. XX*

"Hit send," she said, putting her phone back onto the nightstand. Hillary stretched out and lay back down on the bed to watch television. She found one of the true crime shows she would watch in bed whenever she stayed at a hotel. Hillary would do that when she was home alone at night. Alfie did not like those shows and would say, "These shows are so morbid. Then they always make the husband out to be the bad guy." She would laugh at him and say, "Well, if they kill their wife, they are the bad guy."

Hillary punched the pillow and put it under her head. "I don't need him to tell me about my process. I know how to write an article, and I don't miss my deadlines." She hugged the pillow and said, "There aren't any deadlines when you're a freelancer. You can do whatever you want. That's why I'm up here, cleaning out a dead woman's house. I'm not even a writer right now. I'm a housekeeper." She wiped her eyes. "I don't tell him how to be a doctor or a good grandson." Hillary exhaled and looked at her darkened phone screen. "I'm too tired to write anyway."

*Hillary was dreaming and was back in Nana's house. She recognized the oak wood vanity in Nana's bedroom, as she lay down in Nana's bed. She felt constricted by the blue floral comforter and sheets that were on her body. She was able to loosen the light blue cotton sheets enough to free her arms. She looked over to her right and next to her in the bed was Nana Murphy. "Alfie sleeps on that side too Nana," she whispered. Nana was lying still, only her brown eyes twinkled in the dark as she looked around her room. Then there were noises just past the bed posts, and she stopped moving as someone entered the master bedroom. Then the black shape started opening drawers to the dresser and searched for any valuables. The shape was a man, and he moved to rifle through the stuff on the vanity and knocked over the jewelry box. It was full of mostly costume jewelry, but there were a few gold and silver pieces. Nana gasped when he knocked over some bottles and a glass bottle shattered. She covered her mouth and tried to make herself smaller and invisible in the large bed, but when the man in black turned around, he saw her. The man set down his black backpack and walked over to the bed.*

*"Stop. Don't come any closer. Please don't hurt me." She covered herself with the comforter. "I didn't see you. You can still leave. I won't tell anyone."*

*The man came closer and said, "I'm not going to hurt you, Nana." Hillary saw that he had a small orange syringe in his hand.*

*"Alfie, what are you doing here?" Nana sat up in bed, "I thought you were home. Is there a problem with your parents or with your wife?"*

*"No, I just had to see you." He kneeled next to her and took her arm. "I love you, Nana." He poked Nana's arm and pushed the plunger down.*

*"What is that?" Nana Murphy tried to bat his hand away, but the needle had pricked her arm. "I don't need a shot." She slumped and he helped her lie back down. Her lips moved and she slurred, "What was that? Alfie, I don't feel good."*

*"Just insulin," he said as he tucked her in and smoothed her hair. "Shhhh, now you look peaceful. It won't be too much longer."*

*"Alllfieee," she said as she tried to move, but he kept his hands on her.*

*"If you won't stay still, I'll have to use the pillow." He held her down and she just closed her eyes. The tears fell down her cheeks.*

Hillary woke up because of the wetness she felt on her pillow. She wiped her tears as she sobbed. "Oh my God. Did he kill Nana? Could he kill Nana?" After a few minutes, she went into the bathroom and splashed cold water on her face. She cupped her hands to drink some of the tap water. "Oh, I think I'm going to puke." She crumbled onto the floor and curled up to hug her legs to her body. Her eyes were closed tightly and saw her husband's face hovering over Nana's. "Did Alfie watch her die?"

Hillary parked in front of Nana's little white house and stared at the red door. "I definitely have the creepy crawlies. But it was just a dream. I am just imagining things, and I've watched so many scary movies. But there are no such things as ghosts. I watch too many murder mysteries, and it's always the husband. But Alfie isn't the murderer. He's not her husband. Why would he kill his own grandmother?" She unlocked the red door and walked in. "He did it for the money, of course." She shook her head. "Okay, it's eleven now. I'll just go upstairs and check the room. Then I'll go back to the motel. Evidence or no evidence." She locked the door before walking up the stairs, then took a deep breath. The sheriff left the master bedroom door open last night, but it was still dark in there with all the curtains still closed. Hillary had kept the curtains closed from day one. "I don't know if it's bad juju to have open curtains or not when someone dies. But better to be safe than sorry. Or is it something about mirrors?" Hillary closed her eyes. "No, stop it. You're not that superstitious, and you don't know all the things you do for death rituals. It's okay. Okay, let's go." She walked up to the door and looked into the room.

It was the same as the first day, and she had not gone in the room to pack it up or clean during her first days there. This would be the second time she walked into the room and stood in front of the bed. "This is where the man stood and saw her looking at him. This is where Alfie stood." She closed her eyes and shook her head. "Focus. Okay, if he did shoot her with insulin, how would I prove it?" She looked to her left and saw a small white wastebasket. Hillary kneeled down and looked into the white plastic store bag that lined the wastebasket. It was full of tissues and she pulled the small white wastebasket towards her and away from the wall. When it moved forward, she saw a small orange syringe behind it. "Oh my God, oh my God." She fell backwards and sat on the floor, bumping into the bedframe. "It's just right there. What do I do?"

She pulled out her phone and took a picture of it, then replaced the wastebasket. Took another picture of the wastebasket in the room. She then texted the sheriff:

*I was looking in Nana's room, and when I moved this to clean the trash out of it… I saw the needle.*

She hit send with the two pictures she took.

*I just put the wastebasket back on it and I'm going to leave the room alone. I don't know if it is evidence, but I don't think she needed shots.*

She sent that text, then typed:

*I never saw her give herself shots when I visited her.*

Hillary left the bedroom and shut the door behind her. "It was a habit for him to just throw out the trash." She leaned against the door and whispered, "I found evidence that it was a murder. Alfie killed his grandmother. Oh my God, I'm married to a murderer."

She went down the stairs and looked at her phone, it was already five o'clock. "How did that happen?" She didn't have any missed calls or texts, but that wasn't unusual. Her husband really didn't call her much during the day. Then she did tell him that she wanted to write. "I should just go to get some food." She turned to look into the kitchen and froze.

The kitchen table had been pushed away from the basement door. She walked slowly into the kitchen and didn't see anyone in the kitchen. The basement door was shut and the slide bolt lock was hanging by a screw. "Someone was inside the basement," she whispered. Hillary took a picture of the basement door and looked around the door. The only damage was to the lock and where the table was against the door. The table left a dent and the kitchen floor had some dirt on the linoleum. *More clues, more evidence. I will call the sheriff when I get to the motel. No, when I'm in my car.* When she turned around to leave, she bumped into Alfie and screamed.

"Hey, hey, hey, it's me." He hugged her and petted her head with his gloved hands.

"Alfie? What are you doing here?" She looked up at his face and asked, "How long have you been here?"

"I got the weekend free and thought I would surprise you." He kissed her. "I just got here. Plus, if we can get this done, we can just relax during that week I have off." He kissed her again. "Would that sound like fun? A week together? Especially after how crazy the last few months have been."

"Sure." She pushed him away and looked at him. "But isn't it weird to be thinking about a romantic week together, here in your dead grandmother's house?" Hillary watched his eyes darken, so she smiled. "Sorry, I didn't mean to be a downer. I'm just hungry. I was thinking about making some dinner, are you hungry?" She looked around at the empty kitchen, and she remembered that she packed up the kitchen a couple days ago. The plates, pots, pans, and utensils were in boxes in the living room. "Maybe we can get take out or go to a restaurant."

"Dinner? Didn't you eat already?" Alfie looked at his watch and said, "It's after eight."

"What? How could it be so late already?" She looked at her phone and it displayed 8:04 PM. Hillary unlocked her phone and sent the picture of the basement door with the broken lock to the sheriff. "I thought it was like six or something."

"Silly goose." He smiled and said, "It is dark out already." He looked at his phone that had buzzed in his jeans pocket.

She went into the living room and looked out the window. "I packed up almost everything important." She pointed at the boxes in the corner. "These are all the pictures, albums, and a scrapbook I found." She didn't see his black sedan in the driveway. "Where did you park?"

"Oh, I parked by the garage," he stood behind her and said, "It's just hard to see because it's dark outside. Maybe you should get your eyes checked, honey. When was the last time you had them checked?"

She turned to look at him and smiled. "I don't remember." She stepped away from him and felt him watching her as she walked toward the kitchen again. She turned to look at him again and noticed he was wearing a black sweater and jeans. *Why is he wearing a sweater, it's June. Is it that cold outside? I have never seen him wear that sweater before, but it looks familiar. Oh my God, he wears it in the dream.*

She shivered and flipped the light switch on that lit up the stairs and upstairs hallway. "I have been leaving some lights on, so the house doesn't look empty." She sounded nervous, "Hopefully, no one else tries to break in or something. I don't want to run into any bad guys."

"You shouldn't be scared of that, I'm here to protect you." He beckoned her to come to him. "I've missed you. Have you missed me?"

She fell into his arms. "Yes, of course. But it still feels creepy. I mean someone else was in here. They violated this place, I feel like they robbed me."

"Yeah." He let her go.

"Yeah, I mean I cared for Nana too. She was always nice to me." Hillary turned to pick up her keys from the coffee table when she felt something hit her head from behind. She fell forward and her body hit the table. She rolled onto the floor, the breath was knocked out of her. She landed on her side and tried to catch her breath. She looked at Alfie with a baseball bat held over his head and she rolled under the coffee table to get out of the way.

He lowered the bat and tilted his head in a way that used to be endearing to her. He said in his condescending voice, "You know, Hillary, I think you're smart, but you have a bad poker face." He grabbed her arm and pulled her out from under the coffee table. "How did you figure it out?"

"What are you talking about?" She gasped and tried to stop him from dragging her into the kitchen by grabbing the rug Nana had in the living room. It only succeeded in moving the coffee table and Nana's recliner towards her. Her legs were being dragged over the rug, then the hardwood floors. Her exposed skin was burning, but her gym shorts made it easy for Alfie to pull her across the floor towards the kitchen. She had to stop him, he was going to hurt her. She was not going to go into the kitchen, or worse, the basement. The dark, dirty, spider-filled basement. *I hate basements.* She began to scratch at his wrist, above his black leather gloves. *Who wears gloves in the summertime? Killers do!*

"You texted me the picture of the syringe." He tossed the bat that he had hit her with. "I think I'm going to use something else on you."

*Dammit Hillary! You text your killer husband and not the sheriff. Of course you do, it's 2020.*

She couldn't lessen his grip on her arm, the scratches weren't slowing his progress down. *Damn him for working out! I knew I should have started lifting weights more. I should have known if he wasn't working out to cheat on me, he was working out to kill me!* She pulled herself up closer to him as they crossed the threshold of the kitchen and onto the cool yellow linoleum floor. She looked up at her husband, he had stopped to scan the counter for the block of knives. *Who am I kidding, he probably is cheating on me.* She took advantage of the pause to bite into the unprotected outside flesh of his arm.

"Shit!" He screamed and grabbed her hair, pulling her off his right arm. "You stupid bitch!" He growled, grabbing her throat with his wounded arm and starting to choke her. "I guess you're right, I am the bad guy."

She just smiled her bloody smile and struggled to catch her breath. She kept fighting and scratched his face and tried to kick him off her. He shifted his weight to keep her legs down and used both hands to choke her. His arms were longer than hers, so she could not reach his face anymore. Hillary was losing her strength as she lost consciousness and used the last of it to scratch at his bite wound. Fresh blood flowed down his arm, and he had to readjust his grip on her neck.

He watched her face turn red and banged her head against the floor. "You stupid bitch," he kept saying through clenched teeth. Her eyes rolled up and fluttered closed. "Finally." He banged her head against the floor one last time before letting her go. Alfred sat back and watched his wife lying there, she didn't move. Once he caught his breath, he jumped up and went to the sink to rinse his wounds.

"She bit me. She fucking bit me. Shit!" He watched the blood dilute in the water and go down the drain. He started to feel the sting of the other scratches on his wrist and face. He grabbed the chrome toaster from the counter top. He looked at two scratches on his left cheek in the reflection. "Dammit." He turned his face to look at the scratches closer. "It might not be too bad, I am a doctor and can take care of myself." He laughed, saying, "Or Candy will patch me up. She likes my pretty face. Plus, we have to wear masks now. No one will notice any bandages."

He paused when he heard a noise, he inspected the background reflected in the chrome toaster and didn't see anything. He set it down on the counter and turned off the faucet. He saw some blood droplets on the countertop. "I'll have to look for some bleach." He laughed again and said, "The smell of bleach won't look suspicious in a house for sale during a pandemic. This is just perfect." He took a breath and turned around. "Well, almost perfect. What am I going to do with you?"

His face fell when he didn't see Hillary laying on the kitchen floor. First his anger flared up, "Where the hell is she?" Then he smiled and mused, "Maybe this will be fun. She did mess up my face." He opened the kitchen drawers where he remembered grabbing utensils his whole life, "It was my job to set the table." The drawer was empty, he went to the next one. "Empty." They were all empty. "Where would they be?" He didn't bring a knife with him.

"Alfred Duncan Murphy," Hillary scolded from the doorway, "You are making a mess of my kitchen. Never mind the mess you made of my life."

He spun around and saw his wife in the doorway, her head was hanging down, her hair covering her face. Her arms were spread out, blocking his escape out of the kitchen. "Hillary? What are you doing?" He started to walk towards her, he could just have to use his hands, or get the baseball bat from the living room.

She spoke again, her voice husky from being strangled, "Alfred Duncan Murphy, you dare come into my house and disrespect me."

"What are you talking about Hillary? This isn't your house. It's going to be mine."

"Oh, was that your plan? Kill me and get my house and my money." She started to laugh.

"I will kill you, Hillary. Yes, and I will get everything because I am your husband."

"I am not Hillary," she said, raising her head and glared at him with bloodshot blue eyes. She winked and smiled, before saying, "I am your grandmother. You coward. You sneak into my house and murder me in the dead of night!"

"I didn't hit your head hard enough, Hill." He moved closer to her and said, "But I can make it all better. You won't be crazy, if you're dead."

Hillary dropped her arms down and he saw the light flash off the knife blades she held in each hand. She flew towards him and elbowed her way between his arms. Alfie tried to grab her by the neck and she kneed him in the groin. He bent over and she stuck one knife into his chest, then the second knife. She held the blades horizontally, so they wouldn't get resistance from the ribs. She used all her strength to push the sharpened blades through his sweater, skin, muscles, and into his lungs. Hillary didn't need to be a doctor to read Alfie's anatomy books. *Plus, everyone knows where the lungs are and that knives are sharp.* He stumbled back and coughed up blood. He fell onto the kitchen floor. She put a foot between the blades and pulled the knives out.

"I loved you Alfie, I took care of you. I gave up so much for you." She watched him push himself away from her on the kitchen floor. Hillary looked around. "Okay, you're right. You're always right, dammit." She leaned forward and said, "I am not Nana, but I didn't know if I was going to actually be able to do it." Hillary sighed and continued, "But it looks like you're going to die. You deserve it, but I do feel bad that I didn't tell you what Nana told me. But Nana knew that I liked murder mysteries, and I know you don't." She watched Alfie's eyes narrow. "I looked into the missing persons cases and didn't tell you about my suspicions about your grandfather, because I saw him in you. I was afraid that you were going to be like him." She set one large kitchen knife onto the kitchen table. "I had to watch you, after I figured out that he may have hurt some girls. Do you remember the newspapers talking about those missing girls that summer? I found the scrapbook with those articles." She looked at the knife covered in Alfie's blood. "That was your scrapbook, wasn't it Alfie? You are just like him." Hillary shook her head before continuing, "But like Nana, I am a jealous person. I cannot abide infidelity, and you have girlfriends. I know you do!" She gripped the knife in her right hand. "I watched you, thinking you were good and not bad. But thankfully, my eyes have been opened."

She walked over to Alfred, avoiding the growing puddle of blood and his moving hands. "They didn't even know that you are a murderer." She raised her head up and laughed, before saying, "Ha! I thought it was a random break in. But then I saw the basement window. I saw your old skateboard by the bushes. You really don't like to get dirty. You said to me and Nana to use the skateboard when gardening. You said it was easier on the knees and you will stay off the dirt. I also remembered that a skateboard or any tools wouldn't be left in the bushes after weeding. Nana was a neat freak." Hillary waved the knife in the air. "A place for everything, and everything in its place." She kneeled down. "So, then I had to think if you were a murderer. Would you come back to me because you loved me or hated me? But it looks like you're a cheating, murdering, greedy man." She took the knife and sliced his throat.

Alfie stopped moving when the gasping and gurgling stopped. Then the blood stopped flowing, and she took a deep breath. "It's done. It's over." She stood up and stepped back. Hillary placed the second knife on the table and fell into the kitchen chair. Her neck burned and her head was throbbing. She looked at Alfie and cried saying, "It's over."

# I'm Going Home

## Carol Allen

"I'm going home!" Martin walked through the apartment towards the kitchen. His black fleece and his shoes were already on, so all he needed were his keys.

"What are you talking about? You are home." Ashley was sitting on the couch looking at her cellphone. She didn't look at Martin when he walked past her.

Martin shook his head and paused at the kitchen counter. "I can't do this anymore."

"What? I just asked you what you wanted for dinner." She finally looked up at him, her brown eyes met his own darker brown ones. Her smile fell when she saw he was dressed for going out. Just twenty minutes ago, he had been wearing sweats like her. With the threat of snow, Ashley wanted to stay home. "It's just so cold outside." She put on her white and pink house slippers and his grey sweatshirt. Then she sat on the couch and covered up with a fleece blanket she kept on the couch for under twenty degree days like this. She vetoed Martin's suggestion of going downtown, to the diner they liked. "A pizza sounds good, and we haven't had it in a while. Why don't we just stay in? Did you just want the Supreme with a salad or something else?"

"I'm sorry, but I can't look at your face anymore." He put his blue beanie on over his sandy brown hair, moving his hair out of his eyes.

"What the fuck did you say?" She stood up, her black braid flipped over her shoulder as she strode over to the kitchen counter. She pointed her finger at him. "What the fuck is that supposed to mean?"

"I'm leaving. It's over." He grabbed his duffel bag and left his apartment key on the counter. He looked at Ashley and said, "I just don't love you anymore."

He walked out of the apartment and shrugged.

*Maybe it was a little dramatic, but I've wanted to break up with her for a while now. She just didn't pick up on any of the clues. She didn't support me. She made fun of me. I'm going to die, and she just called me a hypochondriac.*

Martin got into his green sedan and drove out of the city. He exhaled as he drove up the ramp onto the highway. He felt free.

*No (annoying) girlfriend, no (small) apartment, no (boring) job. What kind of office has a Halloween party? They didn't have a Christmas party. No one wants to hang out at the office around the holidays. But how professional is a Halloween party? How can you work with someone after seeing them dancing in their costumes? Then there's the alcohol, and having the temp as the psychic. No one wants to see their co-workers drunk. Now, here it is the end of January, and the receptionist is talking about doing something for Valentine's Day. I mean, are we in elementary school? Do we need to have a formal every season?*

Martin didn't hate his job, it was just an office job, and he was responsible for data input. Good Ole Marty just didn't see himself doing that for the rest of his life. What was left of his life, just a few more hours or days or weeks or months? It could be years, but he didn't want to think about that right now.

*Stupid Halloween party. Why did they have a fortune teller?*

At the gas station, he walked around the car, to go into the convenience store, and thought his tires looked good. He almost got a cherry slush drink for Ashley. It was her favorite, any time of year, but he wasn't going back to her. Ashley had wanted to go to visit her parents in a few weeks, but he didn't want to spend his whole vacation in the mountains. Skiing didn't impress him, so he never bought the plane ticket.

***

"You can die in an avalanche, or even fall off the ski lift. Did you see that story in the news? You can even get mauled by a bear," he argued with Ashley.

"Bears are hibernating right now, Marty." She rolled her eyes. "Plus, no one fell off the ski lift, I think they were hanging onto it and were rescued."

"Okay, so they don't fall and die. But do you think you could hold onto the bench and just dangle until you get to safety? I don't think I could just hang there for fifteen minutes or whatever."

"You could do it, and you would help me. You wouldn't let me fall."

"Do you know how much harder it is to grab something when you're wearing gloves or mittens? It would be game over! I'm not going skiing." He crossed his arms. "We might not even make it to the airport. There could be a snow storm, and we can't drive or the plane can't take off. There could be a blizzard on the mountain."

"They are well prepared for winter weather since they are in the mountains." She tried to reassure him. "Look, I booked the flight for February, you know it's when I usually go to my parents' house." She hugged him. "Plus, there are other things to do in Colorado than skiing."

***

He lived in the same state as his parents, but it was about a four-hour-drive in bad weather. So it had been a while since he had gone to his parents' house, but he was now the trifecta of jobless, homeless, and single. "So not a lot of options," he muttered at his phone, it was full of texts from Ashley and missed calls. She didn't deserve him being an asshole to her. He texted, "I'm sorry."

The bad luck and the worrying got worse after that office Halloween party. Ashley couldn't go with him to it, but insisted that he go. "Have fun and get to know your co-workers. We should, like, socialize more. I feel like we only hang out with my friends. Don't you have any friends?"

"Of course I have friends." He looked at his phone and silenced the video he was watching about the local news. "But we have been dating for so long that our friends are our friends."

"I think you should have your own friends." She pursed her lips. "I have my own friends, and you should have some fun."

Martin thought about turning the phone off to preserve the battery, since he wasn't sure if he packed the charger. He decided against it and went into the convenience store for some water and energy drinks. It'll take another three hours to get home, and he could look for a charger in the glove compartment. That would be plenty of time to charge the phone. He picked up two cans of flavored energy drinks. He wasn't sleepy now, but he knew it would be hard, that last hour. That last hour was always the hardest, longest part of the drive home.

He got back on the road, and cracked open the window for the cold, fresh night air. Martin was thankful for the clear roads and little traffic. He was thinking about the last few years as he followed the curves of the highway, and the choices he had made. Maybe he should have majored in just business or computer information systems instead of just a liberal arts degree. He could be a boss now instead of looking for another entry level job. He took a drink of one of the energy drinks.

"But be a boss of what? What kind of business would I want to start right now? Even if I had the money to start a company, what would I even want to do?"

He shook his head, college can teach you a lot of things, but not how to be lucky. The snowflakes started falling and his attention was brought back to the present.

"Great. It isn't slippery yet. Maybe I won't get the worst of the snow." He looked up to the sky and saw the white flakes drift down. "Yeah, maybe I'll be home before the roads really get bad. Maybe I can stay ahead of it. Then I won't hit black ice, slide off the road, and drive into a drift. Then I won't die of hypothermia or dehydration or lack of food, because they can't find my car for days."

Martin shivered and rolled the window closed to keep the warmth in the car. He drank more of the flavored energy drink. Then he slapped his face. "Don't want to fall asleep driving. Got to stay awake. Still got hours of driving ahead of me." He shook his head. "Got to stop thinking negatively." He slapped his face again. "Thinking about how I die won't help me get home safer."

***

After driving for about two hours, Martin stopped for what he hoped was the last gas up for the night. The snow was coating the roads, but it didn't feel unsafe yet. His phone had been screen down on the passenger seat and charging for the last few hours. He unplugged it and checked his texts, then listened to the voicemails. He deleted the messages that Ashley left. They were just sad, and then she got angrier and angrier. There was one message that wasn't from Ashley, but he didn't want to listen to it, so he pushed the end button.

He got a coffee with cream at this stop to warm up a little. Thanks to the first energy drink, he still wasn't tired. He was trying to remember the last time he was home as he waited for the coffee to cool before he took a drink. "I don't need to burn my tongue, and go to the ER for first- or second- degree burns."

*When was the last time I went to my parents' house? Was that before we had moved into the apartment? Has it really been that long?*

***

He went to college in the city, and it was easy to stay there afterwards. There were a lot of job opportunities for students and graduates. He should have done an internship first, but Ashley was going through her post graduate program. So he couldn't pick the lower paying internship and take care of their bills. She was still a student and didn't have a lot of money or time. He couldn't have left the city, if he wanted to stay with her. "How long did I date Ashley?" He didn't remember when they started to be a couple, he met her a week after classes started freshman year. Then they were just together, until tonight, when he left her.

He remembered her staring at him across the lecture hall. Marty was surprised by how bright her eyes were for brown eyes. They were warm, and he couldn't stop staring at her until she winked at him. His cheeks burned, but he smiled and walked over to sit next to her. It was the bravest he felt, and she did make him feel brave. Was that why he loved her? He frowned.

***

"Why am I going home tonight?" He pulled off the highway and grabbed his phone. He looked at the missed calls, a lot of them were from Ashley. Then after he left, he had a missed call from his parents. "Probably mom." But before all those calls, there was an unknown number. The last voicemail was from that unknown number. Martin called voicemail to listen to it, and he heard the man's voice telling him to call the office to make an appointment to go over his test results.

"Is this how I die? Did they find cancer, a blood disease, or the level of cholesterol is so high that I'm going to have a stroke or heart attack, like, tomorrow?"

***

He ended the call and pulled back onto the highway. This was the last hour of the drive, and the snow covered the lanes completely. He had to concentrate and wasn't sure if he was staying in the right lane. He drove slower and had to squint to see where the white lines were buried under the drifting snow.

"I'm just guessing where the lane is. Okay Marty, just stay between the trees. Jesus, good thing the ditches are deep here. I just have to stay between the ditches. Okay, there's a few tire tracks to follow."

***

Martin was trying to focus on the road and not think about how afraid he was of the test results. Martin was almost thirty and was worried about his health, so he went to get his annual physical. But the doctor had said that everything seemed fine, "Marty, you could lose some weight with your family history of heart disease and diabetes. But so could we all, am I right? I mean, it's a struggle for me to even get to the gym." The doctor cleared his throat and said he would do bloodwork, it looked like he should look at his cholesterol since it was higher at his last visit. His doctor had suggested, "Maybe it was time to try some medication? But we'll see what the numbers are first."

"That stupid Halloween party. It got me scared, and I've just been waiting to die. I should have choked on a piece of candy and just died then and there." He exhaled. "If I had a peanut allergy, I definitely would have died. There were so many nut based candies there."

***

The alcohol and snacks were in the breakroom under fake cobwebs and spiders and other decorations that were choking hazards. The Halloween themed music played throughout the office complex and the maze of cubicles was decorated with scarecrows, maize, a few stuffed crows, and straw. He wasn't sure if he had an allergy to hay, or if he was getting a sinus infection, or maybe the flu, and felt his eyes water. He looked for some tissues at someone's desk, when he saw there was a fortune teller set up in the manager's office. He didn't want to go in there either, it was decorated in scarves and mood lighting. He didn't believe in psychics anyways. What could she tell him? Where he will be in five years? Probably in the same cubicle he was in and doing the same spreadsheets on market performance. He took a drink of beer from his red cup. "Dear God, help me," he whispered as he walked around the office. Martin avoided the conference room full of the diehard Halloween enthusiasts made up of dancing ghosts, witches, and masked creatures.

"I am not going to wear a costume," Martin told Ashley before she left the apartment. He was buttoning up his plaid patterned shirt. "I'm just going to wear normal clothes."

"You're no fun sometimes." She stuck her tongue out at him. "Come here," Ashley used some of her eye makeup to give him a black eye. "There, you need something to get you into the spirit of Halloween. I still think you should wear the mask." She held up the wolf mask that he had from last year. She was going to a party with her friends and was wearing the Little Red Riding Hood costume from last year. "It would be nice if you would still be my big bad wolf."

"But it's so stuffy in there," he said, pushing it away. "I could suffocate or trip and fall. The eye holes are not very good. The rubber stinks too. I might be allergic to it. Didn't I get hives the last time I wore it?"

She laughed and said, "Okay, don't wear the mask. I don't want you to hurt yourself. I'll see you later tonight then." They kissed and she pushed him away laughing. "Don't smudge my lipstick!" She then gave him one last kiss and a wink before opening the door.

"There's lipstick on me, isn't there?" he yelled as she waved goodbye.

"Leave it, it looks hot!" she yelled before she shut the door.

In the bathroom, he shook his head and said, "Halloween or not, I am not going out like this." He washed his face and scrubbed off the makeup.

Martin was not the only person who did not dress up for the office party, and he tried to talk to those normal co-workers. He found out they were either too drunk to have a conversation, or they only talked about their job. He finished his beer and tried to listen to the mundane conversation. He wasn't getting a buzz from the beer, he had to decide to keep drinking or to leave the party as soon as he could.

*No, I don't want to drink too much. Or I could keep drinking and get embarrassingly drunk. Maybe I would have fun then or die from alcohol poisoning. If I don't die, then I would have to call a taxi to get home. Or I could get a ride from a co-worker, but I could get kidnapped or murdered by them because they are a secret serial killer. Maybe I get mugged as I leave this building, because I'm an easy target and stumbling around. Or I fall down the stairs and break my neck. I could get stuck in the elevator and not be able to leave until Monday morning. No, I'm just going to stop drinking. I'm going to go home as soon as I can. I won't tell Ashley that I was home by eleven. Yeah, she doesn't need to know that. But I want to be there when she comes home anyways.*

Martin walked away from the boring co-workers to get some water to drink. He threw out his red cup of beer and headed towards the breakroom. He went past the manager's office, when a woman wearing a black eye patch beckoned him. She looked like the redhead from the temp service that started two weeks ago. Martin nodded. "Hi, you're Cindy, right?"

She shook her scarf-covered head and said, "Tonight, I am Madam Gemini." She fanned out a deck of Tarot cards. "Do you wish to have your fortune told? Your palm read?" She put the cards in her pocket and snapped. "Do you want to know your future?"

He eyed her gold medallion and her long purple dress. "Oh, you're the fortune teller and not a pirate."

"This eye is my knowing eye. I only use it when I want to see what needs to be seen." She got close to his face. "I know you are afraid of germs, so I do have hand sanitizer, if you will step into my office."

He followed her into the manager's office. The large illuminated crystal ball in the middle of a white cloth covered table in the corner of the office caught his eye. Some staff meetings were conducted in this office, when there were just four or five people required for a project. The Madam tried to cover up the corporate features of the office with many multicolored scarves hanging over framed certificates and awards and over the few lamps in the room. The computer speakers on the manager's desk played some ambient music. Madam Gemini sat down in a tan leather office chair behind the crystal ball. Martin was offered the other chair and some hand sanitizer. He rubbed his hands together and handed the bottle back to her. She also used some hand sanitizer before putting the bottle away.

She rubbed her hands together. "You can never be too careful. It is cold and flu season."

"Yes, it is." He cleared his throat and suppressed the need to cough.

"Plus, I like the smell of the alcohol." She laughed and said, "I know it's weird."

He shrugged and asked, "So, what do I have to do for this?"

Madam Gemini set her Tarot cards onto the table, next to the crystal ball. "Well, the crystal ball is more or less for decoration. I can read Tarot cards and palms. What do you prefer?"

"I think I will stick with palm reading." He placed his hands onto the table. "I mean, our hands are now sanitized. I am not really afraid of germs, but I do try to stay healthy. I try to work out."

"Sure, sure." She waved her hands over his palms and closed her eye. She hummed for a few seconds then said, "It is okay." Her hands circled above his and he felt a vibration in his fingertips as her hands got closer to his.

*Am I feeling her body heat? Must be. There's no such thing as psychic energy.*

She stopped moving, and he focused on her painted red fingernails. She opened her eye and placed her hands on the table in front of her. "Okay, we can start. Hold your dominant hand out." She held his right hand. "You have an odd life line. It's segmented, like you've had a lot of lives."

Her fingers caressed his palm, tracing all the lines. It tickled and he tried to pull his hand back. Now he was feeling the buzz of the beer and wanted to end the palm reading. She just held onto his hand and said, "It is okay Marty, don't fight the reading."

Martin asked, "Okay, I'll bite. A lot of lives? Like a cat?"

"More like past lives," she mumbled. Then she looked up at him with her brown eye and asked, "Do you have odd memories? Feelings of having done things before or been places before?"

He shrugged and asked, "Doesn't everyone have that?"

"Sure," she said and she looked at his palm again. "There are a lot of people who believe in reincarnation." She smiled. "It's nice to know that you don't really die, but that you come back." She sat up straighter. "I'm going to use my seeing eye." She flipped up her black eye patch, exposing her right eye, and she gasped. "Do you see that man there?" She pointed past Martin and towards the office door.

Martin slowly turned to look behind him and said, "There's no one there. I don't see anybody." He turned back to Madam Gemini. "This is getting too heavy. I don't want to do this anymore."

"Were you ever in the hospital Martin? For a procedure, no, an operation?"

He nodded. "Just to get my appendix removed."

"This man says that you almost died." Her body shook. "He said you were very sick."

"I don't know about that, I was just a kid. But I got an infection." He closed his eyes. "I remember my mom was crying after the surgery."

"You are being offered a great honor. The man in black will tell you when or how." She grabbed his hands and repeated, "When or how?"

"When? What does that mean?" He looked around the office and still did not see anyone else in the room.

"He is holding up three fingers, then one finger," she whispered. "Three. One." She looked at Martin, "You will die around a thirty-one."

"Thirty-one what? Days or months or years?"

"The man is gone." She sat back in the chair and closed her eyes. "That doesn't happen often." When she opened her brown eyes again, they were watering. "I'm not really experienced in palm reading, and I don't get visions very often." She sat up and grabbed his left hand. "I see a good life line on this hand. I think it means that you have a chance." She pointed to his palm and said, "See, it is unmarked." She stood up and moved to stand in front of him. "It's not my place to say this, but a lot of people believe in fate. Whatever you do from here on out, do it with purpose. I think that we all have free will."

Martin rubbed his hands together and stood up to leave. He said, "Okay, good advice."

Madam Gemini kissed his cheek. "Everything is of consequence. Maybe you can succeed or not. It has to be done with no regrets." She started to chant and made a symbol on his forehead with her thumb. "A charm for protection." Then she made a symbol on his right cheek and said, "One for insight." The last symbol was made on his left cheek. "And one for strength." She kissed her gold medallion and warned, "For you are now a marked man."

"Okay, thank you." Martin turned and left the office.

***

*That was the worst day of my life. All I could think of is this how I die? I don't even believe in psychics. But when I asked mom about my appendix, she said that I almost died from an infection. Of course, that has to be why I'm afraid of hospitals, doctors, and of dying. Everyone is afraid of death though, that has to be normal. Or everyone would be adrenaline junkies and risk takers.*

"After that party, I spent a lot of time thinking of different ways I could die. Suffocated by a pillow, falling asleep while cooking, and then a fire starts. Or I could be killed by a hitchhiker. All highly unlikely, but there's West Nile disease, lead poisoning, heat stroke, or a dog attack. Almost everyone has a dog these days. Electrocution; we use so many electronics. I could drown in a bathtub. I could be hit by a bus." He shook his head. "When will I die? He only said thirty-one, it wasn't seconds, minutes, or hours. It wasn't thirty-one days, so now we wait. It could be thirty-one months. Then, I'm almost thirty-one years old." He looked at the digital clock above his car's radio and it was 11:31 PM. "Great, is it going to happen on the half hour? I think that clock isn't right, is it too fast?" He gripped the steering wheel. "I'm almost home." The snow was falling faster and visibility was getting worse. Martin could feel the sedan fishtail when he took a curve too fast. He slowed down and turned on his hazards. "I don't want to get into an accident tonight. Oh shit, today's the thirtieth. So it's almost the thirty-first. Is this when I die? Who was that man anyways?"

He had not seen the man and only pictured Cindy's scared expression that night. He remembered her telling him that he was marked. Martin's hands gripped the steering wheel. "Was there a man who visited me in the hospital? A man in black, would that have been a priest?"

He closed his eyes and tried to remember his hospital stay, but he only remembered his parents as his only visitors. He remembered his mom crying and saying his name over and over again. "Marty, Marty, please wake up. Son, please wake up."

His head snapped up. "Shit, I am falling asleep." He was in the left lane of the road and tried to ease over to the right lane as the car entered another curve. He was frozen and his hands tried to react to the car that was now spinning. He had hit some ice and overcorrected. When he instinctively hit the brakes, the car did not respond. Martin and his car went into the ditch. It stopped when it wrapped around a tree.

He groaned after the impact. He tried to look around, but he could not move. "Everything hurts. Should I even try to move? I might paralyze myself or make it worse."

The air bags had deployed and were slowly deflating, but he was pinned by the steering wheel. He looked forward and watched the falling snow. "It is beautiful."

He should be concerned about, "Where am I? Can I find my phone? Would anyone find me?" But he didn't remember what mile marker he had passed or the last exit sign. He was too focused on the road to read every sign. He couldn't see where his phone was on the passenger side. The airbag was deflating, and he could feel the pressure lessening on his chest. It still hurt to breathe, so he tried to take smaller breaths.

Martin saw a snowflake land on the windshield. "Large and fluffy, probably good for packing and making a good snowball." Then it melted and was replaced by another snowflake. "Just like someone else will replace me."

He started to cry and thought of Ashley. "She's the love of my life." He took another breath and closed his eyes. "I'm going home."

***

Martin walked through the apartment towards the kitchen. His black fleece and shoes were still on. Ashley was lying on the couch, staring at her phone and texting different friends. Then she called Martin's parents, and they said that he hadn't arrived at the house yet. Martin's mom had said, "Ashley, don't worry. The snow is getting worse, so he may be driving slower now. He may not get here for hours. It's still early. You know he's a careful driver."

"Yeah, he is very careful." She took a breath. "Okay, please call me when he gets there."

"Of course," his mom said.

"Ashley," he went towards the couch and said, "I'm back. I wanted to apologize."

She texted, then threw her phone onto the couch. "Dammit, why won't you answer your phone?"

"Ashley, I'm right here." He tried to grab her, but she reached for her phone, and he missed her shoulder. She looked for any missed messages or calls, then got up and went to the bathroom. "Ashley?" He followed her down the hall and stopped in front of the door. He watched her wash her face with cold water. She blew her nose and started to cry again. "Ashley, I'm okay. I just… can you hear me, Ash?" She stopped crying, and he whispered, "Ashley?"

# Sanctum

**JK Allen**

*Content Warning: Violence, Sexual Assault*

My feet ache. That's an understatement. My heels have been bleeding for days, even on the paved roads of the old highways, still the fastest route between the ruins they used to call cities. My journey is turning desperate. With only an apple and a few pieces of jerky left, I know I'm in trouble if I don't find food fast. The trees have overrun the edges of the road, towering over me with their gnarled roots pushing through the cement. This means birds and squirrels, but I don't have any way to make a fire and I won't eat those raw. My best bet is an old market in the city will still have canned food. It's less time-consuming than raiding houses.

I haven't seen a soul since I left. This is good. This is safe. But the silence is starting to get to me. I have talks with myself as I walk the white lines. My footfalls echo out behind me. I begin to count as high as I can to pass the time, starting over when I forget a digit. The walking is endless, and I am covered with a layer of dust and sweat. The constant sun has begun to burn my skin, especially on my nose and cheekbones. It stings when I wipe the sweat away. If I had an extra shirt, I'd make a headwrap, but it's been so long since the last clothes ration, I only have this sleeveless tee. I can't bear to walk in just my bra, so exposed and vulnerable, even though there's no one around. So I bundle my dark hair on top of my head and tie it all in a messy bun. I really should shave it, but it's my one vanity that remains from my old life. Back when I'd be on this highway driving my old Impala, going to the city when it was filled with people and not just silence.

I reach Detroit on the evening of the fifth day. The sun has stopped sweltering and begun to slink towards the horizon. Luckily, it is behind me, so I'm not blinded. I recall my mission, to find friendlies to join our Sanctum, which I never want to leave again. I don't know why they sent me. I'm not good at talking to other people or at making friends. And how am I supposed to weed out the bad ones? These thoughts rankle my stomach and bounce around my brain for a while as I set up shop. I pick a decent looking house, but not too nice. The kind of house a family of four would live in. I gently shimmy the lock and hold my breath as I enter, eyes closing themselves.

It's strange to see all the furniture and belongings left there like some odd museum exhibit. A layer of dust covers everything, and I wander over the family pictures, a couple and two boys in matching blue and red striped tops. The youngest boy shows off a toothy grin, a few gaps in between. Those ghostly smiles haunt me as I raid the pantry. A can of corn, a can of pie filling, and two cans of tuna fish. I'll have a feast tonight.

I make a party of it, lighting candles and eating some old candy I found. I drink my fill of water, bathe, and sleep for eight hours. Now, it's morning, and I have no idea how to complete my mission. I pack up the food, and candy, and a thermos of water into my bag. I don't know if I'll be able to return here.

Still worried about food, I head out to find a market or convenience store. There's a chance they'll be picked clean, but there's so few living in the city now that there's always a chance I'll find food.

It rained last night, so the pockmarked streets are all darkly gleaming. There's the stench of garbage from the ripped, strewn trash heaps rotting next to the road. I stay on the sidewalk, avoiding the curling worms the rain has flushed out.

I hear her before I see her. She's singing "Hallelujah" by Cohen, and it takes my breath away. I peer around the corner and see her standing in front of an old fountain, and I have to blink three or four times because she's controlling the water. Magic. That's the only way to describe this moment. Trails of water leap out of the fountain and dance between her fingers, looping around her hand before elegantly trickling back into the fountain. The water curls around her fingers as she hits each note with her sensuous voice. I have to remember to breathe. My heart thumps in my chest.

Soft amber curls adorn her heart shaped face. Softer than any hair I've seen since before the war and before the great sickness. Her skin is a bronzed ochre, and I am mesmerized by her. I gather my courage and step away from my hiding spot.

"That's beautiful." My voice is a hush.

She is startled, the water clattering back into the fountain, but she laughs. "Thanks."

"We have, um, we're building a sanctum in Chicago. I'd like you to come with me." The words rush out from me, and when I'm done, my face is hot.

Her hazel eyes search my face. "That was sudden." She laughs again, and my heart begins to pound. It is a lovely sound. "Well," she says, looking coy. "Only if I get to stay with you."

My eyes widen in shock, and my face goes even hotter, but I can't stop grinning ear to ear at the thought.

"I wouldn't have it any other way," I cough out.

She picks up a single drop of water and maneuvers it across the space between us. It splashes my nose.

"Can anyone else do that? Or just you?" I ask, wiping the drop away.

"There used to be others. That seems like a long time ago now."

Everything is mired long into the past.

"Do you really want me to join you?"

"It's the only thing I want right now." I smile at her shyly.

She walks up to me, a mischievous glint in her eyes. "Can you keep my secret?" There was such little space between us now. "About the water?" Her hand goes to my shoulder, trailing down my arm. My breath shortens. She smells of roses and musk, and my skin shivers at her touch. She leans in towards me. I close my eyes, and that's when I feel the blade biting at my throat. My heart hammers in my chest.

"Your sanctum sounds nice and all, but I get lots for each person I bag for the Cortez Brothers. Especially females." Now a rope is being wrapped around my wrists. I open my eyes and look at her, tears falling freely. "Should have stayed there, sugar." Her voice is now harsh.

She's right. She tugs on the rope, and I stumble forward to follow her. I should have stayed in Sanctum.

***

What will they do to me? Why do they pay more for females? My stomach clenches, and I bite down on a scream that's been trying to escape since she tied my wrists. She drags me down the road. I can't manage more than a shuffle.

"What's your name then?" she calls behind her. I have no desire to find my voice. Not for her. "Mine is Sadie. Didn't tell you earlier. I got bad manners, you'll have to forgive me." She laughs lightly and something goes steel inside me.

"You know, I'll have to tell them Cortez boys something. They won't care that you've gone mute. Means no backtalk, no sass. They like 'em quiet. But not me. They like me for different reasons."

I refuse to stare at the back of her head any more. My scowl drops down to the ground where the faded yellow lines slowly tick by. I feel the sun beating down on my neck and shoulders. It's comforting to feel its familiar touch. We pass houses, faded stop signs, and rusted lights. What's going to happen to me? It's enough to unseam my mind.

She directs me to an old warehouse. I am rooted to the ground as she knocks on the door three times, then twice. My breath catches in my throat. Someone opens the door and she tugs on my rope.

"Got a good one, young and pretty."

"Sixty days ration," the middle aged man with a scar under his eye says after barely looking me over.

"She's worth at least 100. Just look at her with her hair down and her top off."

"Seventy tops. Take her inside."

Sadie yanks on my rope, and I stumble while she laughs. The warehouse is dark and musty smelling. I cough as she leads me to the janitor's closet and locks me in. I sit on the floor defeated.

Why do they pay more for women? The thought haunts me and rattles around my skull, making my pulse race. Why do they pay more for women? I know why. Tears seep from my eyes at the thought. I stare down at the knot that binds my hands together. It's bulky, but that doesn't mean it's impenetrable. I can untie that knot. I go to work with my teeth.

My lips are raw and my teeth ache, but I get the knot loose, pulling the rope off my wrists. They sting, but that is nothing in this circumstance, so I ignore the pain and try to think. I hear footsteps approaching and wrap the rope around my hands. I stand to the side of the door and wait.

The door opens, and the man with the scar enters. He makes a confused sound, and I jump behind him, wrapping the rope around his neck. He bucks, but I hold on, rope twisting into my skin. I bite down hard on my lip, the sharp, coppery taste of blood filling my mouth, and use my dead weight to choke him. He makes awful gurgling noises, and tears stream from the corners of my eyes. Finally, he slumps to his knees, then forward onto the ground. I wait one agonizing minute before I release my hands. He doesn't move.

I search his body and find a gun. I stare at it until I figure out how to turn the safety off. I'm no pro at this, but I don't need to be. I take the rope just in case, wrapped around my shoulder.

I'm in the middle of the hallway. Four rooms stand between me and the exit. I force myself to walk to the first room. The light is off, and I see stacks of boxes. Sadie was getting paid in rations. Maybe these hold food. My mouth salivates at the thought.

The second and third rooms are devoid of people and boxes, just full of machines I don't recognize. I hear voices ahead of me. I hear Sadie laugh. I clench my jaw.

There are two guys wearing flashy clothes and one guy with a gun. I aim and shoot, a red flower blossoming on his chest as he goes flying sideways away from me. Sadie drops her drink, pink alcohol in a chilled glass. They have quite the setup here. The two men reach into their jackets, so I aim and shoot again, holding my breath. The first bullet misses, but the next gets the first man in the gut. The second is pulling out a gun, and I aim for the middle of his chest. I get him right in the throat. He falls to his knees choking.

"What the hell do you want?" gutshot asks, a sheen of sweat on his face. I say nothing, just stare at him. His eyes are a golden hazel, glimmering in the light. I train the gun on him.

"Honey, did I underestimate you," Sadie says with a laugh. Hatred bubbles in my belly, and I swallow hard.

"Take off your shirt," I say.

"Honey, if that's what you want—"

"Take it off and throw it here," I interrupt. I don't want to hear any more of her nonsense.

"Sure thing, doll." She strip teases it off, but it has no effect on me, even when she reveals she has nothing on underneath.

"Look, I'll give you whatever you want. Food, water, whatever you want," the man rushes out.

"Where?"

"Right here. In the other room. I can show you."

"Then I can help myself."

"Wait—"

The bullet finds his head. I turn the gun on Sadie.

She begins fondling her bare breasts. "I know what you want, sugar."

"I want you to die," I say and watch her face change. Her hand flexes and the spilled liquor rushes towards her. One sweep of her hand and it douses my face. I flinch and the gun shifts right before I pull the trigger. I pull again and hear an empty click.

Sadie rushes me, and we both go down. Pain sparks where I land and races up my back. She is clawing at my neck and shoulders, wherever she can reach. I slam my fist into the side of her face again and again, and she rolls off me.

I scramble up and run for the dead guy's gun, the first guy I shot. She's pulled out a bottle of water from somewhere, releasing the liquid so that it hangs in the air in front of her. I point and right before I shoot, the water rushes towards me and douses the gun. I pull the trigger anyway, and she takes a step back, looking down at the blood spilling from her chest. She looks at me then falls. Silence echoes around me.

I search the other bodies and decide to trade my gun for a different one. Mine is all wet, and I don't want the parts to corrode.

I take her shirt and go into the room full of boxes. The boxes are stuffed with food, cans, and boxes of things I haven't seen in years. I pull off my sleeveless tee and wrap it around my hair, swapping it for Sadie's. I find my bag and begin filling it with food and bottles of water. I'll need enough for a five day walk. Sanctum, I am never leaving you again.

***

I can't just leave all this food. So I break into a house down the street and stash several boxes there. I work up a sweat doing this. The day is already hot, sweltering sun high in the sky. I'm glad for my head wrap and my new shirt. A pang of remorse tears through me as I see Sadie falling to the ground again, and I squeeze my eyes shut hard.

She deserved it, she was selling me to the Cortez boys. My eyes fly open as my heart pounds, remembering being tied up in that closet. Walls closing around me. I see sky, expansive and cloud free above me. I feel for the gun in my waistband before I can take another step forward.

I step out onto the road, shouldering my pack. The road is crowded with cars left over from the flight, where everyone tried to leave for somewhere safe, but no one had anywhere to go. There are remains in a lot of the cars. It's been years, so only bones with bits of dried flesh stuck to it remain. The skeletons are in disarray as they fold into themselves. Most of the bodies liquified quickly in the hot sun. I remember the stench, like a nightmare. Very few people actually made it out. They cordoned off the cities to try and contain the outbreak, but it spread faster than a wildfire. The Great Sickness took out 70 percent of the population the first year. I lost my parents that year. My sister, Marie, didn't die until a few years later. When the Great War had begun. There is too much history. I blink my eyes to clear them.

I've barely walked a block, lost in thought. The cars are lined up like dominos, and I walk by them refusing to look inside. A sigh escapes me, so I take in a deep breath. That's when I hear the footfalls right behind me. My hands fly to my gun, but I fumble with it as I turn around. Finally, I get a grip on the gun and swivel. I stop when I see who is in my sights. A girl my age with large blue eyes that pierce me and a scar on her face, and a ten year old girl hiding behind her. Her hands fly up by her head. She holds a knife in one hand.

"We didn't mean to startle you."

"You should be more careful," I say, eyeing her blade.

My chest is heaving, and I lower my gun slightly, as I stare at the girl with a scar. It curves down under her right eye, trailing down her cheek. Who knows what these girls want from me. They could be just like Sadie. I let my guard down with her and almost ended up sold to the highest bidder for God knows what. I have to be vigilant even though they look harmless. Well mostly harmless. Yesterday, I would have been sold as meat. I can't let that happen again. Blue Eye's hands shake as she holds them up, turning her body to shield the little girl from my view.

"What are you doing here?" I ask, trying to keep my voice steady despite my pounding heart.

She has dark hair, like mine, which makes her eyes stand out even more. I see fear and something else, something more like desperation.

"Please, we're just hungry. Hannah hasn't eaten all day." Her voice breaks, and she swallows hard.

Hannah peeks out from behind her for the first time, and I see a face full of freckles and blonde braids that curl into tufts at the end. She has the same heart shaped face Sadie had, and she has Sadie's vibrant hazel eyes. The air leaves my lungs and my hands shake. The gun rises a little as I remember the feel of ropes against my skin.

"We don't want to hurt you."

The little girl steps forward, the sun highlighting her, and I see how pale she is. This, with the blonde hair, reminds me of how unlike Sadie she is. Her little frame trembles as she looks at me. "Please," her voice is so small.

"Let me put this away. We don't want to hurt you," Blue Eyes says and tucks the knife back into her pocket. I lower the gun to my side.

"Follow me," I say, turning back. I don't want to give away my safe house where I stored the food, but I can't bring them around the bodies at the warehouse, so I head towards the house.

At the house, I stick my gun back in my waistband. "Come on," I say, conscious of the sound of my own voice. "There's plenty of food in here."

They linger in the doorway. Blue Eyes clamps her hands down on Hannah's shoulder, biting her lip.

"It's mostly canned food, so you know it's not poisoned," I say looking down.

"I don't think you're going to poison us," she says softly.

"The gun is only for protection."

"Same with my knife. We don't mean you any harm."

"Then have some food." I wrack my brain for the right thing to say. "I like sharing. I know what it's like to be hungry."

"Thank you." She lets go of Hannah, so I open a box and place it in front of the girl.

Her hazel eyes go wide, and she gifts me with a full-toothed grin. I can't help but smile myself. I bring out the candy from my bag and add it to her pile.

"Candy! I can't remember the last time I had candy!" Her voice is clear as a bell, and her excitement is contagious. "Mirabel, come eat."

"You eat first," Mirabel says with a laugh.

"Go ahead," I urge.

She tears into a can of pineapples, savoring the sweetness with her eyes closed. I paw through the box for her, placing cans on the table in front of her. Slowly, Mirabel makes her way towards us. She picks up the closest can and starts eating. I drink water as I watch them. Who knows when the last time they had a good meal was, a feeling I know all too well. It does feel good to share my food with them.

"Well," Mirabel says, putting the can down. "You know our names now. What's yours?" She arches her brow and smiles at me.

I swallow. I have no reason not to tell her, but feel I have a spotlight on me. "My name is Ash."

"Ash," she says nodding. "Nice to meet you."

"You too."

"Is it short for anything?"

I don't want to reply. "Ashlynn."

"That's a pretty name," Hannah chimes in between bites of candy.

"Thanks." She grins again. Her teeth are tinged blue.

"How long have you been in the city?" Mirabel asks.

"Just a couple of days."

"And you have all this food?" She cocks her head.

"I came across it."

"We've been in the city for years now. But it hasn't been easy."

"You've had to deal with the Cortez brothers."

She stares at me mouth agape. "How did you know?"

"I met them."

She looks at me in shock, but then nods. "They have people all over the city. You can't trust anyone."

"They are dead." She stops in her tracks. "Why did you trust me?" I ask her, crossing my arms.

"Because you looked as scared as I felt."

She looks at me steadily, her blue eyes striking. Her lips are a soft pink. My heart skips a beat.

"Why are you in the city?" I ask.

She shrugs. "Easier to find food and shelter. In the suburbs the houses are too spread apart. And it's harder to get to the stores." Hannah has finished eating and curls up right on the floor. Soon she is breathing softly, asleep.

"How did you two find each other?" It's clear they're not related, but have been together for a while.

"I found her on the road crying. I didn't know how long she'd been walking, but she was alone. Only seven years old. I couldn't leave her. She's been with me ever since."

This feels true, and I feel the muscles in my shoulders relaxing. Maybe these two are the reason for my mission.

"Would you like to go somewhere safe?"

She stops and stares at me. "There is no safe place."

"We're building one. In Chicago. We call it Sanctum. I was sent here to bring people back with
me."

"To Sanctum?" Her brow furrows.

"We have food. And we grow it. Our leader is named Chase, and he leads the Council who votes on how we live. We even have a security team."

She rubs her arm. "And we can just join?"

"If I decide you will, yes."

"What do you need to know to decide?"

"That you are as scared as I feel." She smiles at me. "Will you come?"

She contemplates me before saying, "Yes."

"Then wake up Hannah, and let's go."

I go through the house until I find a backpack. I pack a couple shirts and enough food for Mirabel and Hannah. She fills their canisters with water. It's a five day walk, and I am eager to get home, back to Sanctum.

***

I don't fully breathe until we're out of the city. The wind rustling through the trees that line the highway sounds like freedom after the claustrophobic events of the past couple days. I rub the chafed skin on my wrist as I watch the leaves dance. I remember the kick of the gun each time I discharged a bullet.

"How long will it take to get there?" Hannah stops skipping to ask.

"Five days."

"That's a long time."

"We'll help you," Mirabel says, ruffling her hair.

Two hours later, and Hannah needs a break, so we stop and eat. I stare at the dipping trees as we lunch. It's so green.

"Have you ever walked this long before?" Hannah asks between bites.

"To get to Detroit, yes."

"Was it safe?"

"It was." She nods her head and goes back to her corn.

"Tell us about where we're going," Mirabel asks.

They both stare at me, so I clear my throat. "Well, it's called Sanctum. There's a great, big fence around the property to help keep us safe. We grow fruits and vegetables to eat."

"What kind of fruit and veggies?" Hannah looks at me with eager eyes that makes me smile.

"We grow apples, tomatoes, onions, potatoes, and herbs to cook with."

"Cooked food?"

I laugh. "Yes, we always cook dinner."

"I can't wait to get there." She rubs her stomach and laughs.

"How many people live there?" Mirabel begins to clean up.

"Only about thirty or forty. We all work in the garden and take turns cleaning house. We have a security detail to keep us safe, and Chase runs the Council which makes our laws."

"Laws?" Hannah asks.

"Rules."

Hannah scrunches up her face. "Are the rules hard?"

"No. Don't hurt anyone else and everyone helps. Those are the main ones."

Her face goes serious. "I can do that."

"I'm glad."

"It sounds wonderful," Mirabel says. "I'm surprised there aren't more people."

"We're still young. And you'd be surprised by who doesn't want to follow the rules."

"Not that surprised." She arches her brow. I'm reminded of Jonas and his unruly crew and how they're always pushing at the rules. And all the people we've had to turn away because they wouldn't follow them. The scar on her cheek is a pale pink, smooth and not raised. I tear my eyes away from it, wondering how she got it.

"Alright," I say, standing up. "Back to walking."

I am reminded of how lonely my walk to Detroit was. As I ran out of food and blistered in the sun. That walk had been so tortuous. As afraid as I was then, I would have welcomed another person. Now I feel so different. People mean danger, and I keep looking around us, praying I don't see another figure.

Hannah sings made up songs as she rambles along. Sometimes Mirabel joins in, so the songs must be familiar to them. I'm just glad for the voices, and that I'm not just out here counting to myself. My mind doesn't feel like fracturing. But the extra sound does make my heart beat a little faster.

The day is uneventful, and I'm grateful for that. We don't meet anyone on the open road. Mirabel and I take turns giving Hannah a piggy back ride when she gets too tired to walk. It reminds me of when Marie was younger. She loved piggy back rides and would beg me for them all the time. I would spin as fast as I could just to hear her shriek with joy, her curly brown hair flying around us. Carrying Hannah is hard work, but we need to make good time, and I don't mind. Sometimes I find myself believing it's Marie on my back, despite the fact she'd be too old for this now. But I have to think of now. It's too dangerous until we're safe inside the compound. Only then can I finally relax.

We get ready for bed. I give Hannah some peaches as a treat. She curls up next to Mirabel who strokes her hair. I take off my head wrap and let my hair down. The night is sweet, with a cool breeze blowing through my hair. It feels magnificent, I can't help but smile at them.

Hannah falls asleep immediately, but Mirabel and I stay awake, looking at the stars. There's millions of them out here in the open. I remember driving the highways as a child, finally being able to see the stars away from all the lights of the city. It always seemed so magical.

"Do you remember what it was like before?" Mirabel asks.

"What do you mean?"

"There used to be so many lights. When it all changed, I was so scared of how dark it was at night. Now it's so natural, but I always remember how dark the night really is."

"I remember the lights," I say looking at her. It seems even darker now that we've said the words. In my mind, I see lighted windows in a row of houses. Everything is bright and cheery and safe. Out here in the dark, I suddenly feel out in the open with a target on my back. "We should keep watch. You sleep first. I'll wake you in a few hours. Get some rest."

"Oh, okay." She lies down and snuggles up to Hannah.

I go back to watching the stars as the night swirls around me.

***

We're in Illinois and making good time despite Hannah's little legs. The day is winding down into evening and the temp drops at least ten degrees.

"Let's build a fire tonight," Mirabel says, dropping her pack and wiping the sweat from her brow. Her hair is slicked to her long neck, and I reach over to wipe it off. She shivers.

"Sorry," I mumble, flexing my hands at my side. "I don't have anything to make a fire with."

"We do. Just gather the kindling and some sticks."

She winks at me, and my face goes hot. I immediately turn and head for the trees. My steps crackle as I collect some dry leaves and sticks to burn. Hannah runs back and forth carrying a stick at a time. This makes me smile.

Mirabel goes to work with the kindling in front of her, placing small sticks in a cone above the leaves, like a teepee. She pulls out a zippo and before long, we have a cozy fire in front of us that we all crowd around.

"Mirabel, tell us a story," Hannah says, hugging her knees to her chest.

"Well," Mirabel clears her throat, "the only good stories I have are the ones about my brother." She looks at me sheepishly before continuing. "His name was Tommy, and he was the sweetest. He was two years older. I remember when I was seven, we moved to a new house that had a pool. I was so excited, but I hadn't learned how to swim yet. I would go in the shallow end and hold onto the edge and kick my feet, but I couldn't float.

"One day my dad got sick of me trying and failing and grabbed me out of the pool. He picked me up and threw me into the middle of the deep end. I tried to swim, but I kept sinking. I was thrashing so hard I couldn't see anything and was running out of air. All of a sudden, I was pulled up just as I was starting to pass out. Tommy had run from the house and jumped in with his clothes on to save me.

"I was so afraid of the water I wouldn't go near the pool for a month. When summer started, Tommy taught me how to swim and overcome my fear while dad was at work. He was the best big brother."

Everything is quiet for a moment. The fire pops, and Hannah leans against Mirabel.

"You must miss him," I say.

Mirabel nods, wiping an eye. "We lost him in the first year. Wasn't long after that I left home and went out on my own."

I look at her differently. She chose to be alone. To survive on her own without anyone who had her back. That takes strength. Strength I didn't realize she had. But who was I to talk? The only strength I had was a gun I'd stolen from a corpse.

Mirabel adds larger sticks to the fire as Hannah settles down. I know she will be asleep in minutes, and I wonder how she can do it. Out here in the open. But she's exhausted from all the walking. Doing her best not to complain about it either. My feet ache, and I'm getting blisters on my heels. They'll be bleeding soon. I hope I can get some new shoes in Chicago. Hannah and Mirabel probably need some too.

"You're quiet tonight," Mirabel says, poking the fire.

"Sorry, I'm not the best at making conversation. I'm not good with people really." I look down at my fingers and pick at my nails.

"I wouldn't say that."

I raise my brow. "Oh really?"

"Hannah likes you."

"Hannah probably likes everyone."

Mirabel laughs. "She doesn't like everyone. She's terrified of most people, but she feels safe with you."

"Must be the candy," I say with a smirk.

She scowls. "I'm being serious."

"Thanks, I'll feel better once we're safe inside Sanctum. I never should have left there."

"Why did you?"

"To find people like you and Hannah."

"And what happened?"

"I met a girl who sold me to the Cortez brothers." I remember the rope around my wrists, biting into my skin as I shuffled along. Then I see Sadie as I shoot her, as she falls. Her face showing her pain and shock. I shiver.

Her voice is low. "How did you escape?"

"I untied myself and killed the man they sent to fetch me. He had a gun, so I took out the rest. Including the brothers, I got lucky."

"That couldn't have been easy," she says, brow furrowed.

I ramble, "I didn't have a choice. They were going to traffic me."

"I would have been so scared," she says, rubbing her arms.

"I still am," I say with a shrug.

"I think you were very brave."

I get flustered and my face goes hot again. "You would have done the same."

"Well, thanks to you, I'll never have to find out. So thanks for that."

"No need to thank me. It just happened."

We stare at each other over the fire, the flickering flames bathing her face in red light. I can barely see her scar and am struck by how young and carefree she looks without it. Like it somehow ages her and paints her as cynical. I wish I could erase it.

"Shall we keep watch tonight?" she asks with a smile.

"Sure." I smile back. "You sleep first. I'm wide awake."

Mirabel wakes me at dawn.

"Ash," she hisses. "Wake up. There's someone on the road."

I bolt up and nearly headbutt her. "Where?"

She points and I see him. Closer than I would like. A lone man walking towards us with quick steps.

"We're leaving. Now," I say harshly.

We grab our packs and Mirabel wakes Hannah, gently but tersely.

"Run. We need to keep some distance between us and him." I take off and take Hannah's hand in mine. We run at the fastest pace I think Hannah can handle for a while. We don't want to burn out, and there's still at least a day before we reach the city.

I look back and see he's loping after us. What could this man possibly want? I squeeze Hannah's hand and run a half-step faster.

We run for miles. Until I can no longer see him, and then some for safe measure. Hannah is gasping for air and dragging her feet. She can't handle any more now.

"Water break," I say, panting and coming to a stop.

"And food," Mirabel answers. "We haven't eaten yet, and it's late morning."

"Quickly," I concede. Hannah collapses on the road. "Drink water, Hannah."

She nods and takes her bottle from Mirabel, who begins opening cans. We slurp down some food, and I push them back on their feet.

"I'm still too tired," Hannah cries.

"I'll carry you, and then we'll walk for a while," I say, handing my bag to Mirabel. "Come on, up you go."

I crouch, and she jumps on my back. "Pretty soon, you'll be too big to do this," I say, taking my first step with her added weight. It's always the hardest.

We walk in the rising heat. Last night was cool enough for a fire, but now, with the sun beating on us and our hurried pace, we are soon drenched in sweat. I go as far as I can with Hannah, but the heat from her, and the weight of her, is making me light headed.

"Another break," I gasp out.

"I'll take her," Mirabel says, digging for water.

"I can walk now," Hannah says with a smile.

I turn and do a 360, looking for any sign of the man we saw before. I take a deep breath when I see we are alone.

"At least we're making good time," I say between gulps.

"You shouldn't have carried her so long. You need your strength." Mirabel puts her hand on her hip and purses her lips as she looks at me.

"I'm fine. Next is your turn."

She nods. "It sure is."

Hannah screws up her face. "I can walk for a while, just all that running was hard."

"It was hard, honey. But you did such a good job." Mirabel brushes the hair out of Hannah's face and flips her braids back over her shoulders. Hannah just beams at her. Mirabel is so good with kids.

We travel at a fast pace all day and make it to just outside the city. I want to keep moving even as night falls around us, but Hannah is dead on her feet, and

Miri and I aren't far behind. We make camp and sit down to eat.

"Drink lots of water. You've got to make up for all the sweating you did today," I say as I stretch my legs.

"Stretch too, Hannah," Mirabel says, going through the food. My legs are burning, my thighs and calves especially. I stretch, and Hannah mimics me, giggling. I make funny faces at her.

We eat and settle down for the night. I can't stop blinking and yawning. Mirabel notices.

"You get sleep first. I'll wake you in a few."

It's all I can do to nod. I'm asleep within minutes.

I wake to an absolute panic. Dawn is infusing light into the sky, steel grey turning to a cornflower blue. I jolt up and see him immediately. In shouting distance. My heart slams into my chest.

"Get up now," I shout, and I swear I see him snarl at me.

We all leap up and start running. This time I don't give a damn about pacing ourselves. But Hannah can only run so fast.

"Wait," he screams after us. "Stop, please."

It motivates me to run harder. Mirabel and Hannah are just a step behind. But it's like I can feel him right behind me, breathing down my neck. My feet ache, but I speed up again.

"We can't go that fast," Mirabel rushes out. I stop completely, cursing myself. I can't leave them behind. I let them pass me and run with them in my sight. My body is telling me to run as fast as I can, but I fight it, swallowing down the panic.

"I need help." His voice carries towards us, and I shudder violently. He's too close for comfort.

"Keep running," I say without hesitation.

Hannah looks at me terrified, but nods. I chance a look behind me. He's a big guy. Built, not lean like most survivors. He looks like he's always had food and a couple of people to punch around. He's in his thirties, with black hair. He shouts at me, but I swivel back forward.

We near the city. I don't want him following us to Sanctum, so I decide to take us to Shoe Warehouse for new shoes and socks. When we get there, I'll pull the gun on him, and then we'll slip away to safety. I run the plan by Mirabel, and she agrees to it.

"I'm so glad you have that gun," she says in a small voice.

We veer off the highway and enter the streets of Chicago. My home for the last seven years. We run in the middle of the road to avoid the abandoned cars, and I rush us to the store. Every shop has long been broken into, but there's plenty of merchandise left over. People only steal what they need.

We burst through the doors, and I immediately go for my pack. I find the gun and drop the bag, pointing the gun at the door.

He walks in, head down and panting, His eyes go wide when he sees what I'm holding.

"I don't want any trouble," he says, holding his hands up.

"Then quit following us."

"I just want—"

"I don't care what you want," I snap. "Leave. And I better not see you again."

"But, I—"

"I said leave," I scream.

He jerks. "Okay, I'll leave. I just wanted your help."

"We don't care what you want," I repeat.

He glares at me, then turns around slowly and leaves. We all stand stock still for minutes after the doors close. Finally I can breathe, and I lower the gun and put it in my waistband, turning to the others.

"Who wants a new pair of shoes after all that walking?"

"I do!" Hannah jumps up and down and spins to survey the store.

"Here, let me help you," Miri says, and they head towards the kid's aisles.

I find a nice black pair for myself and start grabbing socks. Socks are always needed. I put on a fresh pair and my new shoes. They feel so luxurious after all that running in my ratty old ones. I smile for the first time in days.

We leave the store cautiously, looking everywhere for that guy, but he's nowhere in sight. We walk quickly, but don't have it in us to run. I take a slightly circuitous route there, but we make it to the chained fence perimeter of Sanctum. It's disguised as a construction site. Larry opens the doors right up for me.

"Your mission must have been a success. You brought two right pretty ladies here with you."

We enter the gates, and I introduce him to Mirabel and Hannah. I throw my head back and breathe, deep breaths that break the tension in my chest.

"I am never leaving here again, Larry."

"That bad of a trip, huh?"

"We even had some psychopath chasing us for the last two days."

"How did you shake him?"

"With this," I say, holding up the gun.

"Turning that in, ain't ya?"

"Yes, of course." Mirabel gives me a look. "Part of the rules. Only security has guns."

Larry is locking the fence when I hear footsteps. I spin around, it's the psychopath from the freeway.

"Please help me," he pants out.

***

He avoids my scowl, pinning his piggy eyes on Larry's face. He's even bigger up close.

"Please, help me," he says, linking his fingers through the fence.

"What's wrong?" Larry asks, hand on his holster.

"What isn't wrong? Everywhere I go, there are people trying to kill me. I can't live on the streets anymore. It's too dangerous."

"That's not our problem," I snarl, and he gives me the meanest glare. I can feel his anger from here, and I know he's no good. "Larry, give me back my gun. I'll get rid of this creep."

"Don't listen to her. Let me inside, will you?"

"Larry, you can't," I plead, turning to face him.

He runs his hand over his grizzled beard and eyes me. "You know what our mission is."

"Not this guy. We don't know he's safe. In fact, I know he's not safe. He chased us for two days."

"You wouldn't help me."

"Help you with what?" I demand as I whip around. "What the fuck were we supposed to do for you?"

"Well, you obviously have a safe space here. I need a safe place to live too."

"You are not safe. You don't have any right to be here."

"I have a right to be anywhere I want to be."

I laugh. "Maybe things used to be like that, but they aren't any more."

"You will let me in," he threatens, baring his teeth.

"Alright you two," Larry chimes in, "calm down both of you. Mister, why should we let you into this place? Do you even know what we are?"

"I don't know, but it's somewhere safe, isn't it?"

"We have laws you have to abide by."

"Fine, I'm just sick of being shot at whenever I meet someone out on the streets."

Larry scratches his chin. "I'll get Chase. See what he says."

I scowl and kick at the gravel.

"Who's Chase again?" Miri asks softly.

"Our leader," I mumble.

"You don't think he'll let him in, do you?"

"I really don't know." My stomach sinks at the thought this man might get into Sanctum. I can already tell there's no way he'll follow the rules, and it's clear he has a thing against me. What will I do if he does get in? I suppress a shiver. I will not look weak in front of him.

I glance at him, and he smiles lewdly at me. I pierce him with a look of pure hatred, and he laughs.

"You don't frighten me, girly," he says before spitting to the side.

"Don't listen to him," Miri says, putting a hand on my shoulder. It calms me along with her soothing voice. I look at her and smile.

My head itches, so I unwrap my hair and let it down. Miri runs her fingers through it to straighten it, and it feels so good I close my eyes and sigh. I wish I could stay in this moment forever.

"Hello, Ash." Chase's voice breaks my reverie, but I welcome it. I open my eyes and embrace him. "I'm so happy you made it back safely," he whispers in my ear.

When we pull apart, I grin at him. His curly blond hair is tousled as usual and his green eyes are warm and smiling.

"This is Mirabel," I say, gesturing to her. I pull Hannah in front of me, "And this is Hannah."

"Hello, and welcome to you both."

"What about me?" psycho says from behind the fence.

"Don't let him in, Chase," I beg, grabbing his hand. He looks at me confused.

"We want new members," he says softly.

"We want safe members."

"You don't believe he's safe?"

"No," I say firmly.

"Look, I don't know what her deal against me is," Piggy Eyes starts.

"You chased us for days. Who does that?"

"I wanted to talk to you. I needed your help."

"You keep saying that, but you still haven't even said with what. Check him, and I bet he has a weapon."

"To defend myself."

"So you chased us for days with a weapon. Yeah, you sound pretty safe to me."

"I wasn't going to hurt you."

"I don't believe that for a second," Mirabel says suddenly.

"We can't let you in if you're a danger to others," Chase says.

"I'm not! I have a weapon only for self-defense. Even she has a gun." He jabs his finger at me.

"He doesn't even know what we are. Why does he want in so badly?"

"I don't understand why he's being so persistent," Mirabel says, looking down.

"I just want to be safe. That's all."

Mirabel clears her throat. "I don't think he's safe either."

"We can't deny him just on that," Chase starts. "We can let you in on a trial basis."

"You can't." My voice goes high.

"You must follow all laws and do as you're instructed," he continues. "You will be monitored, and any infraction will mean immediate expulsion. I think these terms are a fair compromise for both sides. Larry, let him in."

"You're making a mistake," I say to Chase, tears in my eyes.

Chase puts his hand to my cheek, but I turn away. I hear the lock open, and the scraping that means the gate is opening to let that creep in. I squeeze my eyes shut and breathe through my mouth.

Someone grabs my hand, and I look up to see it's Miri. She entwines her fingers with mine. I'm shocked, but I give her hand a squeeze. She squeezes back. Hannah steps behind us as he walks in.

"What's your name, stranger?" Chase asks.

"Marcus." He strolls in, head high and chest puffed out.

"Got to check ya," Larry says, putting his hand out to stop him.

Larry pats him down before pulling out a large hunting knife. I swallow hard at its size. Larry goes to put it in his pocket, but Marcus grabs his arm.

"What are you doing?"

"Regular citizens ain't allowed weapons. Only security detail can carry 'em. Rule number one."

"It's just for defense," he scowls.

"You want to break the first rule. Get out of here and good riddance," I say.

He glares at me, but lets go of Larry's arm.

"How do I join the security detail?"

"The Council decides that," Chase says. "Come, let's get you all settled

We turn and follow Chase to the living quarters. Girls are on the left, men on the right, and family rooms in the middle.

"Do you want a family room?" I ask Mirabel quietly.

"No, I want to be near you," she says, and I flush, her hand warm in mine.

"I'll take Miri and Hannah to the room next to mine," I say to Chase.

"Alright. Marcus, follow me."

I don't want Marcus to know where we sleep anyway. I help them get their room set up. I give Hannah some paper and some crayon nubs so she can draw pictures to put up on the walls. Mirabel and I make up a large bed for the two of them. It makes me think of my own empty bed. But at least they're right next door.

Chase comes back with two copies of the laws and a pamphlet on how Sanctum is run. Hannah takes her copies with such solemnity it makes me laugh. She reads through it slowly before returning to her crayons.

Chase leaves when they have no questions, telling me to give them the grand tour. He gives us three days to rest after our trip before we have to start doing shared chores together. I tell them I need a nap.

"Sleep here with me. Hannah will be fine for a while coloring," Miri says. I can't find my voice so I just nod.

We climb into the bed, and she wraps her arm around me. I have to consciously force myself to relax each muscle she touches. But once I'm relaxed, it feels good. Warm and comforting and familiar. It reminds me of Marie cuddling up to me in the middle of the night after a bad dream. It feels so right, my breath catches in my throat. I cough, feeling awkward, but place my arm over hers and close my eyes. I feel her breath on my back and the tension from the mission and everything that's happened finally breaks, and I drift off, happy.

Miri shakes me gently. "Dinner time," she coos in my ear. In a sleepy haze, I flip over and hug her close, burying my face into her neck. She laughs, and I realize what I've done. My face goes a deep red, and I come up for air.

"Sorry," I mumble.

She boops me on the nose. "Sorry for what, silly?"

All I can do is smile.

"Come on, it's dinner time, and Hannah is super excited for a cooked meal."

"Okay, I'm coming." I rub my hand down my face and stretch. "You're lucky I'm starving," I say with a smile before joining them at the door.

"I can't believe we get cooked food," Hannah chirps.

"Come on, little bird." I take her hand. "Follow me."

I lead them to the mess hall. Hannah talks nonstop about the food she remembers from before. I smile at her, and she beams at me, and warmth blossoms in my chest. I ruffle her hair and take a seat.

I'm used to sitting alone, but now I have Miri on my left and Hannah on my right and even Larry sits across from us. The kitchen crew begins bringing out the food and setting the tables. Soon we have a simmering stew on our table, a bowl of rice, and steaming asparagus sitting before us. I make Hannah's plate, mixing the rice into her stew for her. Her eyes are wide and shining as she grabs her spoon.

"Eat a lot, little bird," I stoop down to say with a grin.

Miri makes plates for both of us as we watch Hannah eat. She curls her fingers around the spoon.

"It's so good," she says as she moans, eyes shut.

"It is really good after nothing but canned food on the run," Mirabel agrees after a few bites.

"Those kitchen queens sure do pretty fine by us," Larry says, downing his stew.

I am happily lost in this moment until I feel his eyes on me and the smile dies on my lips. I look right and immediately spot him glaring at us. He's already found his kin in the group, Jonas and his gang.

Jonas is the meanest kind there is. He would kick a puppy just to laugh at it. He's been bucking against the rules and trying to turn people against Chase since day one. And a few of the rebels stick to him because they don't like the rules. There's only six of them, but I can't understand why Chase won't kick them out. Seeing Marcus at their table makes my stomach churn. I give him a death glare, then turn back to my table.

Mirabel tucks a strand of hair behind my ear. "You called me Miri earlier today."

I am locked in her gaze. "Oh, did I?"

"I haven't been called that in years."

"I'm sorry," I say, looking down.

"I liked it." I look into her blue eyes that are so piercing they take my breath away.

I smile and release my breath. "I like it too."

"Like what, pretty lady?" Marcus plops himself in front of me, pushing Larry to the side. I have to suppress a shudder of disgust, but it's written all over my face.

"What I like is none of your business."

"It could be." He leers at me, and I swallow bile.

"It really couldn't though."

"You know, this place is nice and all, but you're missing a few key ideas."

"And I bet you got some."

"I sure do. This is about our survival, after all. It's not enough just to eat a hot meal. We got to think of repopulating the world and building a militia, not a puny security detail."

"Our detail does just fine," Larry says with a cough.

"Repopulating the world? You mean forced mating," I say. "Do you imagine this is something we women want? Or is it just about pleasing men, 'cause I can tell you exactly what to do with your dick and your ideas about procreation.'

"I like them feisty," he says, then licks his lips.

"Any part of you that touches me, you're going to lose."

"Where's all this kinda talk even coming from?" Larry asks, jutting his chin out. "We don't force people to do nothing they don't want to do."

"Unless it's a law."

"You don't like our laws, you leave," I snap.

"Laws can change. So can where you sleep." He leans in, resting his chin on his interlaced beefy fingers. "Just so you know, Ashlynn."

"Say my name again, and I'll cut out your tongue."

He reaches his hand towards me, fingers close to brushing my cheek. I slam down my fork where his hand was moments before. It bites down deep into the wood of the table.

"You just wait, girly. You just wait." He stands and stalks back to his table with Jonas.

"Are you alright?" Miri asks, placing her hand on my arm.

I'm trembling. "Can you believe what he said? Forced mating? A militia? We can't let this happen."

"Maybe you were right about him," Larry says, giving me a sympathetic look.

"What did he mean by mating?" Hannah asks sheepishly.

"Forcing women to have babies with men." Her eyes go round. "Don't fret, little bird. That won't happen on my watch."

"Or mine," Larry says, rubbing his chin. "Or Chase for that matter."

I reach across and clasp Larry's hand. He's a good guy.

"I don't know about you, but I'm still beat. I think my bed is calling me." I say looking at Mirabel.

"Oh, okay." Miri starts to stand. I push her down into her seat.

"You two don't have to sleep this early just because I am. Talk, get to know some of the people here. You know the way back to your room, right?"

"Yeah, okay. Good night, Ash."

"Night."

I watch the stars as I make my way back. I feel exposed being alone, but I shake off this feeling and breathe in the cool breeze playing with my hair.

I pause at Miri and Hannah's new room, smiling at the colorful drawings Hannah made. I crawl into my own bed in my plain room. My life was so drab and empty, but Miri and Hannah have brought me color and music and a lightness that feels like flying. I burrow into my sheets, pretending I'm holding Miri, and fall asleep within minutes.

***

I am locked in that closet. Eggshell white walls closing in on me. My heart thunders in my ears, racing along like a bullet train. Panic rises, and I can't breathe. I'm gasping, and the rope around my wrists keeps cutting deeper into my skin. I hear footsteps approaching and turn to face the door, backing up into the wall. The door opens and it's Sadie looming over me. She leers at me and pulls out a gun, placing it against my temple. It's cold and hard against my skin. I squeeze my eyes shut and bang.

My eyes fly open, and I'm drenched with sweat. I sit up, gasping for air. Everything is dark and silent, and I close my eyes, breathing it in, waiting for my heart rate to slow. I see Sadie's face again, a smirk turning up one corner of her mouth. It hits me that she's gone forever, that I'm responsible for that. I choke back a sob.

But how many people had she hurt? How many had I spared by stopping her? Back in that moment, it had seemed like there was no other way. Had I been wrong? No, if the tables had been turned, I'm sure she would have killed me.

I flop back onto the bed and stare at the ceiling. I think of Sadie moving the water from the fountain with her magic. Magic that had only come about recently. When the Great Sickness came, we discovered some of us were resistant to the strain. The magic was tied to the same gene, but only showed up in the children of two recessive gene-carriers. It was something people were still trying to understand. Some were even taken from their homes for their ability in an attempt to make them into weapons. Really, Sadie had been careless to do that in public. But she had been under the protection of the Cortez brothers.

Soon, the room begins to lighten, and I decide to take a bath before the others wake up. I light a large candle, grab my towel and soaps, and make my way down to the tubs on the first floor.

I'm feeling much better after my bath. Combing out my hair, I braid it one on each side. I wash my clothes in the tub before getting dressed in them, grateful it's warm enough to do so comfortably. By now, dawn is breaking, and pale pink streaks across the baby blue sky.

I sit in my room and wait to hear any noise from Miri and Hannah's room. I stretch and pace the room, trying to stop my mind from whirring, of thinking of Sadie, and Marcus who is now a very real problem. His words from last night haunt me, and my stomach sinks at the thought.

Finally, I hear stirring in the next room and make my way over. Knocking quietly on the door, I feel suddenly self-conscious and clear my throat as Hannah throws open the door.

"Good morning," she cries and embraces me. I blush, but hug her back.

"You're up early," Miri says standing.

"How did you sleep?" I ask, fiddling with the end of a braid.

"Really well," Miri says, coming to the door. She smiles softly, and I feel a tingling in my center.

"Let's grab some breakfast, and I'll show you around."

We wander the garden, which is where I usually work. I like the work, like the feeling of my fingers in damp soil, like seeing new life sprout daily. I take Miri and Hannah over to my favorite fellow gardener, Abigail.

Abigail is our oldest member, being in her fifties, but she's spry and hardworking and clever.

"Now what do we have here?" she says standing, wiping dirt from her sun-warmed, brown hands. Her eyes crinkle as she takes us in.

"This is Mirabel and Hannah," I introduce them to her with a smile.

"I'm Abigail, nice to meet you both. Now, when did you get home?"

"Yesterday. We get a couple days off before I'll be back on work detail. Think you can use these two?"

"Seems like we have enough people to do our thing, but they do need more people in the kitchens. Can you girls cook?"

"We'll be happy to help wherever we're needed," Mirabel answers, and that makes Abigail beam.

"You're most welcome here, child. Yes, we are glad to have you. How did you all meet?"

"I was actually leaving Detroit. I thought I had failed my mission when I heard a noise behind me and there they were. We got acquainted over a meal, and they decided to come with me."

"And we're happy they did." Abigail bends down to Hannah's height. "And how old are you?"

"Ten-and-a-half."

"Oh my, you are getting big then. Would you like to help me plant something?"

Hannah nods and they get to work, digging in the soil.

"Hey there," Chase says, strolling up to us. "How are you getting settled?"

"We're doing great. It's so nice not being on the roads anymore."

"We're happy to have you. And we hope to keep expanding. There's so many that need a place like this."

"Do you have room for many more?"

"Our setup is ideal for a great many more than we have. After that, satellites could be set up in different locations. We just want to find a system that works for people, unlike our former government."

"That's very noble of you," Miri says.

Chase blushes and rubs his neck.

"Oh, I wasn't teasing you," Mirabel rushes to say in a flutter.

"It's fine." He gives her a crooked grin. "Just trying to do my part."

"And Marcus says he wants to force people to procreate," I say bluntly.

Chase looks up with a frown. "Larry told me as much. He's doing a lot of talking, that Marcus is."

We stand next to a row of buckets filled with water for the plants, and Hannah tugs on my arm.

"Hey, Ash, want to see something?"

"Sure."

Hannah takes a step away from me and holds her hand out in front of her. "Watch this," she says and flips her hand up. The water in the buckets rushes into the air in one motion. My mouth falls open. She resembles Sadie as she smiles at me, her hazel eyes glowing. Flicking her fingers, the water rises along with her movements. I realize she must totally trust me to show me her magic so openly.

"Wow, that's amazing, Hannah," I find my voice to say. She grins widely, moving her hand in a circle so that the water loops around high in the air.

"Have you always been able to do that?" Chase asks, voice high.

"Ever since I was little," Hannah replies.

"You are quite something, child," Abigail says before clasping her hand over her mouth.

Hannah returns the water to the buckets, and then beams at us. The weight of the trust she has placed in me keeps me rooted to the spot. She is in danger now.

If anyone would have seen her, the consequences could be dire. I can't let that happen.

We leave the garden and tour around the compound. Later, Miri and Hannah decide to have a bath, so Hannah fills the tubs as I get them soaps and towels. I wait for them just outside the door, laughing as they splash, and giggle, and joke around.

The rest of the day is uneventful. Like most days in Sanctum.

***

We start our work details, me in the garden, and Miri and Hannah in the kitchens. We meet up for dinner and recreation time. Miri and Hannah adjust well, and Hannah seems to be flourishing. She is open and talkative, and engaging with others. She reminds me of Marie more than Sadie.

Weeks pass in this way, until one day, Hannah comes to visit me in the garden.

"I can help water the plants," Hannah says with a giggle, making the water rise out of the buckets. "I can do it much faster, anyway,"

The water rises into the air and loops around us. That's when Marcus walks by and glares at us. Hannah is making the water circle us now, and I want to scream at her to stop, but he's already seen, and his shock mirrors mine from days before. A man like him can't be trusted with this. He could try to manipulate her, try to make her into a weapon. I will never allow that.

"That's great, Hannah. Why don't you water the plants now?" I say as cheerfully as I can. Inside, my heart is racing, and I feel a sick jolt of adrenaline. Protecting her won't be easy, but I have to do it no matter what. She trusted me with this.

She waters the plants and rushes over to give me a big hug. I squeeze her back, trying to reassure myself that everything is fine. Abigail gives me a look, but I can't decipher it with my mind racing like it is.

"Thank you for helping, Hannah," Abigail says, and it brings me back to the moment.

"Can she do it again?" Marcus stalks towards us, breathing heavily. "Can she do that thing with the water again?"

"That's none of your business," I snap.

"It's all of our business. Do you know what she could do?"

"Nothing for your benefit."

"My benefit is all our benefit."

Chase walks by and hears the commotion. "What's going on here?"

"That's none of your business," Marcus spits.

"You're not the leader here," Chase says quietly.

"Says who? There's quite a few folks here who think I got better ideas than you."

"Only a few. Doesn't change anything."

"It could." Marcus spits. "And we could use her."

"You're not going to use anyone," I say, pushing Hannah behind me.

"She's right," Chase says. "You're not in a position to do anything."

"Let's vote on that."

"Vote on what exactly?"

"Who should be in charge and what we should do with that little girl."

"You have no chance," Chase says, curling up his lip. "But I'm not afraid of you. We'll call a meeting."

Everyone gathers in the mess hall. People mill and mutter under their breaths to each other. Jonas's faction is spread out at other tables, whispering urgently to the others, trying their best to get them to join their side.

It can't work. Chase is well-loved and a good leader. He's fair, and honest, and hardworking. He helps with chores. He has to win. It's bad enough Marcus got in at all, but there's no way he can become the leader. I can't even think about the possibility without getting sick to my stomach.

"Thank you all for coming," Chase addresses the crowd. "Now, I have served as your leader since you voted me into the position originally. We've recently had a newcomer that would like to challenge me for the position. I don't have to cater to his whims, but he is convinced this is what you, the people of this commune, want. So we are putting this to the vote. Who would you rather have as leader, me or Marcus?"

Marcus stands. "Thank you for the introduction. Yes, I am new here, but I am not new to this life. I am no stranger to our reality. Broken up, fighting each other to survive, population dwindling. But here we are safe. And here we must begin rebuilding. It is not enough to just eat. We need to repopulate. Men should be assigned partners for that purpose. And we need to do more to secure our safety. A security detail isn't enough, we need to build a self-reliant militia to protect us. And some of these laws are too stringent. No personal weapons? No extra food? These are unreasonable, as is your leadership. Great things would happen with me in charge. Thank you."

Marcus sits down with a smug smile, and everyone starts talking at once. My stomach twists.

Hannah is sitting next to me, looking miserable.

"They'll vote for Chase, won't they?" she asks, eyes wide. "That bad man won't win, will he?"

I put my arm around her shoulders and pull her close. "I'll never let anyone hurt you," I say fiercely. Mirabel holds my other hand.

Someone goes around passing out folded pieces of paper and pencils stubs for us to vote with. On the center table, there's a wooden box for us to place our ballots in. My hand shakes a little as I take Miri's and my ballot and place them in the box. I walk past Marcus with my head high, refusing to look at him.

An agonizing fifteen minutes pass. Hannah burrows into my side, biting her nails. Miri sits stick straight and doesn't move. I hardly breathe until Stan walks up front, the tally sheet in his hand.

"By a landslide, Chase remains our leader," Stan announces. Jonas slams his fist down on the table and Marcus looks murderous.

"What about the girl?" Marcus shouts, and Hannah goes still by my side.

"As our leader—thank you, folks—I have decided that it is not an issue, and we will not discuss it further. Thank you all. Dinner will be ready soon. Why don't you all enjoy some free time until then.

People clap and smile at the reprieve from work and disperse.

"Let's go color," I say to Hannah. She needs to be distracted, and there's not much for kids to do here. She still has paper and crayons in her room. "I need some decorations for my room, and you did such a good job with yours."

"Okay," she says, subdued. My heart aches a little to see her affected, and I fight not to scowl.

This is Marcus's doing.

In their room, I sprawl on the bed and Miri joins me.

"When did you get to be so good with kids?" she asks while Hannah hums.

"I had a little sister, though I am very rusty." I laugh a little.

Miri flips onto her side to face me. "Tell me about her." She pauses when she sees my face. "If you want to," she rushes to add.

"Sure, just not much of a story teller. She was four years younger than me and just like the sun.

She was so bright and cheerful and outgoing. She called me the moon because I stayed up late and was quiet and brooding. But she always said we belonged together. We did a lot together. She was my best friend. I had her until the Great War, then out of nowhere she got sick. It was just like with our parents." My eyes tear up and I swallow hard. "They went so fast. I couldn't believe how fast they went."

I can't stop the tears that fall, and Miri slides over to hold me. I haven't cried in years, and all the turmoil from the last few weeks finds its release. I start sobbing, but Miri is holding me and I regain composure.

"I'm sorry," I say, but she kisses me, and I'm lost in the warmth of her arms and the soft touch of her lips. She deepens the kiss and I turn into her, pressing my body into her. She moans, and that's when I stop.

"Hannah's here," I mumble, red-faced.

Miri laughs and kisses me once more, lightly. I reach out and gently trace her scar. She's beautiful, more so with that scar.

"Are you done crying, Ash?" Hannah asks. "I don't want you to cry."

"I'm done crying. Sorry if I worried you."

"It's okay, I was just wondering if it had to do with that bad man. He lost though, didn't he?"

"He did, and we're very happy about that. He won't bother you."

Hannah makes me three drawings and helps me hang them in my room. Then we all go down for dinner. Hannah skips in front of us as Miri and I hold hands. I have a newfound buoyancy since Miri kissed me. I'm happier than I've been in years.

Tonight, we have grilled chicken and vegetables and canned peaches warmed with brown sugar. Hannah can't remember what chicken tastes like. I serve her a heaping portion and watch as she takes the first bite.

"It tastes so good," she squeals and begins shoveling her food down.

"Slow down," Miri says, fixing our plates.

"A little to celebrate with," Chase says, holding up a jug of liquor. "Abigail's made punch to go with it."

Everybody cheers and gets a cup. I'm adamant about Hannah not getting any, but Miri lets her taste hers. I give her a death glare, and then go back to dinner.

The three of us eat in peace. I completely ignore Marcus, even though I can feel his eyes on me. His time here now feels numbered, and I am glad for it. People get cup after cup and the mood is high, festive, and loud. After dinner we sit and talk to Abigail and some of the others, but I get tired fast and decide to go to bed alone.

I fall asleep within minutes, but am roused when someone crawls into bed with me.

"Mirabel?" I mumble, eyes still shut, and that's when I feel his hand running up my thigh, going under my shorts. I kick my legs out and try to sit up, but he pins me down. I can smell his BO and the booze. My eyes shoot open, and I turn to see his face. Marcus is trying to molest me.

"Get the fuck off of me!" I yell as loud as I can.

He pins my arms down and climbs on top of me.

"Don't touch me. Let go of me," I scream.

"I'll shut that pretty mouth of yours," he says in a husky voice and goes to kiss me. Revolted, I turn my face away.

"Get off me!"

He pushes my arms down with the crook of his arm, pinning me helplessly and starts groping me with his free hand. He laughs as he stares down at me.

"Fucking pervert. Stop touching me," I shout at the top of my lungs. I hear a pattering of footsteps and soon

Chase and Steve from security are pulling the sweaty pervert off of me.

"Ash, are you okay?" Chase asks, helping me to sit.

"Nauseous, but I'll survive."

"Marcus, you have violated our laws and are immediately expelled from our commune effective immediately. You must never return."

"You can't keep me away."

"We can. You will be escorted from the premises first thing tomorrow morning. Now lock him in the bunker for the night."

Steve leaves with Marcus in tow, and I take a shaky breath. I feel dirty, violated, and my heart is still pounding, my stomach is queasy, and I feel close to tears.

"Are you sure you're alright?" Chase pushes a lock of hair behind my ear.

"I just need to calm down." I brush away a tear. "I'll be fine. I promise."

"What he was doing was despicable."

I nod.

"I'd like you to be one of those that takes him out into the city."

"If that's what you want."

"It is. Are you up for it?"

"Yes, we need to do a supply run anyway. Hannah will need school supplies, and we all need more clothes. We'll multitask."

"Sounds like a plan. I'll find you in the morning."

I sit in bed without moving. I can still feel his hand, hot and rough, on my skin. Miri runs into my room and crouches next to me.

"I just heard what happened." Her hand goes to my cheek. "How awful, are you okay?"

"I'll survive."

"I've already told Hannah I have to sleep with you tonight."

"You didn't have to do that."

"I'd never be able to sleep alone after something like that. I'm going to hold you and help make you feel safe." Her eyes are earnest as she searches my face.

I kiss her, and she returns the kiss. "Thank you," I whisper once we break apart. We get situated in my bed and, before I realize it, I'm asleep.

***

I dream of rough hands grabbing me, rotting breath in my face, and a man laughing. I jolt awake, but Miri's arm is there around me and brings me back to reality. She murmurs in her sleep, and I flop back down on the bed, turning my face to look at her. Her hair isn't curly, but it's not straight either. It kinks in tangles that frame her face. I can't see her mesmerizing blue eyes, but I see her dark lashes that flutter slightly against her cheeks. Her pale scar trails from her eye down her cheek. Her lips are soft and pink, and I long to kiss them. How did I ever find Sadie beautiful compared to her?

I think about the task before me, of getting rid of Marcus in the city. We'll take him along a rambling route to the other end of the city, hopefully getting him lost. Then we'll tie up one of his hands with a bunch of knots so he can't follow us back. We'll be on a supply run anyway. I need to get Hannah school supplies.

There's a teacher store I know along the way. Mirabel will come of course, she won't want to leave me alone with him. Of course, we will have some of the security detail, with us. But I have to prepare myself for Marcus's leering and the things he will say to get under my skin. My skin crawls just thinking of it.

The sky lightens, and I slide out from under Miri's arm. She scrunches her nose and then turns over. I'll let her sleep a while longer. I pull out my journal from its hiding spot in my closet and document everything that has happened. I try to be as clinical as possible, my tears have already been spent and the deeds done. I do have to pause when I write about Sadie and again for what happened last night, but I make it through dry-eyed. Hiding my journal again, I notice the sun has risen. I rouse Miri.

"About time to go," I say with a smile.

She stretches and yawns. "I'll get Hannah ready for the day. We can drop her off in the kitchen."

Chase stops by my room with a cup of coffee in his hand. Coffee is a rationed good and his only vice.

"I thought about today, and I won't feel okay about it unless I go with you."

"You know you don't have to."

"I will feel better if I come."

Braiding my hair to the side, I make small talk with Chase until Mirabel reemerges with Hannah.

"Am I really getting school supplies today?" Hannah jumps up and down.

"Yes, you are. And we're getting new clothes too. You'll be good while we are gone, right?," I ask, grabbing my backpack to fill up.

We take Hannah to the kitchen queens and all assemble outside the dorms. The three of us and Steve and Darren from security with Marcus in tow. He scowls until he sees me, then grins, looking me up and down.

"You can't get rid of me, sweetheart."

"We are in fact getting rid of you, right now," I say, stepping forward. Darren gives Marcus a shove, and we all start walking.

Larry lets us out of the compound. Chase ties a bandana around Marcus's eyes and we begin meandering the streets.

"You know you won't be able to keep me away, sweetheart. I'm coming for you."

"Larry has a gun just in case you try."

"After all the fun we had last night, that's how you talk to me?"

Chase slaps the back of Marcus's head, and Marcus guffaws. "Watch your mouth."

We walk into the center of town close to the teacher store when a dozen people burst onto the scene. They're disheveled looking, long, ratty hair and ripped clothes as they make their way towards us, sneering.

"Look at what we have here," one grizzled man says then spits.

"Take this blindfold off me." Marcus grunts. Chase yanks it off his head. The mob moves ever closer.

Five of the mob are holding baseball bats and things like lead pipes, one holds a hammer, and the rest have knives they all pull out.

"We're going to have some fun today," a woman with matted black hair says. "It's your lucky day, folks."

"We don't want any trouble," Chase says as Steve goes for his gun. They see the gun and the first man who talked charges, blade held high. Steve shoots him and chaos ensues. Chase hands Marcus his monstrosity of a hunting knife and Marcus runs straight at a man with a baseball bat. He ducks under a swing and plunges the knife upward, raising the man two inches off the ground. I rush forward to stop the woman from attacking Miri, putting everything I have into my sprint. I somehow slip under her and turn sideways as her pipe swipes downwards towards me. I exhale and punch her in the nose as hard as I can. I hear a sickening crack and she crumbles. Marcus shuffles off to the side. Steve and Darren take care of the rest.

Miri grabs me and hugs me as I struggle to breathe.

Marcus turns to look at us, a strange smile on his face. He strolls towards us and reaches

Chase. His hand rises and he slits Chase's throat in one smooth motion. I scream and rush towards them.

He punches me in the face as soon as I reach them, and I'm reeling. His fingers wrap around my throat in a bruising grip. Pain sears, and I gasp for air that suddenly isn't there any more. Clawing at his hands, I kick out hard, but I'm growing weak. Black starts at the corners of my vision and begins to crawl inward.

Miri appears and stabs Marcus in the back, a cry escaping her. He flings his arm back and sends her to the ground, but I grab the knife and yank it out. I'm going numb, so I have to move fast. I plant the knife deep into his neck. Hot blood splatters my hand and face. We both fall at the same time. Miri crawls to me.

"Are you okay?"

I'm coughing too much to answer, so I try to nod. I roll on my back and stare at the clouds drifting by so peacefully. Chase. The thought hits me like a punch to my gut. He's gone. That animal killed him. The tears come then, rolling down my cheeks.

"Get up, Ash," Miri demands. I can't, so I reach out my hand and grab hers. She clings to me, nails biting into my skin. "You have to be okay."

"I'm okay," I croak, and a sob escapes me. "I'll be okay."

Miri strokes my hair, and I swallow hard. I can feel the bruises on my neck. I'll feel the pain of this instant long after those bruises fade.

We can't stay out on the streets like this. Not after the mob. We move the bodies under some bushes and say our goodbyes to Chase.

We get school supplies and clothes, but everyone is subdued and skittish. We make it back to Sanctum as quickly as we can.

Everyone gathers when they hear the news. Larry approaches me with a frown. "Chase was a good man. We're gonna need someone else like him. Someone like you."

"I'm nowhere near as fair as he was. Nowhere near as good."

"Near enough," he says, clapping me on the shoulder. "Near enough."

"I should be the next leader," Jonas cries out way too soon.

"No one here wants that," I reply.

"What, then it should be you?" He laughs. "What do you know?"

"No, it shouldn't be me. It should be Abigail. She's wise, fair-minded, and smart enough to guide us. We should all vote on this, but I nominate her."

"Here, here," the crowd agrees.

It's almost unanimous. Abigail wins. "Thank you all. I can't replace Chase, no one can, but I will do my best to honor his memory," she says, quieting the crowd.

Everybody claps. Miri comes over and hugs me tight.

"I'll miss him so much," I whisper, tears in my eyes.

"I'm here," she says.

Hannah comes over to us and embraces us both. "Are you okay, Ash?"

"I'm okay, just hard to talk," I say, squatting down to her level. She heard about the attack before we could shield her from the truth.

"I wish I had killed Marcus," she says grimly.

"Killing isn't an easy decision. I'm glad you haven't had to kill anyone yet."

"Do you feel bad because you have?"

"It's complicated. I've only killed when my life was on the line, but it's never easy."

Hannah nods, recognizing the wisdom of my words. "I just want you to be happy."

"It will take time. I'm really sad my friend died, but you and Miri make me really happy."

"You make us happy," Miri emphasizes.

I look into her sapphire eyes and kiss her, but pull away after a minute. Hannah needs reassurance right now. I bend over and hug her close to me. "Everything will work out okay, little bird." I stroke her blond hair. "And we'll be happy."

She looks up at me and finally smiles. "Can we go through my books now?"

"Sure." I grin.

The three of us make our way to Hannah and Miri's room, smiling and holding hands.

# It's Not Scary If It's Home

**Carol Allen**

Gary finished mowing the side lawn and wiped his brow. He started to use a bandana as he got older, when the humidity was too much for him. Today, he kept the red bandana in his pocket, but on really sunny days, it was tied around his neck. The humidity made his sweat soak his t-shirt, and no cloth around his neck would stop that from happening. He should have used the riding lawn mower and took it easy today. But this was how he stayed active, he was getting too old, and his knees wouldn't allow for a lot of physical activity. His achy knees were more accurate than any weather forecaster, and he waited until after the morning rain to come over to the master's house. Thankfully, the sun wasn't brutal at four in the afternoon when he started pushing the mower. Gary thought he should start wearing a big straw hat to keep the sun off his face and neck. The thought made him feel older and he whispered, "I have got to get out of here."

He nodded to the tall, thin man standing on the porch, running his hand through his sandy brown hair. The man's name wasn't important, he was one of the many who had stayed in the master's house. There would be new people in the house soon, and he was too old to keep the names straight. Nor did he want to remember their names, it was bad enough to remember their faces. The man ran down the porch stairs and joined Gary as he pushed the mower towards the shed. "Is everything okay?" Gary asked the young man.

"No. Uh, yes, everything is fine. It's just that," he struggled, then asked, "Is it really okay for us to stay here?"

"Yeah. Oh yeah. It's no problem. The owner has like five houses. So he only comes up once a year, if even that." Gary took off his faded blue baseball cap and wiped his forehead with his tanned arm. His white shaggy hair dripped with sweat and he thought he should get a trim, but he found this style made him look the part of a caretaker. Plus, the barber had left his shop to his son, and Lord help him, Junior wasn't as good as his daddy. "It would have been a shame to let you—and your family—a real shame, to have you guys out on the streets in times like this. Especially with your little girl."

"We appreciate it too. Is there anything we can do, to repay you?" He adjusted the collar of his blue polo shirt. The humidity was thick, and the young man had sweat beading on his forehead and upper lip. "We don't have much money, but I could pay you something."

Gary shook his head and did his speech. "I'm just being the caretaker, sir. I'm really just a glorified gardener, and the boss pays well. If you all can just keep the house clean, that will help me out a lot. And let me know if there are any problems in the house." He winked and said, "Like anything with the plumbing or any repairs needed, but I don't do any dusting."

"Oh yeah, sure." The man exhaled and nodded. "We can do that. We can clean up after ourselves. I don't think we will need to stay for too much longer. It's been great to just sleep in a house and be safe."

"Sure, it sounded like you guys traveled for a while. Take this time to rest, and feel free to eat anything in the kitchen. I usually help myself to the perishables when there aren't any guests." He laughed. "But it is easy to go to the grocery store."

"Yes, thank you." The man put his hands into his khakis pockets and turned to walk back towards the house.

Gary said, "One last thing, I would stay out of the master bedroom too. There are a lot of other rooms to sleep in. Just keep that shut door shut." Gary adjusted his hat and pushed the lawnmower into the shed after the man nodded. Through the shed's window, Gary watched the man walk into the house and heard the screen door slam shut. He whistled a tune and left the mower near the door. "Next time I'll use the riding mower to do the job in one day." He closed up the shed and walked to his blue pickup truck.

The only gas station in town was on his way home. He passed it, coming into town on his way to the master's house, and then to go back to his cabin in the woods. Gary filled up four gas cans—five gallons each—and his truck. He had been friends with the station's owner, Pete, since high school, and Gary would tell him that the gas was for the lawnmowers. If Pete even asked, he should be used to him filling up the gas cans since he became a caretaker. Anyways, Pete was always behind his counter.

Early on, he was watching his television until the big broadcasting stations went static. Since the major cities went down, Pete was manning the radio, dialing through all the stations, listening for any updates. "I think they said something about an attack. I think there was an attack, and that's why the power went out," Pete said as he dialed through the radio stations. Pete then asked Gary, "Could it be another terrorist attack? I thought they had reinforced the power grid after the east coast lost power for a couple weeks in the early aughts."

"I really don't know, Pete." Gary watched some of the townspeople walking down Main Street through the window. He noticed a few outsiders walking toward the bed and breakfast. It looked like a group of college-aged friends. He hoped they would be able to stay there.

"I thought I saw an explosion on the news before the power went out. It looked like it was another sky-scraper, like where the studio is filming." Pete stopped spinning the wheel on the radio and turned it off. "I'm tired of the static. I think the unknown is the worst part of this."

***

The few people that walked into town didn't have any new information. They were just leaving the cities for the quiet country or small town. The cities were dangerous—just full of people—unsafe with fewer resources to fight over. Some were heading north, and the travelers would say, "Maybe it'll be better where it's going to be cold in the winter. There's still time to prepare for the winter, it's still early." But there were no answers to anyone's questions, and there was no news in town. The ones that were left in town would stay away from the travelers, the strangers. Then there were the other travelers who were going south to avoid a cold winter. They would whisper to each other, "What about food? What about the snow? I don't want to freeze to death."

The town had been almost empty from outsiders since the colder spring. The main road was littered with cars, SUVs, and trucks that have been pulled off to the shoulder and abandoned. They had run out of gas or couldn't be driven because of the traffic that packed the roads. Now they were all empty from the out of towners, who just left to go back to their cities, where they thought it would be safer in the beginning. When the electronics went out, the rest of the outsiders left after Pete cleared the road with his tow truck.

Then the power was restored, and the small town life continued. But there were no television stations, no mobile phones, no radio station broadcasts nationally. The local newspaper tried to tell the people about different causes. The first explanation was an attack from a foreign enemy, an uprising from an anti-government group. Pete thought that would explain the explosions he saw. That would also explain the lack of communications available or lack of news. Then the newspaper thought it could be a new flu virus that was going through the population. But it was all speculation, all rumors, and life went on in the town.

Pete didn't think the flu was the cause. "I don't think that would cause the power failure," he said.

The travelers either stayed for a few days or moved on after filling up their bags with supplies. No one could offer any news, just to say that the town or city they left didn't feel safe anymore. "Better to stay put," most of the town had concluded at the end of the first month.

***

Gary's mom lived in a small apartment for seniors about two hours away. Landline phones had been pretty reliable, and he had been able to talk to her until two weeks ago. There was a busy signal or just the automated answering system for the first week. Then the phone would just ring for minutes and minutes. When he tried to call her again on the phone at the gas station, there was no dial tone.

"I think I will go check on her," Gary told Pete after he hung up.

"Really? Do you think it's safe to leave town?" Pete scratched his head of salt-and-pepper hair. He kept his hair short because he didn't like wearing hats. Pete still went to the other businesses in town. He was not like

Gary. Gary didn't trust anyone, just Pete, and just barely.

"The road looks clear for miles out of here. I don't know. I've had no problem when I drive in from the cabin."

"That's driving like twenty miles versus two hundred. Who knows how the road is to get into the actual city?" Pete shook his head. "Or even how things really are out there. I mean what is this virus thing they keep talking about? Do you think the city isn't dealing with what we are?"

"That makes me want to check on my mom even more." Gary wiped the back of his neck with his bandana. "I don't see a lot of travelers. But the ones that do, wander in then," he waved his hand and said, "wander back out."

Pete leaned against the counter and asked, "Do you think it'll be okay to leave? Just leave?"

"I just cut the grass, so it should be good for at least a week or two. Then you could direct a few people to go over to the property while I'm gone." He scratched his head then said, "If the road is bad, then I'll just turn back. I don't expect to be gone for long." He cleared his throat. "There's a family at the house now. That should hold them over."

Pete shook his head and hit the countertop. "What did we sign up for?"

"It's us or them," Gary said, grabbing a six pack of beer. "We have to survive."

"But a deal with the devil?" Pete shuddered. "I don't know anymore."

"Take care, Pete." Gary left thirty bucks on the counter and listened to the bell ring as he pulled the door open. It might be the last time he visited this gas station.

He drove down the main road out of town. This was the same road that would take him to the city, but he turned off onto a dirt road. It had a few cabins that were along the dirt road, and his was at the end of it, deep into the woods. The road turned into a trail that would go to the river and follow it for miles. Gary liked the quiet of the woods, and in the years he lived in the cabin, he never had visitors, other than Pete.

After he parked the truck next to the cabin, he took two of the gas cans out of the truck bed. Then he opened his garage and put the gas cans into the back of his Jeep. "This might be better for the road trip than the truck." He also put some groceries into the back of the Jeep, then locked up the garage. He left some empty gas cans in the truck bed and grabbed the beer, before going into the cabin.

Gary entered the locked cabin and unlocked the front window. He opened the shutters to let the fresh air in. He didn't like to be so open during these times and draw attention to his cabin, but he liked to hear the birds and the sounds of the woods. Gary opened a can of beans and made a ham sandwich for his dinner. He looked out of the window when he heard a vehicle drive up. It was Pete's red sedan, which he parked next to the truck.

Gary let Pete in, they sometimes ate dinner together, but he was surprised to see him so soon. "What brings you by, did I forget to pay for something?"

Pete shook his head before he sat on the chair opposite him with a sandwich and a beer. "Are you really going to go to the city?"

Gary nodded and scratched his leg. "Yeah, I think I'll leave in the morning or the next day. My knees don't hurt, so it shouldn't rain." He took a big bite of his sandwich.

Pete looked out of the window. "Do you think the city is better off than we are? I don't know if having more people around is better."

"Oh, I really don't know." Gary leaned back in the wooden chair. "I tried to get information from my mom, but she didn't leave her apartment." He took a sip of beer then said, "I even tried to talk to her nurse before the phones went out, but she said she was staying in the complex with my mom because she was scared of the gangs."

"I just don't know what is happening in the world." Pete shook his head. "Did you think this was even possible? Actual monsters."

Gary looked down at his hands. "We had to do what we did to survive."

"I know." Pete looked at the empty beer can in front of him, then reached for another. "I didn't think that we would be here, six months later."

"Why don't you just enjoy that beer, Pete." Gary stood up. "I'm going to walk the perimeter. You can stay tonight, if you want."

Gary left the cabin and walked towards the trees, there was a mixture of maple and pine. There were a few oak trees as well, and he headed toward one of them. He looked around before he climbed the tree where he had his blind. He wasn't an avid hunter like his dad, but he kept up the maintenance of the blind. He used it to look at local birds and kept a pair of binoculars in it. He also kept blankets up there, since he sometimes stayed in the blind all night. Most days, he felt safer when he could be hidden in the trees. Before Pete came over, he had decided to stay up there tonight. Now, he had a bad feeling. "Would Pete tell on me? Did he tell the master that I was leaving?"

Pete didn't know that Gary had a deal with the master, he had promised to be the caretaker until he had given the master one hundred people. The family of three put him at his quota or close. "And it only took me about six months to do it." Gary looked at his cabin and the door stayed shut. That was the secret, make the house a home, he told himself. "It's not scary if it's home." He took on the project to fix up the old house on Main Street. He was able to furnish it with the help of the townspeople. "We were all in it together. It was the town that voted to keep the master happy." There were a few dissenters who did not attend the meeting. They left town after the meeting, after the vacationers. Gary didn't think there were other places to go. "If the monsters are here, they are probably in the other towns and cities. It was the monsters that were killing people."

He covered his body up with the blankets in the blind. He wasn't a hunter, but he tried to keep the blankets in the elements to help disguise his scent. He didn't want to scare off nature. But this would help him. "Maybe they won't be able to smell me. It's been six months and he thought he had left them just around a hundred people. It had to be at least ninety-nine." He leaned against the tree and tried to get comfortable, it was going to be a long night. Would this make it one hundred? "I think so."

He was worried that he would be the next one to meet the master. That's why he preferred to stay in the cabin. The shutters kept him safe, he could leave them closed and locked, and the monsters wouldn't be able to get him. Initially, he worried the blind was a risk, but they didn't seem too interested in getting rid of him in the beginning.

*Before we knew they were here. Before we knew what they were feeding on.*

***

Gary was bird watching, he had climbed into the blind before the sunrise that morning. He didn't see the monsters come into town, he was looking at a cardinal. He liked to see the little red bird, against the snow covered pine trees on a still, cold early spring morning. "But they didn't see me either."

It wasn't until he went into town that afternoon that he saw the beginning of the exodus. The few out of towners were driving out. There was an ominous fog that hung in the air, so everyone drove slowly. The church bells were ringing, and people were standing outside, looking toward the white building. "Were they calling a meeting? Was there a weather emergency?" Everyone was asking questions, but hesitant to go into the church.

"I don't like the looks of this fog," Pete had said to him after he parked his truck near the gas station. "Did you hear about the missing couple last night?"

"What's going on?" Gary stood next to Pete. "Did you say missing people?"

"Yeah, I'm surprised you didn't see the search party out by your cabin. I guess, a man and woman were hiking in those woods and didn't come back." He looked at the crowd growing larger. "I think they tried to look for them yesterday, before it got dark."

"I didn't see anything." Gary ran his hand through his white hair. "I was birding and didn't see many birds. I definitely did not see any people."

"I don't know if that's going to be the search party, but I guess we should go check it out." Pete shrugged and crossed the street walking toward the church.

Gary joined him, and so did some of the other townspeople on the sidewalk. They crowded the front door and heard the man in the suit say, "There they are! Come on in! Come on in! All are welcome!" He gestured for people to take a seat among the pews. "See Father, I told you they would come."

Once the pews were full, the bells stopped ringing. Everyone was quiet, watching the short man in a grey three piece suit. He was talking with the priest and the mayor. The mayor stood up and asked for attention by raising his hand. No one had made a noise since entering the church, something felt different; not safe, electrified. The mayor had to clear his throat many times before he could speak, "Everyone, I'm sorry I have bad news." He looked at the town with tears in his eyes. "I'm afraid we are going to have to make some tough decisions. We have a visitor here, I'm going to let him talk and explain."

The man in the grey suit smiled a big smile, then said, "Well, thank you, mayor. I have a proposal, once I tell you the details, you will have ten minutes to confer. Then I will need an answer. This is a democracy, so a majority of votes rules. Then once the decision is made, the terms will have to be adhered to." He paused, then asked, "Do we have an agreement so far?"

The mayor nodded in consent.

"Well, folks," the man continued, "It seems like there is going to be a change in how things are done. You will have changes that are going to be made less, if you agree to my terms. I can guarantee that your lives will be mostly as you're accustomed to. That means, a continuity of services, like electricity and water works. The local grocers will continue to be stocked. There may be some interruptions in these services, but you have my word that things will be restored as soon as possible." He had been pacing in front of the crowd and now paused. "All I ask is for the house on the hill and a caretaker."

There was a collective sigh and the crowd murmured, "A house? That's all?" Everyone was asking, "What house does he want?"

"What happens if we don't agree?" Mr. George, who retired from the bank, asked.

"The effects of the world will come here to this little town. Your town." He pointed to the man who asked the question. "Old timer, do you know what happened after the depression?"

The man nodded, he had lived through the aftermath of it.

"That will happen here. Not only will there be no food or electricity, but no contact with the outside world." He looked at the people. "So, I leave you to decide on an agreement or not. I will give you ten minutes." He sat down in a chair next to the mayor and smiled at the crowd.

The mayor and priest stood up and walked to be in front of the pews.

"What is going on mayor?" The principal of the elementary school stood up to ask. "What is going on?"

"Well, Marjorie, we heard that something is going on in the cities," the mayor said. "The news was reporting about some kind of virus leading to a lot of people in the hospitals. Then there were reports of a run on the grocery stores, and some damage to property. This was on the morning news until things went to static."

"I saw that on the news too," Mr. George said. "Something was happening in a few of the big cities on both coasts too."

"There was an explosion that I saw on the news," Pete said and scratched his chin. "I think there's some kind of attack."

The mayor raised his hand, asking for silence. "I'm not sure what is going on as of right now. But we are all here, and we are safe. This gentleman said that he could help us out, with keeping the supplies going. He can keep the town going. We just have to agree to his terms."

"How can he do that?" A woman with two small children asked.

"I think he's wealthy," the priest answered. "He said he owns many chains of stores, and that's why he can help us. He can get us supplies and food."

The local realtor asked, "What does he want? Which house?"

"He said he wants the house on the hill, is that the big white house?" The mayor looked back at the stranger.

"Yes, with the wraparound porch," the man in the grey suit answered. Then he stood up. "I'm afraid that I need an answer. Shall we vote?" He stood in front of the mayor and the priest. "You two have to vote on the matter." He looked at the crowd. "Let's have everyone who agrees to raise their hand." He smiled and raised his hand, his long nails looked blackened despite his immaculate appearance.

The townspeople slowly raised their hands, and it was unanimous.

"Good, good." The man smiled widely and he seemed to have more teeth than normal. "Now, I need a volunteer. I will need someone to be a caretaker of the house for me." He looked at the crowd. "I need someone who is handy and reliable."

People shifted in their seats and cleared their throats, but no one raised their hand. Women with teenage boys kept their arms around them. They wouldn't volunteer their sons. Gary looked at the crowd and saw a few of the men contemplate the choice. He saw that Seth, the local high school biology teacher, was raising his hand. Gary beat him to it and stood up. "I will do it. I just have one question."

"Go ahead." The man smiled wider, and seemed younger than he did at the beginning of the meeting. His hair looked darker, instead of having grey hair and beard, it now seemed black with a few grey hairs.

Gary asked, "Does the job pay anything?"

"I may not pay a regular salary, but there are certain perks." He stepped down from the altar area. "That is, if you volunteer of your own free will."

"I agree." Gary felt a shock of electricity go through him when he shook the man's hand.

It would be later, after the house was cleaned up, that the true deal would be made. Gary was told he was to let people stay in the house. Then the man, who he would call "master," would return weekly to, in his words, take care of the people. Gary's weekly responsibilities were to clean the house and keep the lawn manicured. The perks were, he could eat any food that was in the kitchen and help himself to any of the items in the house, including what was left by the house occupants. It took Gary a couple weeks to figure out that the visitors who went into the house would never leave. It took the town a few more weeks to figure out the same. Some of the families who attended the meeting decided to leave after a couple months, including the mayor. He wondered if they made it to the city. Some of them had called when they made it to the next town, but the calls stopped after a couple weeks. Gary guessed that other towns had made similar deals with the master, and that maybe it wasn't safer outside of town. He couldn't tell anyone what happened in the house at night, since he was never on the grounds once the sun set.

Gary definitely didn't tell anyone about the real deal he had made with the man in the grey suit. The man arrived after the house was repaired and the paint had dried. A black Lincoln pulled up and the driver opened the back door. The man stepped out wearing a different suit and mirrored sunglasses. His shiny, toothy smile showed his pleasure with the house. "This is exactly what I wanted. You did a fine, fine job." He was looking at the curtains and the sofa cushions. "Ah Gary, this is nice. Did you have your wife help you decorate?"

"No sir, not married." Gary followed the man's path through the upstairs rooms.

"That might not be an entirely bad thing, Gary." The man laughed. "I mean, women, you can't live with them, right?"

Gary was too nervous to laugh, he just nodded.

"Aww Gary, I didn't realize you were a feminist." He frowned and raised his hands up. "I apologize. Please, don't be offended."

"A joke is a joke." Gary shrugged. "Is there anything else that you needed?"

"Well, this is definitely a good start. So, of course, you will be in charge of the upkeep of the house and the lawn." The man went downstairs and into the kitchen with Gary following behind. "The kitchen pantry should be kept full of food and the refrigerator. I will keep a tab at the grocer's, and you will keep any guests of this house fed. You also may keep any food items you want from the house." He spun around. "Waste not, want not." Then he stepped out the back door and went down the few steps into the backyard. "This is nice. I think families will like it here. Maybe we should get an outdoor grill and a patio furniture set."

Gary nodded and wrote down those notes.

"I don't love the flower situation here," he said, pointing to the few plants that lined the back of the house, "but that can be taken care of later. We can't expect perfection all the time."

"Sir?"

"Nothing, pay that no attention." He looked around. "There is a nice peacefulness here. I mean, there's a quaintness to this town. I mean, it's so quiet here, but if I were to scream, do you think anyone would hear it?"

"That would depend on how loud," Gary answered. They were at the edge of town, on the hill after the downtown stores gave way to neighborhoods. "If it was loud enough, someone might hear it."

"Do you think if someone were to scream inside with the windows closed, they would be heard?"

"Again, if it was loud enough." Gary looked at the man. He tried to read the man's face, but he could only see himself in the mirrored sunglasses. He cleared his throat and tried to look less worried.

"Well Gary, why don't we leave a window open in the house." The man turned and headed towards the front lawn.

"All the time sir?" Gary followed and asked, "All year?"

"Well, let's just say yes to that for now." He chuckled. "Safety first."

The master didn't return for weeks, and the house was empty for those weeks. Gary kept the kitchen stocked and lawn mowed. Then the travelers started coming into town. Most of them stayed in the hotel for a few days and moved on. There were issues with the electronics, so people weren't driving into town anymore due to lack of reliable gas stations. So in the beginning, there were waves of people just walking in groups. They would stay in the hotels for days, and as they rested, they would talk to the townspeople about how things were. Things were friendly until the money ran low, or out. Then the hotel was no longer fully booked, and the travelers were camping out in the abandoned vehicles. They wouldn't stay in town for too long, just long enough to fill up on supplies. There were some families with younger children that would accept Gary's offer to stay in the large house. He told them about the fully stocked kitchen. He refused payment, as the master had required. His only job was to stop by to take care of the yardwork and to make sure they were alright.

Gary was happy to help the families. The house was full of life, and the children were able to play on the lawn. They really started to look happy after a few days of rest and food. The first two families had been neighbors and travelled for a few weeks to reach this town. They were going to try for the coast, the cities were scary they had heard. The stores had run out of food early, and it was too dangerous to be out after dark. But they hoped a small town by the ocean would allow for fishing and warmer weather. Gary would later talk to his mom and tell her to stay in the apartment. She reassured him that she was taken care of and had enough food.

The families were in the house for about a week before they were gone. Gary drove up with a few new toys for the kids. There were different toys for the two girls and the three boys to play with, maybe a little old fashioned with dolls for the girls and cars for the boys, but he was a middle-aged man with no kids. He drove up expecting to see them on the porch, enjoying the warm weather for a spring day, but there was no one. He parked the pickup truck and walked into the quiet house. The spring door slammed behind him, and he looked at the empty living room. There were a few books on the couch, probably left there by one of the children. There were more books on the coffee table, and an empty coffee mug left by an adult. He saw some dishes in the kitchen sink, but nothing out of place. He went up the stairs, "Hello! Anyone home?"

The doors were all open except to the master bedroom, that one was always closed. The beds were all unmade. "So they slept here, where are they now?" Their belongings were in the rooms, he could see the clothing they wore in the closets, dresser drawers, and strewn on the floor. The kids' rooms were a little messier, but there were no people in the house. He closed some of the windows on the upper floor, "It was supposed to rain later that day." But he kept the kitchen windows open as he washed the dishes. He spent most of the day mopping, vacuuming, and cleaning the bathrooms.

After he ate some leftover fried chicken he saw in the fridge for lunch, he went upstairs and took the clothes and ran them through the washing machine. He thought he would just wash their clothes and pack them. They weren't going to stay forever, but he had hoped to see them before they left. Then he changed the sheets on the beds, they would be washed after he was done with the clothes.

After he removed the clothes from the dryer, he brought the basket into the living room to fold. He was surprised by the master. "Sir, I wasn't expecting you today."

"Oh, Gary, you did a fine job this week." He patted his belly. "Just above my greatest expectation. But I do think you are being an overachiever. What is going on with this pile of clothes?"

"They belong to the guests, I was just going to pack them up. I don't know where they are, but if they are going to leave, I wanted to help them."

"Oh Gary, they won't be needing those where they are. I guess we can donate them to some charity or someone who needs them." He buttoned up his blue suit jacket. "I will be going, but if I were you, I would get this house ready for the next guests."

"Yes, sir." Gary watched the man leave.

The same routine happened a few more weeks before Gary understood what was happening. He started to dread going to the house on the hill. He was happy to see the travelers on the porch when he parked. He wanted to warn them about the master, but he didn't know when the master would appear. Even if he had advanced knowledge, what would he tell them?

"You have to leave this house, or else!"

"What? Or else what?" They would've asked, and he didn't have an answer. He didn't know what happened to the others. They just weren't there. He tried to find them. He would walk through town and see if they were in the diner or the library. Maybe they just left town. But none of the families left with the luggage they came into town with. He would look for signs of them as he drove home at the end of the day, and the next day, when he drove into town. But there were no signs of them. He even looked for clues of something horrible in the house, but it was just as clean as a house would be with a family living in it.

After a few months and almost twenty families, Gary had the courage to ask the master about what he was doing.

"What am I doing? What do you mean Gary?"

"What am I doing here? Why am I letting these people stay here? Where do they go? What are you doing to them?"

"Gary, I will tell you if you really want to know." The master was wearing grey again, not the three piece suit, but a grey suit.

Gary was reminded of the first meeting with the man because of how he seemed to look younger during that meeting. The master looked even younger today, the grey hair was almost completely black now. The beard, a trimmed goatee, did not have any grey in it anymore. The man smiled his too big smile and Gary shivered.

"Gary, I know you volunteered for this job, but what if you and I came to some sort of agreement. Going forward."

"What kind of agreement?"

"You seem to have a head for numbers, and you don't seem very happy with your job here. Am I right?"

Gary nodded.

"I thought you were a smart guy. That's the downside of being smart, you can be too smart for your own good." The man sighed and sat down on the couch. "Well, Gary I won't tell you what you already suspect. But I propose a quota. Your numbers are great. You have exceeded my expectations, but what I find is there will be a lull eventually. It is inevitable, that is why I travel so frequently." He sighed again. "But I digress," he smiled then said, "So, the new agreement is once you have delivered to me 100 guests, I will release you from the job of caretaker."

Gary sat down opposite the man in a brown recliner. His mind calculated the months he had already been there and the number of people... it was two months and twenty families. It wouldn't be an impossible number to meet. Maybe it would take another six months or so. Could he keep doing it for that long? Would he be able to keep doing it for the rest of his life? Did he have another option?

Gary stood up, "I agree."

***

"A deal with the devil is right," Gary muttered. Then he pulled the blankets up over his head, it was getting chilly now that the sun was setting. He tried not to make too much noise when he saw Pete step outside the cabin. Pete looked around then lit a cigarette and sat on a plastic chair next to the cabin. "Smoking will kill you, Pete," Gary whispered. He looked around the property and didn't see anything suspicious. "If it's quiet after a few more hours, I'll go back inside." Gary rubbed his eyes and said, "Maybe I'm being paranoid." He watched Pete go back inside the cabin and turn on the lights. "Close the shutters and lock the windows, Pete," Gary whispered as the crickets took over and the night went on. Gary started to nod off and was awakened by the sounds of fluttering.

It sounded like a lot of birds flying by him, but he didn't see that in the woods. There wouldn't be a big flock of birds in these trees, maybe by the lake, but that was miles away. He blinked and let his eyes adjust to the dark as he looked around his property. He looked at the cabin and saw the light coming out of the open window. "He didn't close the window," Gary whispered and held his breath. He guessed that Pete had fallen asleep waiting for him, since he didn't see any movement in the cabin. Then he heard the fluttering again and saw a dark figure fly from the trees to the open window. The master was illuminated when he looked into the open window. There was no mistaking the master's dark hair and taste in suits.

Gary watched the master crawl over the window sill and enter the cabin. He was startled by the sight of a man moving so unnaturally, and who seemed to slither through the window. Gary closed his eyes briefly, then opened them to watch the shadow of the master move over the grass. It was like watching a shadow puppet show. Gary could see the shadow of Pete in the chair and the master walked up behind him. Pete didn't have a chance to react before the shadow of the master grew in size. The master's mouth gaped open and Pete disappeared into the master's shadow. Gary now knew what happened to all the guests that had stayed in the house on the hill.

He covered his mouth with both hands. He couldn't risk exposure. He closed his eyes and tried not to grieve for his friend at this moment. The silence should have been comforting, but he had to assume that the master was still in the cabin. Gary did not want to open his eyes. He was afraid that when he opened them, he would see the master's large smile in front of him. Time passed and there was a fluttering noise. Then the crickets returned, and Gary opened his eyes. He saw nothing but grass, trees, and his empty cabin. "Why didn't you close the window?" Gary rubbed his eyes and tried not to cry.

The next morning, Gary ate some more beef jerky as he stayed in the blind. He thought it was still early enough to leave town and put a lot of miles between him and the house on the hill. Gary had spent all night counting all the guests he had encouraged to stay in that house. The number had to be a hundred by now. He had hoped that Pete wouldn't have been a part of his quota. But he was right to be worried. Maybe he would not be able to leave town. Maybe the end of the job meant the end of his life. Could he negotiate a new deal? Did he want to have a new deal?

Gary stretched out his legs and started to take off the blankets when he heard voices coming down the trail. He froze and listened to see if they would continue down to his cabin. The first of the group he saw was a tall man in jeans, a green flannel shirt, and a black beanie. He held a stick in his right hand and walked onto Gary's property. He watched the man walk up to the cabin and look inside the window. "Just take the car keys and drive away," Gary whispered. He knew Pete's car keys were on the table. "Or they were there when I last saw them. Hell, you can take my truck. Just get out of here." The man tried the door and it opened and he disappeared for a few minutes.

Gary prayed until he saw the man run out and yell, "Elise! Girls! Come on out!"

"Shit," Gary cursed under his breath. He watched the rest of the family of three walk toward his cabin. The wife was a pretty, thin woman, also in jeans and wearing a brown sweater. Her blonde hair was in a braid and she held onto her little daughter's hand until they crossed the threshold. "The girl looked like she was only eight." Gary whispered, "Close the window if you're going to stay." He looked around the blind, and found his cooler in the corner. There were some bottled water and a couple bags of chips in it. He took out a bottle and drank some water. "It's going to be another long night." He moved to the back of the blind and watched the cabin. He saw some smoke coming out of the chimney. "They're probably eating my food," he said to himself and took another bite of the jerky. "I should have grabbed a beer to go," he whispered and closed his eyes.

Gary spent the day recounting the guests that he had let stay in the master's house. He had made tick marks on the notebook that he normally used to write down birds he saw. But over the last six months, he was keeping count of his guests. His ticks were men, women, kids that wanted shelter from the road, and food. They were families, couples, and friends that were trying to find a new home. He had to add the latest families, the family of three last week. That was a single father with two teenage kids. This week was a family of three, a couple and their five year old daughter. Gary made a tick mark for Pete and started to count the tally again. He was at ninety-eight. "Shit," he cursed again and looked to his right. His father's rifle was in its case there. He unzipped it, took out the rifle, and inspected it. It was loaded and he looked through the telescopic sight at the cabin's door. He took a breath and took the safety off.

The time went by slowly and he couldn't see into the cabin. He imagined that the family ate, then bathed, and slept. That's what they all did in the master's house. Gary almost dozed off when the man went out the cabin door and walked to the back of the cabin. The wife followed him and they were talking. Gary strained to listen. He heard the man say, "We could stay, but I think someone lives here."

"There's no one here though," the woman said. "I mean, why is it just open?"

"They could be somewhere in the woods, but will be back by tonight." The man picked up a few logs. "I think we should keep on the main road. There's probably a town and we can stay there tonight."

"I'm just so tired of this," the woman said, wiping her tears away.

The man put his hand on her shoulder. "I know. But we didn't make it this far to start giving up, right?"

"Why did we leave?" The woman had her head in her hands.

"Things were getting dangerous. You know that."

"I do." The woman nodded. "I know."

"We had to leave or they would make me join them." He kissed her. "I couldn't do that to you and the kid."

She nodded and wiped her face again. "Okay, we can try the town."

"Okay, I'm going to put some of these by the fireplace. I'll leave some money for the food we ate, and then we can blow this popsicle stand."

"Okay, I'll get the kiddo ready." The woman walked towards the front of the cabin and went inside. The man continued to pick up some firewood. Gary took a breath and aimed the rifle at the man's back. He pulled the trigger and the man collapsed onto the ground, yelling. The woman screamed and went to run out of the cabin. Gary shot at the ground, near her feet and she stopped and ran back into the cabin. The man yelled and tried to get up, but could only flip onto his back. The woman went to a window in the back of the cabin and opened it.

"I can't get out," she yelled to her husband.

"It's okay. I'm okay," the man told her, "I just can't feel my legs right now." He rolled onto his side to look at her through the window. "Just stay calm. Pack a bag to be ready to run."

"I don't want to leave you," she said before crying again.

"It's okay. Just let me think." He pulled himself closer to the cabin. "But you got to get ready to run, if this guy comes in."

"Okay, I'll pack the bag." The woman went away from the window and Gary could hear her talk to their daughter. The man continued to pull himself closer to the cabin, but stopped when he felt weak from the blood loss.

Gary didn't want him to suffer, but he couldn't let the family leave. Gary just hoped that he hadn't spoiled the man too much for the master. "Just in case I need three more."

# Jacob's Transition

## JK Allen

Jacob awoke with a start. He had been having the most vivid dream, nightmare really. Likely a punishment from his father. All because, well, Jacob's father was the first greater demon. He had been an angel, beautiful to behold, then fallen to the lowest realm. His alabaster skin turned to the color of corpses, his wings blackened. Perdition was a dry and dusty place, and his father was chained there for all eternity in the pitch blackness. A desert of choking rust, surrounded by his demon minions. He had time to mess with his son and he did.

Jacob took a shower to rinse off the sweat and tears that fell in the safety of his private bathroom. Shaking off the remnants of the dream in the hot spray of water. If Marta were to ever see such a show of weakness—of human emotion—the other half of him he was constantly fighting against and suppressing, then she would punish him in crueler ways than even his dear old dad. Marta was the only constant in his life here in Bend, Oregon. He lived here and made his money here until it was time to return home, to Lockewood in the sleepy midwest. She was tasked with raising him to be able to fulfill his destiny. To be able to free his father and release a demon army on Earth the likes no one had ever seen. But unlike a mother, she was cold and unfeeling, a cruel teacher to be obeyed. So cold she chilled his half-human blood sometimes.

Here was the place his gang operated, and they did well. Making him money and providing him with victims to take his feelings out on. He was coming into his own manhood now, and starting to push the boundaries with Marta and the men. He wouldn't just blindly follow his father or Marta's instructions forever, after all.

And he had a victim to torment now. Just, he didn't want to.

Tara Teegan was a sweet girl, by most accounts. The kind of gal you didn't mind meeting the parents. Well, not that Jacob had ever had any in his life in a real, meaningful way, but if he had, he'd love to bring Tara to dinner. A sweetheart in public, but fun when she got to let her hair down. She was the perfect mix of spunk and sweet. And Jacob loved that about her. It reminded him of himself in some ways, of his struggle with being half-human. Jacob liked many things about Tara. Even after she had started to run errands for his boys down at the gang. She was supposed to be their good luck charm. But she got pulled over and searched, and well, that did no one any good.

The obvious plan was that Jacob was to make her disappear. They would find her body maybe in a few weeks, looking like she had run away and run afoul of things. Or perhaps like she had killed herself. It didn't really matter as long as her lips could no longer move to testify against the family. Jacob briefly considered disfiguring the girl, taking away her ability to communicate, but that seemed too cruel. He was fond of her tongue, with her sassy comebacks and lilting voice.

Marta stormed into the room where he was playing a video game half-heartedly.

"You know you need to kill girl. Why you hesitate? She is pretty, that why?" Her eastern European accent was thick in her anger.

He rolled his eyes. "Oh, as if that would matter."

"You can't marry her. You must wait to marry. You know this. The angel's daughter is meant for you."

"I know. I just wish…." He shook his head. He would never finish such a dangerous thought.

Marta spat on the floor. "You are weak." There was venom in her voice.

"Why can't we use our judge to throw out the case."

Now it was Marta's turn to roll her eyes. "Over her? Pathetic."

Jacob got up and paced. "That's what we pay the police and lawyers and judges to do."

"Why you no want to kill her?"

He stood up tall, facing her and giving her a dark look. "Leave me alone."

For once, she didn't question him further. She scoffed but left the room.

Jacob needed to find a solution that would bring him peace of mind while still saving face. Judge Johnson was in his pocket and always owed them a favor. He had a gambling problem, and they helped fund it.

But Marta was dead set on not letting him use this connection. Just two days later, when Jacob was to have a meeting with the judge, he heard the news. Tara had been found in the woods, brutally ripped apart by wild animals. There would not be an open casket. Demons did not leave a pretty corpse.

His heart felt ripped to shreds in his chest, and he left without a word. Tears of anger and grief mixed hotly on his cheeks as he ran out of the building and into the woods. See if Marta's henchmen would do a damn thing to him. They would pay for what they did to her. Martha included. They would learn not to act without his approval again.

He wiped his eyes and drove to the warehouse where the gang hung out. It would be easy to dispatch them all. Well, all besides Marta who would be at the house. She would learn her lesson by having to replace the men. But it was easy to replace underlings when you could promise them what only Jacob could. Preternatural powers as changelings. If you were chosen, you would gain superhuman speed and strength, along with regenerative abilities. It wasn't something to scoff at. Neither was retribution.

Fifteen minutes after he arrived, Jacob left the scene. Having watched the small blaze turn into a raging inferno. He was satisfied hearing the screams of pain and terror of those trapped inside. Of course, he had left no exits available. They would join his father in Perdition. Jacob had no regrets as he glanced at the fire reflecting in his rear-view mirror as it disappeared into the distance.

*If you are interested in Jacob's story, check out the An-gelborn series by JK Allen, rereleasing soon!

# Fairy Tales Can Come True

**Carol Allen**

"A fairy godmother sounded great. It was great to have someone in my corner for once in my life. But now, I have an ungrateful family. I'm supposed to write my last Will and Testament and have them happy for me to die." Susan was throwing wet tissues into the trash. She didn't care how her make up looked, but she still looked pretty even with the tears. Her blue eyes were just sparkling through the smudged mascara and black eyeliner.

"Just don't tell them about the will," the dark figure said from the corner in a deep voice.

"Why do I even have to do this? I'm not old or sick. Am I?" She pouted, her lower lip out like she always did when she wanted her godmother to soothe her.

"No, of course not, dear. Would I come here to hurt you?" The small dark figure flitted out of the shadows.

"Why are you here? I wasn't crying before you arrived." Susan dabbed her eyes again with a fresh tissue. "And I wasn't asking for anything."

"I always show up, precisely when I am supposed to." The dark fairy floated closer to Susan and sat in the chair in front of the desk. Sometimes the fairy's wings were visible, but after a few flaps the black wings were tucked away. The fairy godmother tilted her black head and looked at her pointed black nails. "You need to update the will anyways, you are no longer married and you need to make sure your daughter is provided for."

"Fine," she said as she crossed out her ex-husband's name and left all her assets to her daughter. "That should do it." She stuck the will into a new envelope and put it in the desk drawer. "I'll go to the lawyer tomorrow. Is that everything I needed to do?"

The fairy lilted, "I know you are upset about the divorce, but you cannot have what you desire."

"I know, I know." She put her head in her hands. "I know the magic only goes so far."

"Well, I need something from you to get you what you really want." The dark fairy waved her black hand and shrugged.

"I thought you just said I couldn't have that." She folded her arms.

"Remember the day your daughter was born and how happy you were?"

"Of course, the best day of my life." She played with her pearl necklace absentmindedly. It was her mother's necklace and Susan wore it almost every day.

"Remember what you had to do for her?" The dark fairy blinked its black eyes.

"Yes, vaguely." She sat back in the leather office chair. "Do I really have to do that again to get my husband back?"

"Yes." The dark fairy tented her long black fingers and nodded.

"Then the bitch can have him." She shook her head and her blonde curls bounced. She smiled with her red lips. "I'll just take his money."

"No, you are missing the point." The fairy stood up and floated to be next to her. "You cut that young maid's heart out as a gift for your daughter."

"Yes, you told me I had to." She remembered the fairy circling the young girl's chest. "You said cut here and that you will do the rest to save my daughter."

"Your daughter was dying, she needed a heart." The fairy touched her shoulder, her expensive silk blouse was thin and the heat from the fairy radiated to Susan. "You wanted a daughter and you paid the price."

"Yes, I do whatever you ask of me." She was comforted by the warmth of the fairy.

"So, what did you pay for your husband? What did you pay for your lifestyle?"

"Is that why my marriage did not last?"

"In a way, my child." The fairy floated to the bookcase behind them and looked at framed pictures of the family. "You are a beautiful woman, I did not have to encourage your husband to fall in love with you."

"I just wasn't beautiful enough to keep him."

"Susan, don't feel bad. You were never going to be enough for him, my dear. Some men do not stay faithful to any woman." The dark fairy floated to the window and looked out over the city. "You do need to pay for your lifestyle. That was the wish I granted to you all those years ago."

"What do you want me to do?"

"I cannot say, you will know when the time is right." The dark fairy blew her a kiss and vanished.

***

"I don't know what to do." She looked at the permission slip her teenage daughter handed her.

"It's easy, mom, you sign it." Her brown eyes looked up at her mom and she smiled.

"But a class trip to go skiing? What kind of trip is that? It doesn't sound educational." She tried to look stern, but could not hold in a giggle as she looked at her teenage daughter's facial expression. "So this is just over the weekend?"

"Yeah, a four-day-weekend. We drive up north on Thursday morning, then drive back on Sunday night. So can I go? All my friends are going!"

"How much is this? Did you talk to your father?"

"He said I can go." Audrey looked at her plate and picked up a carrot stick.

Susan worried about her daughter's eating habits, it was hard to be sixteen and trying to fit in. She looked at the paper and listened for the crunch of her daughter taking a bite of the carrot. Once she heard it, she took a breath. "Wow, this is a lot of money."

"Come on, mom." She rolled her eyes and looked so much like her father. She also had his brown hair that her daughter wanted to highlight. Audrey was always saying, "You're a pretty blonde, why can't I be?"

"Did he say he would pay for your trip?" Susan picked up a pen and tapped it on the countertop.

"I didn't ask, but I'll text him right now." She picked up her cellular phone that her father did pay for. "But mom, can I get a new outfit?"

"Sure, if your father pays for the trip."

"He said he would, but he wants to talk to you." Audrey picked up half of the ham and cheese sandwich and took a bite.

"Just finish your lunch." Susan signed the permission slip and said, "It would be nice if you can run the dishwasher, Rose won't be in until Monday."

"Is everything alright?"

"Yes, her daughter is sick, so I told her to stay home this weekend." She looked at her daughter. "Anyways, she's our housekeeper, not our slave. It wouldn't kill you to do some chores now and then."

"Whatever, mom." Audrey rolled her eyes again and answered another text.

Susan left the kitchen and went up the stairs to her bedroom. She glanced at her phone when it lit up with a message. Her daughter sent her a link to an order she placed for a couple new sweaters, jeans, and a coat for the ski weekend. She smirked and paid for the order with her ex-husband's credit card.

"He said it was for emergencies, well, this sounds like a shopping emergency." She laughed.

***

Susan had just hugged her daughter that morning and watched her get on the bus for the ski trip. She had made Audrey promise to at least text her that she was alive, every day, multiple times a day. Susan felt sad to be alone in their house for the whole weekend, but maybe she would be able to get some work done. The fairy godmother said she had wanted this lifestyle, so she had to work to maintain it. She was in her home office, looking at the numbers of her lifestyle website business. She wanted to gain more advertisers and needed to show them her membership numbers and her views were worth their business. She was almost done with typing out the business plan and proposal when her ex-husband called her.

"Should I answer? It'll probably be another fight." She almost hit decline, but stopped herself from swiping left. "Or it could be about Audrey." She swiped to accept the call and said, "Hello, Roger, this isn't a good time."

"It's never a good time for you, Susan," Roger said, then sighed. "I wouldn't call if it wasn't important. Just give me five minutes of your time."

"If it's important, of course I can talk, Roger," she sighed and said, "I just don't want to fight."

"Well, I'm not sure I can promise that we won't fight, but we have got to talk about some of these expenses."

"Roger, she's your daughter too. You have to be responsible for some of the costs of taking care of her."

"Fine, so I paid for this trip, I also pay child support. I can't be expected to pay for everything. What are these four outfits? Susan, that credit card is supposed to be for emergencies only." He sighed and said, "I will have to end that line of credit, if it is going to be abused like this."

"Abused? Roger, your child needed some warm clothing for an outdoor winter activity. Is she supposed to freeze?" She clenched her teeth. "You never denied your daughter anything before. What is going on? Are you having financial trouble?"

"No, everything is fine." He sounded tired.

"So the dealership is doing well?" She smirked as she thought of how many times he had said that everyone wanted an SUV, and it was easy to upsell them.

"Maya is pregnant," he whispered, "I have a new family that I have to start to take care of now, Susan. Now, I will always take care of Audrey, but I have to take care of my new family."

She counted to ten to control her emotion. "You better take care of Audrey. How is she going to feel knowing her dad abandoned her for a new baby? Maybe how I felt when you left me for a new woman."

"Susan, don't do this." He exhaled. "Look, I am not going to cancel the credit card, but can you please just use it for emergencies? We agreed on that months ago."

She gritted her teeth. "Fine Roger, I'm just trying to make sure our daughter is taken care of." She ended the call. Then she took a deep breath and picked up the phone. She texted Roger, "Can we talk tonight?"

He replied, "No, I'm not home. I'm at my parents' until Saturday."

She looked at the phone and closed her eyes to summon her fairy godmother.

"Yes, my child?" The deep soothing voice came from the corner of the room.

Susan looked at her godmother floating towards her. "Will she be home tonight?"

"The new woman?" The fairy petted Susan's head.

"Yes, that other woman." Susan turned off her phone and kicked off her high heels.

"Yes, she will be home alone tonight." The fairy floated over to the desk. "Are you going to make a new wish? Or do you need this?" The golden dagger was presented to Susan, just as it was when she needed a heart for her daughter. The dark fairy held it out to her with both hands, and Susan accepted it by picking it up by the handle.

Then Susan went to her bedroom. She put on some black boots and looked at herself in the full length mirror. She was wearing a navy sleeveless dress. "This should be fine." She took off her jewelry and put her blonde hair up into a ponytail. Susan grabbed her old wool coat from the closet near the front door, then drove over to the house her ex-husband shared with his new girlfriend. She parked on the street and walked to the front door. Audrey's house key allowed her to unlock the door. Once inside, she took off her coat, leaving it on the recliner by the door. Susan made it upstairs before the girlfriend came out of her bedroom wearing one of Roger's pajama shirts.

Maya's eyes widened in surprise. "What are you doing here Susan?"

"Hi, Maya." She kept her hand behind her so Maya couldn't see the ceremonial dagger the fairy had given her. "I just have to do something real quick, then I'll be gone. Out of your hair. Is this Audrey's room here?"

"Yes, if Audrey needed something, she should have called." Maya looked frightened. "You shouldn't have come over, Susan."

"Well, you shouldn't have fucked my husband, but we're all past that now," she said through a strained smile, "After you."

Maya shook her head. "I'm going to stay right here. I'm calling Roger." She took out her phone and Susan knocked it out of her hands. Then she pushed Maya down before she could react. In the fall, Maya hit her head against the doorframe. Maya moaned in pain, and the dark fairy appeared. The dark fairy circled Maya's heart and Susan stabbed Maya with the dagger. Susan asked, "Why do you need her heart now?"

The dark fairy smiled and for the first time Susan saw her godmother's sharp small white teeth. "I need to feed, my dear. I always start with the heart." The fairy took the heart out of Maya's chest and hunched over it to eat. Susan stood up, still holding onto the dagger and turned around. She slowly went down the stairs and was stopped by the sight of Roger. "Roger, what are you doing here? I thought you were at your parents' house?"

"I wanted to come home early." He looked at the dagger in her hand. "What the hell are you doing here? Where's Maya? What did you do to her?" He tried to look upstairs and down the hall into the living room. He wouldn't be able to see anything until he went upstairs, and Susan wasn't going to let him. She planted her feet firmly on the bottom stair and when he approached her she used both hands around the dagger to stab him in the chest.

He staggered back. "What the hell, Susan?" She pulled out the dagger and lunged at him again. He fell onto his back and she straddled him to stab him again. She had stabbed him like she did that young lady sixteen years ago. "What was that maid's name? Cynthia? That sounds right. Did you sleep with her too?"

Roger just looked at her, but he did not say anything. "You don't remember her, do you? There were so many girlfriends, weren't there?" She watched his mouth move and laughed. "You look like a fish," she told him and stabbed him again.

The dark fairy floated down the stairs and stopped Susan's hand. "We don't want to damage the heart too much."

"Of course, I'm sorry godmother." Susan stood up and gave the fairy her dagger. "I think I have paid back my debt to you."

"Yes, you did very well, my child." She floated in front of Susan. "I will take what is owed to me. You can go home and know that all is taken care of, my child."

Susan nodded, put on her coat, and left for home. Once she parked in her garage, she wondered if she would see her godmother again.

"Snap out of it, Susan, you need to get cleaned up." She took off her boots and returned them to her closet. Then she went back downstairs to take off her wool overcoat and inspected it. She didn't see anything on it that would incriminate her. "I should throw this out or donate it." She emptied the pockets and put Audrey's keys back on the kitchen counter. When she went back upstairs and into her room, she took off her navy dress. "There's some blood on this." She started a fire in the fireplace in her bedroom. "Very romantic." She smirked and cut up the dress into strips to feed the fire. "A bath sounds like a perfect ending to this perfect day," Susan said to herself turning the faucet. She didn't get out of the tub until her fingers were wrinkled. Afterwards, she put on her red terry cloth robe and looked at the ashes of the dress in the fireplace. "Now I can turn on my phone." She reclined on her king sized bed. The screen showed that she had missed some texts from Audrey.

Susan read that Audrey was fine.

*Had fun skiing and drank a lot of hot cocoa today!*

Susan replied:

*Great! Sorry I turned the phone off when I took a bath. Talk to you later. Love you.*

There was a missed call from her ex-husband, she wasn't sure of the time he called. "It will look suspicious if I don't answer him." She sighed and texted that she had her phone off when she was in the bath. "Text me later or call me tomorrow, if it's important." She said to herself, as she texted the end of the conversation.

"A glass of wine sounds nice right about now." She went downstairs and was surprised by Rose in the kitchen. "Rose, what are you doing here?"

"I'm sorry, miss. I didn't want to bother you. I didn't know you were home." Rose was clearing out the dishwasher.

"It's okay Rose, I thought you were home with your daughter." She gripped the top of her red bathrobe together.

"I wanted to make sure you were all set with groceries for the weekend. I got you and Miss Audrey some milk and her blueberry bagels. I also brought some brownies I baked for Miss Audrey."

"Oh, bless you Rose." She smiled and said, "Thank you so much. Oh, since you're here, let me get your paycheck." Susan went to her office and wrote out a check for Rose's week of housekeeping. She smiled and whispered, "This is a perfect alibi."

She handed Rose the check and asked, "I was in the bath, have you been here for long?"

"I just grabbed the dry cleaning and sorted the laundry, before I unloaded the groceries. I haven't been here long, Miss Susan."

"No problem, I just didn't hear you come in. Maybe I should have someone look at the alarm system. Did you hear it when you came in?"

"I'm not sure." Rose looked around. "I'm sorry, I have to get back to my daughter."

"Yes, of course." Susan nodded. "Have a good night, Rose."

***

Audrey came home on Sunday as scheduled and hugged Susan when she got off the bus. This made Susan think of when she would meet Audrey's school bus in the afternoon, and they would hold hands as they walked home. She missed those early days, now her little girl was a woman. She kissed Audrey on her cheek, then wiped off the berry colored lipstick. "I really missed you, kiddo. Did you have fun?"

"Yes!" Audrey answered, and told her mom about the ski weekend during the drive home. Then she asked, "Have you heard from dad?"

"No, honey, we don't talk that much anymore." Susan parked in front of the garage.

"It's weird, I haven't gotten any texts since Friday. He usually talks to me every day." Audrey frowned.

"I'm sure he's just busy." Susan shrugged then said, "Maybe try calling him after dinner."

***

Susan was in her home office, finishing up the proposal she had tried writing two weeks ago, when Rose knocked on the door. "Sorry to disturb you, Miss Susan, there's cops to talk to you."

She walked into the living room where two detectives were standing. The shorter one was drinking coffee from her matching white ceramic set that she kept for company. The younger, taller one was holding out his business card. "I'm Detective Klaus, and this is Detective Mason."

She nodded. "How can I help you?" She sat down on the settee and they sat down on the matching sofa. She was happy to see the shorter detective using a coaster, when he set the coffee cup down. *Now is not the time to be a prude, just smile and be a good hostess. You are an innocent woman.*

"I'm not sure how to tell you this, ma'am. But we have to inform you that your ex-husband, Roger, is deceased."

"Wait, what?" She closed her eyes and shook her head. "Are you sure? Was there an accident?" She shook her head again then said, "No, that can't be right." She patted her side pocket for her phone. "Where's my phone? I'm going to call him right now." She went to stand up, but the younger detective held his hand up.

"Please, just sit down." He fixed his tie. "I'm sorry to tell you, but it looks like a homicide."

"Oh Jesus." She covered her mouth with her hand. "Who would do that?" She gasped. "I have a daughter. I mean we have a daughter together, is she in danger? Am I in danger?"

"Why would you say that, ma'am?"

"Well, it's not normal to be murdered. I mean, can you tell me what happened?"

"It appears to be a stabbing. Can you tell us if anyone would want to harm Roger?"

"No, I can't think of anyone. I mean, he's just a car salesman. Unless it was something to do with the business." She shook her head. "I didn't pay any attention to his job when we were married. Then after the divorce, I really didn't talk to him. Unless it was about our daughter of course."

"Is there anything else you can tell us about your ex-husband?" The shorter detective asked.

"I don't even know who his friends are anymore. I'm sorry. I just haven't been close to him since the relationship ended about a year ago."

"This is just a formality, but can you tell us where you were about two weeks ago?"

"I usually am just home, and if I do any running around, it's for my daughter's school activities. I'm a workaholic nowadays. Since I have to take care of my daughter and myself." Susan looked off to the side. "Even though we weren't married anymore, he was a good father. I don't know how I'm going to tell Audrey."

"There's one more question." The shorter detective said. He looked at Susan and asked, "Do you know where your ex-husband's girlfriend could be?"

Susan was confused. "She wasn't at the house? I mean, I thought they lived together."

"No, ma'am." The other detective cleared his throat. "We haven't been able to locate her."

She shook her head. "Like I said, I thought they lived together, but I don't know anything else about her. We just run in different social circles."

"Well, we will keep in touch." Both detectives stood up and she followed them to the front door. Susan watched them get into their car and drive away. Then she went into the kitchen and told Rose about Roger's death. She let Rose hug her and comfort her, while she mentally went through her get away with murder to-do list.

She had donated the old coat, boots, and other clothes of hers and Audrey's last week. So she wasn't worried about anything tracing back to her. She also vacuumed and cleaned her house after Rose had done her usual cleaning. Her only weakness was lack of alibi, but she did have that paycheck to Rose that night. Could that save her? She wouldn't worry about it now.

***

Susan was looking out of the window of her home office and playing with her pearl necklace. She remembered doing this same thing when she was a teenager. Her mom had died when she was two, and her dad had gifted her mom's pearl necklace to Susan when she turned sixteen. Susan had been playing with the necklace when it broke and all the pearls fell around her feet. She was so upset, and was sobbing so much, that she didn't realize her fairy godmother had arrived. She had been afraid of the strange dark creature at first. Susan hid on her bed and when she saw it fly from pearl to pearl, she put her pillow down to watch it. After it had collected all the pearls, it offered to fix the necklace. It held out its small black hand and said she had to pledge her allegiance to the small dark fairy. She had cut her hand and promised with her blood to listen to the small dark fairy.

"Will you always be there for me, fairy godmother?"

"I will." The small creature's deep voice soothed her.

"Are you something I should be scared of?"

"I'm here for you. Are you scared of me?"

"I am. But I think if you're just a small thing, you aren't scary."

"I can change size, but I will stay small if it doesn't scare you."

The dark creature used its black wand to repair the pearl necklace. It floated towards her to return the necklace to her neck. It whispered, "This necklace, like our bond, will never break again as long as I am your fairy godmother."

She would see her fairy godmother over the next decades. The dark creature was the only constant in her life and would not leave her. She took off the necklace and the clasp broke. "Oh, dammit. I thought it was loose." She placed it on her desk. "Maybe I should give the pearls to Audrey after I fix it. She has always wanted Gramma's pearls." She went into her bedroom and changed out of her blouse and skirt. She wanted to work out before Audrey came home, she wasn't sure how to tell her about Roger. She had changed into black yoga pants and a tank top when Audrey came into the bedroom.

"Mom? Are you in here?"

"Yes honey, I'm right here." She stepped out of the closet and saw Audrey standing there with her hand behind her back. "What do you want?"

"I heard about dad. So he's gone?"

"Yes, he is." She held her arms open. "I'm so sorry honey. Do you need a hug?"

"So, did he have a will?"

"Yes, we will be fine though. I have my business too. I'll be able to take care of the both of us." Susan took a few more steps closer to her daughter.

"Do you have a will too?" Audrey stopped in front of her mom.

"Of course, I do." She touched her daughter's face. "You are going to be taken care of, there's no need to worry."

"Oh, I'm not worried." Audrey stabbed her mom in the chest with a golden sacrificial dagger. "My fairy godmother said I will be fine after I do this."

Susan collapsed and looked up at the dark creature floating behind Audrey. "I didn't see you."

"Audrey, my pet, you can go now." The fairy godmother patted her head and Audrey left the bedroom.

"I didn't see you, fairy godmother," Susan sputtered and pulled the dagger out of her chest. The dark creature grew in size and picked up the dagger. Its forked black tongue licked her blood off the golden blade. Again, she saw its sharp white teeth, and again, its tongue flicked out. The dark creature stood up and its black eyes watched her try to push herself away. Her fear of the creature grew and she tried to get away from the large black fairy. Why did she think it was a fairy? It was no longer small, and it didn't have dainty little wings, they looked like leathery bat wings. Why did she trust it all those years ago?

"Did my mother send you to me when I first saw you?"

"No, I came when you called me." The dark creature licked her cheek and she felt the heat from the forked tongue on her skin. "I heard your desires, and I came to fulfill them."

"Why are you here now? The necklace, the clasp broke, is that why?" She was getting weaker and could feel the black creature's fingers in her wound. It was opening the cut that Audrey had made, and the pain made Susan scream.

"I am now bound to Audrey."

# Queenie

**JK Allen**

*Content Warning: Stalking, Violence*

I hated my name. Queen. It was corny and juvenile. It was meant to be stately and regal, but it veered off course into the ridiculous. It made me indignant, and I told my parents all the time that I planned to change my name as soon as possible when I turned eighteen. Mom insisted on calling me Queeniebelle, which was a million times worse. Especially in the south. And why name me after a royal title? I was nothing special. Well, I found out when I turned thirteen, and had my first period. That's when everything changed.

"Mom! Mom! Something's wrong!" I screamed, my breath hitching as I watched my hands. They shook and shook like pale leaves. But that wasn't the worst of it. I could feel my head contorting, the bones shifting and pulling uncomfortably. I lost my vision for a minute before it came back sharper than before. Then my sense of smell sharpened painfully, so I could smell my blood and the sweat under my arms. My hair was suddenly slicked to my face with sweat, completely flat, and I slowly realized it was a completely different color. My curls gone, the red gone, instead I was left with blonde locks that were straight and sleek and thick. No frizz to be seen. I screamed and called for my mom again.

Me, who had always been your run-of-the-mill type girl, was suddenly the ideal type. Blonde, blue eyed, with a large chest and tucked in waist. I was what many envied and even someone who I had wanted to be growing up as a scrawny ginger with unruly hair and piercing eyes. The rose. But I didn't understand what was happening to me. I only felt fear staring at the golden lock in my now somehow freckle-free hand. Even my fingers were prettier, long and graceful, with perfect spade-shaped nails.

"Mom! What is going on?"

My mother came rushing in, and looked me over once, a wide smirk spreading across her face.

"Why are you grinning at me like that? What the heck is going on?"

"You got my genes alright. Honey, you should be celebrating. The week of your period every month, you will be a beauty! The perfect southern belle. Were-wolves are called cursed, but our curse is a blessing. We get to be everything we want to be a week out of every month."

"So that's why you're always gone? Because you change too and look different?"

"Oh honey, it's more than just looking different. Don't you *feel* different?"

"Yes, I suppose I feel different. I can smell better and see better. It's like my senses are heightened."

"You won't get sick ever this special week. And you will discover the perks of looking like this. Don't worry. Your life is about to get a million times better. Now take a shower, the change is always sweaty."

I still didn't quite comprehend what was going on, but I could smell the sweat all over me, so I jumped in the shower. It was a shock when I got out and saw myself in the mirror.

I always had a kind of pinched look to my face, with my angular pixie chin and features, but now my face was sculpted by the gods. I was really beautiful. And my heart sank. I had never felt so ugly in my life before.

***

The years went by in a blur. I missed school regularly now, as I was a different person once a month. I also lived a completely different life that week. My mom took me shopping for extravagant clothes, and introduced me all around debutante events. I was on birth control so I could control when I had my periods, and my mom planned my whole life around those "special" weeks. And I hated it all. I was miserable. It was obvious my mom favored my new look and life more than she ever loved me for myself. And she was just as bad, syncing her period to mine so we both would be glamorous. I felt like she was my pageant mom, who was making up for lost time.

Then I fell in love with Jared. But of course, he only saw me when I looked like a model. When it was effortless for me to be breathtaking, but so fake I couldn't stand any of it. I wanted love for who I was, not who I could be one week a month. This really was a curse, no matter what mom said.

Jared was in love with me, but not the real me. Belle was a different girl that I didn't even know. My skin crawled when I felt her taking over. Then I got the first note from my secret admirer. I wanted to rip off my skin when I read that note.

*Dearest loveliest Belle,*

*Now that I know you exist, I am finally alive. I live for you, You are exactly what a woman should be. I know you're only sixteen, but that's legal marrying age, we just need to get your mom's permission. I love you and can't wait until the night you are in my arms for the very first time.*

*Your secret admirer*

I screamed and ran and showed my mom the letter. She was delighted.

"Oh sure it sounds a little creepy, but it's harmless. It's because you're so beautiful when you're Belle."

"He knew my name and that I live with you, mom. What else does he know about me? He could be stalking me, mom. This is horrible:"

"Oh, calm down. He won't actually do anything. These types never do."

"What do you mean? Stalkers are insane!"

"You dont know he's a stalker. He's probably seen you debut or around town."

"You never take anything seriously."

"I do, how else could we afford our lifestyles? I take my gifts very seriously. And so should you. Let's see, we need to start a skincare routine. It wouldn't hurt. And we can post about it on Pixcha."

And so the note seemed to not make a dent at all in my mother's life, but it haunted mine. The nightmares started immediately. And then more notes came in. Notes proving he was watching me. That he knew parts of my routines. I began to fight mom about going out any more. I didn't want to give him a chance to see me.

But then things started to look better, mom got a new richer boyfriend and we moved to a new condo. She only saw her boyfriends when she was changed, so she would really make the big bucks. She said they liked being kept waiting and would lavish her with gifts so she wouldn't forget them the other 3 weeks.

The notes stopped for a while, and I felt like I could breathe again. At least for a couple weeks. Then they found me again. This time they included pictures of me they had taken when I was out in public. My stomach dropped. Jared was in some of the pictures, and I worried. I showed him the letters and the pictures, and he got a serious look on his face. But then he just laughed after and said there was nothing to worry about. I believed him, but only because I wanted to. Maybe I was overreacting? No one thought it was anything to worry about. But two days later, his body was found under the train tunnel, and his face had been slashed horrifically. I cried for hours, then went to the police.

***

"Tell me your name again," the detective asked, giving me a sweet smile. He looked young, maybe twenty-three, and had dimples. He seemed like he could hardly keep eye contact with me. This was different, usually people would stare at me.

"It's Belle. Belle Byrne." That's the name my mom told me to go by when I was transformed. It was an old family name they kept up for descendants who got the blessing.

"And what brings you in today?"

I sneezed. It smelled awful in here. A mix of many people's body odor and fear. And strong cologne. I rubbed my nose with a tissue and began. "Well it's about Jared, and also about me. You see, someone has been stalking me, and I think they had something to do with Jared's death."

"How do you figure?"

"Here, these are all the letters I've gotten. Only last time I got pictures too. Pictures including Jared. We were hanging out you see. I'm really scared."

"Were you two in a relationship?"

The smell of anxiety was the worst smell of all. It overpowered me for a second.

"We were close friends, but just friends." *Not that I wanted to be just friends. But Detective Jones didn't need to know that.*

He smiled wide and finally looked me in the eye. "Well then, why are you scared? You haven't done anything wrong. No need to be scared."

"I don't know who this guy is. He is obviously stalking me, then I hang out with Jared and he ends up dead."

"You have no proof the two are connected, but if it makes you feel any better, I can come watch you at your residence for a while. Monitor and protect the perimeter."

"You're not too busy? It'll only be for a few days."

"Are you going somewhere?"

"Yeah, I'm only here like a week every month."

"Why is that?"

"Just how our schedule works out."

He looked like he wanted to ask more, so I quickly gathered everything up. "I really gotta go now. My mom is expecting me."

"About that patrol."

I nodded, eager to be out of this place. "Oh yes, I wouldn't mind having a cop around if anything bad happens. I appreciate it."

"I appreciate you."

I smiled at him, though it didn't reach my eyes. He looked a little too eager to help out, but I was used to this by now. But I did feel some sense of relief, so I shook his hand and left.

*** 

It was my last night here. The next day I would change back on the way home and mom would too. We would stop at the same hotel for a shower and food. Go in looking like two beauties, come out looking like our regular selves. Then we'd get into our regular car, Mom paid extra to be able to park her nicer car here, and we would go back home. Back to my plain self. The self no one loved. Even I began to wonder if I still loved either selves. It was exhausting, and with the loss of Jared, I was beyond in the pits of despair. I didn't think anything would get me out of it. Mom had just left to do some last minute dating before we returned to our mundane world, when a knock on the door startled me.

Groaning, I checked my face in the mirror before answering. I had been crying, so I couldn't hide the redness, but I fixed my smeared makeup as best I could and ran to the door. I was surprised and a little deflated to see Officer Jones in his uniform.

"Hi, mind if I come in? I'm a bit parched, and well, thought I'd check in on you and see how you're doing."

"That's very kind, but my mom just left."

"Well now, if you can't trust a boy in blue…" he began.

"Of course, come on in." I stepped aside to let him in. He passed by awful close, and I got a noseful of his cheap cologne. Stifling a cough, I closed the door. I turned around to follow him in and my nose found his chest. "Excuse me, I can get you a drink, if you'll excuse me."

He paused a moment, then backed up with a blush. "Sure thing. Any ole thing is fine. Don't go to any trouble for me."

"No trouble at all." I could hear my grandmama chirping in the back of my head. *Be wary but always be hospitable. Don't do anything to bring shame upon our good name. Be a good host and get the man a drink.* "Would you like a *drink* drink, something stronger I mean? We have some bourbon we save, for company of course."

"No, no," he said with a chuckle. "On duty. Wouldn't be proper. Sweet tea if you have it."

"Of course." I grabbed a clean glass and put some ice in it before filling it with the tea. Sweet tea was a staple of the south. We always had at least two pitchers full in the fridge. Mom was a sucker for it.

I walked towards him and handed him the tea. Then beckoned for us both to sit opposite each other, him on the loveseat and me on the couch.

"I just wanted to see how you were faring. I know it's been hard for you. And you are going to be leaving soon. Where are you going again?"

"You're very kind. I am doing the best I can. Can I get you a bite to eat?"

"No, miss. But where did you say you were going?"

"I don't recall that I had said."

"Aww, don't be like that. You can tell *me* where you are going. It's my job to keep you safe."

"I'll be perfectly safe there," I mumbled, taking a drink of water I had next to me.

"Now you're just playing hard to get." He frowned and it sent shivers down my spine. I noticed a funny smell in the air then. It reminded me of how guys smell when they like a girl.

"I'm not playing at anything. I think if you don't mind, I'll cut this visit short. I'm very tired, and I have to lie down."

"Now, now. I'm not going to let you go now that we are so close."

"What are you talking about?"

"I'm talking about us. Don't you recognize me?"

"Yes, you're the officer I talked to at the station."

"You haven't seen me before that? God knows I've seen you."

My stomach dropped, and I felt faint. Like I really would pass out like some damsel in a movie from olden times. I shook my head to get myself together. I was in the house with the stalker, with a lunatic. Alone.

My mind raced, and I did remember glances of him. A blond man in a red hat at the baseball game. A man with a book covering his face at lunch. Someone bumping into me as I passed him with friends….

Goosebumps broke out all over my skin, and I thought I would be sick.

"See you do remember me." He stood up grinning triumphantly. "Because you feel it too. The connection between us. It's just too strong to ignore.

"I've been patient the last two days. I had to stomach so much not to come to you the last two nights. Knowing you were just feet away, waiting for me."

He began to walk towards me. I fumbled for words. For a plan. Nothing came to me. I stood abruptly.

"I forgot something in the kitchen," I shot out like a robot, then turned and walked squarely towards the kitchen. He didn't stop following me. All I could think of was, *get to the knife block before he does something. Knife block. Knife block.* The words ran through my frantic mind as I slowly sped up each step. Trying not to be too obvious.

"There's no point now in waiting any more. In denying ourselves what we both want and feel. I know.

That's why I came in as soon as I could. I began to wonder if your mom was ever going to leave, but of course she did."

"Yes, just for a minute though. She should be coming home soon."

"Oh we aren't staying here. You and I have places to be."

"What sort of places?" I slammed into the countertop and reached forward.

"What the hell are you doing?" He growled, grabbing my hair and yanking down hard. My fingers slipped off the handle of the knife I was reaching for. But I groaned and pushed up against the pressure, grabbing a knife and swinging it behind me in a single arc of light.

"You slut!" he screeched, letting go of my hair and holding his now bleeding arm.

"I'm not going anywhere with you while I still have breath," I spat out.

"Well, we will just have to change that."

He lunged for me again, and caught my knife in his palm. It went straight through, and he screamed. Shocked, I let go and ran past him into the living room again. He had pulled out the knife, but it must have smarted something fierce, because he bellowed. But he caught up to me, wrapping his good arm around my waist. I thrashed wildly, and somehow managed to smack him right in his injured hand. He yelped and let go of me. I ran to the door and out into the street. I heard more than felt the gunshot that followed me. But it was effective in stopping me. My legs gave out underneath me, and I hit my head pretty hard. The darkness swallowed me up after that.

***

I woke up in the hospital to a nurse checking my vitals.

"Hey, hun, it's good to see you awake. Your fiance has been so worried. Such a nice man, he hardly left your side at all."

"He's not my fiance," I struggled to get out. "I wouldn't stab my boyfriend."

"No use talking till some of the drugs wear off from surgery. So brave how he saved you from a stalker who shot you and brought you to the hospital himself. Oh don't worry," she said, finally noticing my distress, "your surgery was minimal and you'll barely notice the scar."

What they didn't know was that I had healing powers right now. I was the height of vitality. I could even feel the effects of the drugs wearing off. I closed my eyes and listened for him. To see where that bastard was.

"That's it, honey, you get some rest. I'll let your beau know you are awake."

I nodded and waited for her to leave. Taking a deep breath I ripped out the IV in one yank and turned off the machine so it wouldn't beep. Everything hooked to me came off, and I threw the blanket off my legs. One of them was heavily bandaged, but I could feel it healing quickly. I trusted that process and leapt off the bed.

I grabbed my shoes which were conveniently left for me in a cubby by the bed and ran down the hall. I just turned the corner when I heard his steps making their way towards the room. I waited just a moment to put on my shoes, and re-tie my gown. Then as soon as I heard him go in my room, I ran as fast as I could past the nurses station and out into the rest of the hospital. I was too fast for anyone to catch me, and before I heard him shout, I was already flying down the stairs towards the front exit. I burst out into the parking lot and felt his eyes on me. But I didn't even look back, I just ran as hard as I could for as long as I could.

Luckily it was spring, and someone had their clothes on the line hanging out to dry outside. I got dressed in a backyard and found a pay phone. I asked some poor lout for change and he was more than happy to oblige and buy me a Coke. I called my mom.

"What on earth is going on?" she demanded.

"The cop is my stalker. He tried to abduct me. I fought him and got out, but he shot me."

"Oh my. Well, I'll pick you up now, where are you?"

"Are you alone?"

"I will be when I get you. The week is almost over anyway. We need to get out of town soon."

I trusted mom had the ability to get away. I told her where the gas station was and waited. I watched each car like a trained hunter would watch for their prey. I noted each car coming and going. I saw my mom's SUV approaching when a car pulled up right next to me. I smelled him as he rolled down the window to yell at me to get inside. I made sure my eyes locked with my mother's. She gave me a single nod and smiled, a predatory smile. I returned it and got into the car without a word.

It must have been his off duty car, since it was an old sedan. Nothing fancier than power windows. It was loud and smelled disgustingly of him and his cologne. He kept his sweaty uniforms in here far too long, and I kept my attention on not gagging the whole drive. Mom followed behind, he was too distracted to even notice he was being tailed. He thought he was the mastermind of this evening. Too bad for him he was about to be upstaged.

We drove into the country and pulled into an isolated cabin. This must be where he planned to take me for his perverted plans. Well, not today. Today, I would have my way with him, not the other way around.

He opened his door and ran to mine to open it for me. Maybe he thought I would run, but I had come to a realization along the ride. I needed to kill this fucker, and there was no better place to do it than here. Isolated and secluded, his own property, it was the perfect spot. And mom would realize that as well.

I let him open the door for me, and held out my hand for him to help me out of the car. He smiled widely and gripped my hand in his sweaty one. I got out of the car very demurely, glanced once past him to see my mom parking the car in the treeline where it wouldn't be seen. I took a few steps with him to give myself some space to fight, then paused, looking him in the eye.

"Nár chuire Dia ar do leas thú," I spat out the old Irish curse.

Then I punched him in the throat as hard as I could and swept his legs from under him.

I was on top of him in a second as he gasped for air, punching and tearing away at his hair and skin with my nails. Mom joined with a baseball bat and finished the job, screaming "Tribute!" as she bashed his head in. He was a sight to be seen when he was done. We were sweaty and covered in blood, but I felt myself relaxing in a way I hadn't since the stalking began.

I could feel the change happen, my face felt pulled then pinched and the world dulled around me. At least I had my powers for when I needed to defend myself and end this scum. But something was nagging at me.

"Mom?"

"Yes, dearest?"

"Why did you yell 'tribute' when you killed him?"

"We give all the deaths to the great queen who blessed us as tribute to her to keep our powers in our bloodline."

"Do we need to kill many people?"

"Just the ones who don't understand the word 'no,' darling. Scum like this one."

I thought about it for a brief moment, then nodded. It didn't seem like a bad deal to me anymore. A black bird flapped in the corner of my eye, and I turned my head to see a water spigot in front of the cabin and pointed it out to my mom. We would clean up, and then we would change in the car and head back to our real home. The one none of these men knew anything about.

# Moonlight Transformation

## Carol Allen

The full moon was a few weeks ago, and it always made little sense to have that be the requirement for transformation. Why would a very illuminated nightscape be required for a nocturnal predator to reign? Why would sight be more powerful over scent with an animal that is known for its sense of smell? Then that kind of animal would just hunt during the daylight. The kind of animal she was, preferred the darkness to surprise her prey. Even on a cloudy night, the full moon glowed in the night sky, behind the mist.

It was a beautiful sight that night, a harvest moon. The amber moon loomed large over the riverfront and was distracting. Lunatic was a synonym for insanity. The idea of an out of control monster, driven by the cycle of the moon was insanity. That monster would be caught, would be found out. Everyone sees the path of a tornado.

*Wonder if people can see the disaster that is my love life? Did they know that you cheated on me? I can't believe that I didn't see it. That I didn't smell her? Or was that denial?*

Jane sat in her black sedan parked outside the other woman's riverfront condo. She had followed her now ex-boyfriend when she found out there was another woman. The literal lipstick on the collar could not be denied. He had been careful until then. She went through his receipts and credit card bills. They didn't meet in local hotels from what she saw. Then he must have wined and dined her with cash or another credit card. *Did he use his company card?* They worked together, so traveling out of town together must have been nice. He told her he hated all the time away. *The liar.* He had complained about the endless time wasted at the airports and the banality of the hotel rooms.

*Banality, who says banality these days? Is that what made her drawn to him? He did like to say big words. I appreciate intelligence, but abhor deceit. How long had he been cheating? It had to be months. That's when the travel started. Who would notice a hotel room, when they are out on the town cheating on me?*

She watched them through the windows, the open concept made it easy to watch them eat dinner. They used the kitchen table for the meal. He actually poured wine for her, then himself. But when he was at my place, he would just eat on the couch. The crumbs drove Jane insane, because she would be the one to clean up after him. She bit her lip when she saw him put his dishes into the dishwasher, "Another thing he never did at home." They sat on the couch to watch a movie. She watched the back of their heads as they talked through the scenes of the action movie.

*We were supposed to watch that last week. He's such a selfish prick. I guess this is their date night.*

Jane drove away when they started to kiss. She didn't need any more confirmation of his indiscretion. Now she had to wait the two weeks for the new moon to come out. The darkest night. That is the best time to be out. To hunt. A new moon is the time to transform.

The next time she parked in front of the condo, it was a darker night. She saw the dimmed condo and her ex-boyfriend's SUV parked in the driveway. *Tonight is the night.*

Jane pulled away and drove down the road. She parked a few blocks away at a nearby park. She wore all black tonight, black leather jacket, black shirt, and jeans. She pulled on black leather gloves and walked to the condo and used the spare set of keys to unlock her ex-boyfriend's SUV. She touched the garage door opener and it swooshed open. *Only the best, a fast, quiet, smooth action garage door for the happy couple.* Jane walked into the open garage and opened the door to enter the kitchen.

The silence was comforting, and she stood by the counter for a few minutes. She wasn't sure if they were sleeping until she heard the sound of her ex snoring. Jane grabbed a knife from the wooden block on the counter. The condo was very clean, they must spend a lot of time out of town. He was never this neat at her home, but he left his keys and wallet in the same place, on the kitchen table. She smiled and opened his wallet to remove all his money. She knew he usually carried at least two hundred in bills on him, and she pocketed the cash. Then she walked into the living room and saw the woman's designer purse, she dumped out the contents and picked up the wallet. She took out the cash and left the rest. *Might as well make some money.*

But she didn't see anything else of value in the living room. Then Jane grabbed a decorative pillow before going up the stairs. She paused at the open master bedroom and saw the two of them in bed. She listened to her ex's snoring and thought, "He was a deep sleeper, but would he sleep through this?" She would have to be quick. Jane walked into the room and to the left side of the bed.

Jane used the knife to silence the other woman. The woman could barely gasp as her throat was cut, and Jane held the pillow over the woman's face to muffle any noise. She felt the woman struggle less and less, until her hands stopped scratching at Jane's gloved hands. The woman was still again, and Jane exhaled. Her hands relaxed their grip on the pillow, and Jane watched for any movement. A smile grew on her face, and her eyes scanned the bedside table. A diamond ring caught her eye. Jane left the pillow on her victim and pocketed the ring. Then she walked over to the right side of the queen bed.

Her ex had fallen asleep on his side, so his back was to his dead partner, and he was snoring. *He must have taken a sleeping pill.* Jane saw the prescription pill bottle on the bedside table with a half empty glass of water. She put the knife in his right hand that was resting near his pillow and left it there. She watched his hand move and grip the handle before settling down again. *Maybe blood splatter patterns won't matter. Maybe this will be the first time someone can blame a sleeping pill for murder.* Jane left the bedroom and went down the stairs and back out of the kitchen door. She pulled out a black bandana and wrapped it around her gloved hand. Then she opened her ex's SUV driver side door to use the garage door opener to close the garage door. She placed the spare set of keys in the center console, pushed the button to lock the SUV, and gently closed the door.

Jane looked up at the dark sky and was happy to see the stars twinkling. There were no other lights on except the street lights. She slowly walked back towards the park and disappeared into the night.

# Guilia's Kiss

**JK Allen**

Now, Guilia was a lady and treated as such. She was amongst the aristocracy here in Italy, of course she hadn't always been. But smarts and a pretty face could achieve many things, and she married better every time she married, accumulating wealth, houses, and now titles.

She also didn't come empty handed. She brought with her into every house the secret her mother had passed on to her. One that she had refined in the apothecaries she spent time in as a youth. One that she used to make her own legacy, both in money and name. The Kiss of Tofana. She sold it as a perfume to women with rotten husbands. Husbands who beat them. Husbands who beat their children. Husbands who blew their money. Husbands that didn't need to be around any more. Drops from the Kiss could be mixed in with their food or drink. Clear, odorless, and tasteless, it mixed well with anything and mimicked a natural illness. It was her favorite kind of kiss to give, one so well deserved.

One drop and the headaches came, perhaps an upset stomach. Surely feeling a little rundown.

Two drops and the vomiting began. Violent and sweaty.

Three drops and the victim was bedridden besides trips to the lavatory.

Four and the bell would ring its somber tone at the church on the hill. An unfortunate death and into the hands of the Lord we pray.

The whole thing worked out swimmingly well for Lady Guilia. She had her own income and renown amongst her peers. She knew things that had been in the family for generations, and she was teaching them to her daughter. She made sure to only be responsible for the death of bad men. She would listen to the sob stories, weighing out his fate, his decision, like Anubis with his feather. She was a witch, so she knew the three-fold rule. If her magic ever came back to her, she would die, maybe even her precious daughter would lose her life as well. Cut down in her prime like a frost on a blossoming rose bush. Guilia couldn't let that happen.

She went to tea with a new client that had been referred to her. A Missus Florentine. The missus had a mark badly covered under her eye and a split lip. Typical to those that Guilia spent her days with. Her heart clenched as she contemplated the sad sight. Florentina as she called her in her head, was a pretty woman, with plenty of life and vitality left in her. Many reproductive years she could spend with far more pleasant company. She could hardly blame her for darkening her door. Black hair like the shade draped over cerulean eyes. A stunning combination unfortunately marred by the bruises of an angry, immature man.

Distracted by these thoughts, she barely heard the sobbed confession of Florentina, who had a dulcet voice that seemed to almost hypnotize Guilia as she munched on a delicate pastry, minding the powdered icing.

"I'm sorry, what was that again?"

"Oh, just that Giovanni comes home at such different times. He wants dinner ready and warm, but I never know how to time it."

"Of course, dear. With no warning of when he will be home, how could you?"

"Two nights ago, dinner was ready but cold. Last night, it wasn't ready. I don't know what to do any more. I fear I have lost myself completely."

"Do you like perfume, my dear?"

Florentina looked up with a sultry smile, understanding shining in her eyes.

Guilia stirred her tea. "You were referred to me, no?"

Florentina nodded, eyes shining. "Yes, by my maid. A Missus Georgio Gregori."

"Ah, yes. A kind and strong woman." She nodded her approval and began to explain her wares and the precautions she was to take to keep them all safe. It was an important speech, and Florentina listened most dutifully. But it was the beginning of the end. For Florentina was lying, and fortuna always pays her debts.

Two weeks was all Guilia knew of peace. If you could call it that. Black crows haunted her dreams, screaming obscenities at her as she ran in the rain, through a fog so thick, she couldn't see beyond her outstretched hand. Always, it was with a panicked feeling in her breast, that she could not seem to breathe, that she could not see, that she could not escape the crows that flocked behind her. If you could call it peace, it was what she had. And she knew the call of the crows meant more. It was the only peace she was to have left in her life.

She sent her daughter away. She would spare her daughter her own fate, if she could. Guilia gave her money and jewels and a new name with a wealthy relative in Spain. She took the family book. The one called Of Shadows. With shadows written in an elegant silver scrawl. Guilia's own grandmother had bound the book herself, filling it with knowledge. She cried to see it leave her house, but if her daughter were to survive without her, she would need it. Guilia had use for nothing now that her end had been heralded.

She received the letter from the Pope on an ordinary morning during her breaking of the fast. It seemed that the cream on the strawberries clotted and spoiled just at the sight of the parchment scroll. Her finger burned on the wax seal and she barely saw the words etched onto the parchment. Death, her death was being called for. Torture to find out how many victims her witchcraft had claimed. She would proudly say they numbered 600 or more. She was proficient at what she did.

So how had she gotten caught? Florentine was a good man. A helper in his community. And the missus hadn't spaced out any drops, just given him half a bottle with wine at dinner. An obvious poisoning. It was as if she wanted both her and Guilia to meet a bitter end. They assuredly would if he truly was a good man.

Magic is not black or white inherently. But kill a good man, and face the consequences.

She was summoned the next day. She wore her best. Best gown, best jewels, best crown. Guilia wore a kohl eye like the Egyptians and the red lip as of a sweetened berry. She was beauty immaculate. If she were to die, she would die as her best self.

They threatened her with torture, but there was no need. Guilia kept records, you see, of the hundreds of men whom she had been the cause of their demise. And she had recorded every treacherous reason. She read out each story of abuse before their deaths were tallied. It took three days to get through it all. But she was in her glory. Never before had Guilia felt so alive, now here she was testifying before my death of the crimes she had committed. With each word, her heart grew lighter. Soon it would be lighter than a feather. Guilia was ready to die.

They decided to set Guilia on fire. She would at least take her wealth and status with her. In her livery and jewels, she climbed on top of that pyre and stood, head held high, as they lit the coals beneath her slippered feet. As the wood burned, and leapt to life, it ate at her and she began to sing. An ancient song in their family tongue her mother's mother sang when she sang young Guilia to sleep. She was above screaming. Guilia would greet her ancestors with honor and with their words. She sang as the fire bit at her skin. She sang until the smoke smothered her, the wounds on her legs too far gone to feel anymore. She saw her mother waltzing towards her, cloaked in black, hand outstretched, reaching for Guilia. As if to claim a kiss from her.

# Another Year

**Carol Allen**

*Content Warning: Kidnapping, Some Violence*

"Another year, another birthday."

The beauty routine was the same, she would gently pat the creams around the eyes, onto the forehead, and over the rest of the face. Then she placed another cream onto her neck and décolletage. The routine ended with lotions on her arms, legs, and hands. She inspected her face and saw the gentle wrinkling of the skin around her eyes.

"Crow's feet," she hissed, "the never ending battle."

She tore open a sheet mask and put it over her face, then walked out of the bathroom into her master bedroom. She lay down on her bed and put her silk covered pillows under her head. It was supposed to help with wrinkle prevention and also be nice on her hair. But it was a constant battle to stay young and beautiful.

"Damn gravity and sunshine." She closed her eyes and tried to meditate. She had to repeat her mantra to try not to wrinkle her face. "Can't smile or frown or you will get wrinkles. Can't smile or frown or get wrinkles."

She took a deep breath. "Another year, another birthday." She shook her head and looked at her reflection in the mirror. "The wrinkles are going to get deeper." She was entering another decade and the grey hairs were multiplying. "Stop stressing, or you will get more grey hairs. Stop worrying, or you won't be able to get any beauty sleep tonight."

She sat up and removed the sheet mask. She went into her library and sat at her desk. She knew it was time. The thin skin on the back of her hands was losing its smoothness and a few sunspots started to reappear. The creams and lotions can only do so much. "It is time. It's been another decade." She rubbed the veins on the back of her left hand. "So many decades."

The next night, she put on her black party dress and red lipstick. She looked a little old fashioned. "No, this is called vintage." She blotted the lipstick. She winked her black-lined eye at her reflection. She cackled and said, "What is old is new again."

She loved the style of the sixties and preferred to dress more formally than was customary. She even drove an older car, one from the seventies that only cost her eight hundred dollars to purchase it. A car from the sixties would be her preference, but she didn't want the attention of that kind of classic car. Her Lincoln gave her an excuse of affordability, and she loved the maroon leather bench seats. She couldn't believe her luck at finding an older car with power windows and a bench seat. The old cigarette lighter still worked when she bought it for eight hundred dollars in the nineties and still worked now. She wasn't a smoker, but it was fun to buy a pack once in a decade. Especially back in the eighties, when smoking was still cool. The lighter was useful to occasionally burn a spell or protective talisman. She was still surprised at some of the stuff that she found around her town that would cause her pain or diminish her power.

The children loved to leave little paper dolls at the library, and she would have to quickly gather them and burn them at night. Sometimes she was more scared of the children than the adults. Some of the younger ones could see her true self, and she could send them running with a look. But that was the nice benefit about being a librarian, she was able to destroy any of the books that would teach them how to fight her. How to defeat her. She had worked at many libraries and loved spending her time looking through the basements. Some true treasures were in those dusty basements, and she was able to find an old book of potions in the nineties, in Mississippi. The knowledge in that book helped her perfect the formulas of her beauty creams and potions.

Tonight she drove to the local dive bar she liked to visit. The lighting, or lack thereof, would help her look better. It hid the growing number of grey hairs that were mixing with her black hair that she curled into ringlets. It will also help her to pick a perfect man. *Men were an easier target.*

She sat at the bar and ordered a vodka martini, because she liked the look of her lipstick on the rim of that kind of glass. She played with her red high heels, by slipping one off her heel and letting it hang from her toes. The dropping of a shoe in front of a potential date was something that she hadn't done in a while. She giggled at the comparison to Cinderella when she was younger, now she would have to suppress the eye roll if it happened. But this bar was empty for a Saturday night. There was a group of young men and women near the pool tables.

*Maybe a celebration of some sort.* They were going through pitchers of beers and the girls kept doing shots, so it might be a birthday. She kept eyeing the guys playing pool, watching them over her martini glass. *There might be a potential lone male.* But they kept to themselves and were joined by another group of young people who entered the bar a little after she finished her drink. She ate the green olive and pushed the empty glass away from her.

A man in black was the only other patron. He caught her eye when he put more money into the jukebox. He picked some classic rock songs, the usual songs to bring people to the dance floor from the nineties. The man didn't dance though, he returned to the booth in the corner and nursed his beer. The girls started to dance and sing along to each song. The last song he picked was a real classic, it was a song from the sixties, Unchained Melody. Most of the girls stopped being rowdy and one couple started to slow dance.

She asked the bartender for water and drank it. After she pushed that empty glass away, the bartender returned with another martini.

"I didn't ask for this." She put up her hand, she was thinking about calling it a night.

"It's from the gentleman in the corner." The bartender pointed to the man in black.

"I see." She raised the glass to him and took a sip. A warm feeling, like from alcohol, hit her from the drink. But there was something else in this drink. She would be a little more tipsy than usual if she drank this, but that was part of the game.

One of the guys playing pool put money in the jukebox, and country music filled the bar. She took another sip from her drink before going into the ladies' restroom. She took a vial out of her purse and spit out the drink into it. She had a bad feeling about that man and would look at the liquid in the vial later. He looked puritanical and severe in the black get up. He just needed a white collar to look like a preacher. The man in black had a familiar aura that she hadn't seen in front of her since the days of Salem. His black cowboy hat could have just been subterfuge, but a cowboy would not pick rock music.

"No, sir." She washed her hands after she placed the vial back into her purse. She took out another shade of red lipstick, this one was called "Revenge" and was made from her own special formula that has been perfected over the years, and she had drunk the antidote before leaving home. The premonition of a female could not be underestimated, and she had a feeling someone new was in town. She applied her special lipstick and winked at her reflection. "Game on."

She returned to the bar to leave some money for her drink and a tip. She put on a pair of tan driving gloves as she left the bar.

She walked to her grey car and tried to be graceful in her heels as she crossed the gravel parking lot. She was feeling a little dizzy from the alcohol. She should have eaten something before coming out, but she could just sit in her car if she felt unable to drive home.

The tall man in black walked from behind her car when she reached the driver side door. He leaned against her grey Lincoln and looked at her. She just smiled and used the key to unlock the door. "Can I help you, sir? Or should I just say thank you for my drink?" She batted her eyelashes and smiled at him.

The man just stared into her blue eyes with his own dark ones. He looked older than he was, his blonde hair curled under the hat did not have any grey, but his sparse facial hair had hints of grey. His stern facial expression had allowed deep burrows to make a permanent home between his eyebrows and on his forehead. He kept his thin lips closed.

"So, I guess this is goodbye." She waved and opened the driver's side door.

She got into her car, but then the man shoved her over to the passenger side. He slammed the door shut and showed her a hunting knife he had in a sheath on his black leather belt. He let his jacket fall back into place, covering the knife handle. He held out his hand towards her and said, "Keys."

She calmly placed them in his palm, the adrenaline was sobering her up. "Sir, I really didn't have that much to drink. I can call myself a cab."

The bar was at the edge of town, the south end, the wrong side of the tracks everyone said, and that was why she preferred it. She had hoped she would find an exciting date, and this one had potential. She looked forward to see where he was heading. "I don't know who you are, but you can have the car and my money. You can just leave me here, and I won't call the police. I promise."

He pulled out of the lot and just kept driving, through the now deserted downtown, and did not acknowledge her. He was heading north, to the farmland. She let herself slump towards the passenger side window. "I don't feel right" She closed her eyes and let the man drive.

"You should be passing out soon. I spiked that drink." He said and kept driving.

She stayed quiet until she felt the car start to go over the dirt roads. Her forehead was getting hit by the window with each pothole in the dirt road. She sat up straighter. "What's going on? Where are we?" She looked at the man in black, and when he didn't answer her, she pouted. He was being very boring. She looked at the corn field they were driving next to, it was probably the MacIntyre farm. She liked to drive out to watch them do a little maze for the kids around Halloween. Their hot apple cider was delicious with their cinnamon donuts, and Halloween was her favorite time of the year.

The man pulled off to the shoulder by the woods that bordered the farm. He looked at her and said, "I know what you are. Witch, get out of the car."

She feigned shock, almost comically. "What? What are you talking about?"

He opened the door and grabbed her, pulling her across the maroon leather bench seat. He threw her onto the ground. She was getting mad, her favorite dress was getting ruined and her nylons were ripped. She stood up and said, "Now, I don't know what is going on, mister. But nothing has happened. How about you go your way, and I go mine?"

"Witch, you will go to Hell!" He raised his hand and slapped her. "Where do you want to die? In the field or the woods?"

"The trees." She stood up straighter, adjusted her purse strap, and strode towards the woods.

He followed her as she led him toward a clearing, then she spun around. "Could I have a kiss before I die?"

He was almost nose to nose with her. "Keep going and pick a tree."

She leaned closer and brought her lips just inches from his. "Just one kiss," she whispered. Her eyes glowed in the moonlight. "Just one last kiss."

The man stood rigid, and she kissed his lips. The red lipstick was transferred onto the man's lips. She playfully bit his lower lip.

He winced and pulled back when she drew blood.

He pushed her away. "Damn you." He wiped his lips with the back of his hand, trying to wipe off the lipstick and the blood.

She just sat on the grass and laughed, her own lipstick smeared around her mouth.

"What's so funny?" He took out a white handkerchief to clean off the lipstick from his hand.

She stood up and held her hands up. "Do you want me to help you with that? We don't want the missus to get jealous?"

He paused. "How did you know that I'm married?"

"Your tan line, silly. I'm not psychic." She giggled. "Plus, you're boring."

He stopped wiping his mouth and dropped the handkerchief. He bent over to pick it up, but collapsed onto the ground.

"Oh, don't worry. I'll get that for you." She picked up the handkerchief and rolled him onto his back. "I think it's been long enough." She wiped off the remaining lipstick. Then she tucked the handkerchief into a pocket in her dress.

The man started to foam at the mouth and seize. She searched his pockets and found his black leather bound notebook. "Wow! You sure do your research." She read the many names she had used over the decades, the centuries. "I had no idea that there was any of your bloodline left."

He gurgled and tried to reach his hand up to grab her. She easily dodged it. "You won't be able to talk. I gave you a little bit of your own medicine. Well, a little bit different than what you tried to give me. My formula is more painful."

She pulled out an empty vial and collected some of his saliva and started to chant. "I've taken your voice. You cannot speak." She searched his other pockets and took his wallet. She pocketed the money and looked at his driver's license. "You don't live in this area." She looked at his dark brown eyes, "Are you here alone? Do you have a partner?" He just stared at her. "No, try blinking? Once for yes, and twice for no." She laughed. "Like I said, you're no fun. But I will get the answers I need, even without your help."

The woman in black inhaled and chanted some more. "Some hair, to care." She pulled out a couple of his blonde curls and put them into the vial. His eyes teared up. "Some tears for fear. Ha! I said that one for the band. But I do need them." She added the tears to the vial. She grabbed the handle of his hunting knife. "I'm so glad you're prepared." Then she unsheathed it and took his hand. She used the knife to get some nail clippings. "Some nails, to not fail."

She paused and smiled at the man. "We do like a rhyme. It does make it easy to remember what we need." She pushed his sleeve up and grabbed his wrist. "Okay, this is going to be just a little poke. I'm sorry, but I need some blood." She cut his palm and filled the vial with his blood. She capped it and put the vial into her purse.

The woman put his wallet back into his pocket. "So, I'm going to keep your notebook, but I will let you keep your knife." She stood up and put the notebook into her purse. Then she chanted, and the wind picked up making the trees rock side to side and the leaves rustled. Other noises mixed with the wind, little yaps and howls came closer to the clearing.

"There's my babies." She smiled and looked at the man. "That's the coyotes out here."

She kneeled next to the man in black and whispered, "They like the vermin out here." The coyotes stopped at the edge of the clearing, their yellow eyes watched the woman, and they became quiet.

The woman smiled and chanted some more. "Finally, a life for a life. To be young and beautiful again. I won't tell you how many lifetimes this will be, because a lady never tells her age." She cackled and used the knife to slit his throat and slice open his chest. She sheathed the knife and left the man to the coyotes.

Now that the ritual was over, she went to the center of the clearing and took the white handkerchief out of her pocket and burned it with the man's license. She chanted as they turned into ash and black plumes of smoke, and the man was dragged into the woods. Once the fire died down, she walked out of the woods back to her car.

Satisfied, she drove back to her house. "Now I need my beauty rest."

The next night, she finished hand washing her favorite party dress, and it was hanging in her laundry room. There were a few rips in it. She wasn't sure if it could be repaired. But she would worry about it later.

It was another night, so she used her new batch of beauty cream in her ritual. Now she saw results, the wrinkles actually smoothed out and disappeared. She applied some to her temples and the grey hairs returned to their original black color. "What a difference a new batch makes." She used a sheet face mask and went into her library. She meditated and chanted as she put her spell book in a drawer. "Won't need that for a while."

Out of curiosity, she looked at the man's notebook. She had written his address down on a post-it note. "Maybe it was time to move back to the east coast." She tapped the paper. "He came here from Pennsylvania. That's not too far away." She opened the notebook, it made her think of a Bible. The thin papers were yellowed with age. "It's not as old as me, but a lot of generations have worked on it." This had been the first time she had been this close to the Judges in almost a century. She thought she had gotten rid of the last Judge ages ago. *Well, the last active one I thought. I won't leave any survivors this time.*

After a week, she started seeing the man in black on missing person posters all over town. The first one she saw was on a bulletin board in the grocery store. *So he must have a partner. I don't think it would be his wife. He wouldn't have children old enough to hunt.*

When she saw the posters on the windows of the stores downtown, she decided to tell the police she saw him in the bar. *What would they think if she didn't tell them about it, and the bartender did?* She waited a few days before she went to the police station and told them she saw the man at the bar.

She told the officer that she just saw him sitting at the booth, but didn't get his name. She didn't talk to the man at all. "Maybe because he was married and faithful to his wife." The young officer just took her statement and she shook her head. "It's a shame. He looks like a nice guy to go missing. I hope he shows up soon, his family must be worried sick."

"Yeah, his wife reported it." He shuffled the forms. "He was supposed to be home a few days ago."

She got her keys out of her purse. "Does he have any kids?"

The officer shook his head. "No, just him and his wife."

The woman walked out of the police station and scanned the street. There was a pair of uniformed police officers walking toward their patrol car. Another woman was walking down the street, pushing a baby stroller. She didn't see anyone else sitting in the parked vehicles, especially men in black. She crossed the street and got into her car.

*Maybe it was time to leave town. A new year, a new you.*

"I've always liked the name, Tabitha. I haven't used my name in a long time."

# Shadow Work

**JK Allen**

It was a blustery winter day. One of those days they would note in a Victorian novel. The kind of bluster that demands attention and throws tufts of snow back into the air. My curls were being unruly as usual and tangling in my eyelashes. I threw on my glasses, just to separate them a bit, and that's when it struck me. Something so unnatural, it sent shivers down my spine. Preternatural would be the word for it. Something that was so outside the realm of what is meant to be. Yet I couldn't pinpoint exactly what was wrong. Just the feeling of wrongness that was so pervasive. It settled in my skin as goosebumps and twisted my stomach in knots.

I took off my glasses, to see if it was something I could recapture in a glance. Or see out of my peripherals. Placing the cold metal frames back on my face, I had that sensation again. Eerie, surreal. But no further epiphanies. So I shook my head, feeling my curls bounce, and continued on my way to class.

I was on time for once, something that had been getting easier for someone with time impermanence. But things had been on the up lately. I was really getting somewhere with my music, and even school was easier to deal with thanks to the ADHD diagnosis and subsequent treatment. It was like a switch had been fixed in my brain, and that section finally worked. Lights turned on, sounds happened, wires whirred in the last few weeks. And I was able to function without swimming against the undercurrent. I just moved forward. It was not the only change as of late.

My toxic family had made a sudden 180. They wanted to be in my life and support me. I still didn't trust them, but mom paying rent this month sure helped. And dad showing up with groceries? That was a blessing. I was able to use my money for what I needed, new pedals. And my songs were taking off on the Clock app.

But not everything was perfect. I had forgotten to take my pills before this class and they were running out of my system this morning. Which meant I was fidgeting and spacing out. My foot jiggled up and down, outstretched in front of me. And I watched the movement with detached interest. It was then that I realized, as if hit by lightning, that I did not have a shadow.

I was struck by its absence as I drew shapes between the shadows of the chair legs and desk legs with my finger. In between the towers of the lost city, my body made no shapes, no shades, no shadow. How was this even possible?

I checked everyone else and they all had their own. I thought back to everything I knew about shadows and pulled out my phone to research it, but the bell rang. So I unceremoniously stuffed my shit back into my bag and scrambled out of the room.

I waited until I was home to really look into it. Throwing my bag down on my bed, I stomped over to my desk and my computer. It was time to get serious.

*What are the repercussions of not having a shadow?*

*What does it mean if you don't have a shadow?*

According to the internet, absence of a shadow is the ultimate absence of light. Divine light. Meaning, I didn't have a soul.

I sat with this thought for a minute or two, picking absentmindedly at my cuticles. This news did not devastate me as much as I would have anticipated had I been presented with the hypothetical situation of losing my soul. And I had a good idea where I had lost the damn thing. In my dream. In exchange for all the good fortune I was now accruing.

He hadn't looked like a demon. And being a dream, I suspected nothing. But after some amazing coitus, he asked me what I wanted in life. What my dreams were. I said I want a career in music, to make it. I said I want my brain to function normally, to be able to do school and housework like a normie. That I wanted a sense of family. Simple dreams really, and it was all just talk.

Until he said, "What if I can make it true?"

"What if you can? Doesn't mean you would."

"That's true. I don't have to for free."

"What's the cost?"

He caressed my face, making soft circles on my cheek. I felt the edge of his nails, somewhat sharp but not cutting me. "Something small. Something you don't even believe you have. Your soul."

I smiled, thinking of the possibilities. "So that's it, I give you my soul and you bless my life in every way possible?"

His green eyes sparkled. "Yes. All you have to say is yes."

I remember laughing. This was just a dream, after all. Why not make it a happy one?

"Do you like spaghetti?"

"Yes, it's one of my favorite foods."

"Eat more of it then. Carbs are not your enemy."

Then he had left, whoever he was.

I felt buoyant, ecstatic. I had just had the best orgasm I'd ever had, and now I was dreaming about being a success in life and what I could do when I got everything I wanted. It was elating. I didn't want to wake up when the alarm went off. But nothing could foul my mood up.

It was that morning that I finally got a call back about my medications. My insurance found me a provider that would get me what I needed, and they would cover the costs. Unheard of in this market, but who was I to complain? And the pills worked like magic. I cleaned up my place and my life. Started to excel in classes again. And even started to patch some of my friendships.

Then I made the song that would blow up, while working on a follow up. I wasn't about to be a one hit wonder. And I wasn't about to have only fifteen minutes of fame to myself. I wanted longevity.

And now, here was proof that it was all working. Sure it was also proof I had no soul. But what had my soul ever done for me? I couldn't be bothered.

I sat down to make another song and video it. I just had the best idea for a song. Peter Pan and his lost soul. We would never grow old together. But I was about to grow in wealth and blessings. So be it.

***

The first time my shadow visited me, it scared me relentlessly. Like it was only there to remind me of my former shadow of a self. A loser with no focus or friends. Someone who could barely afford to eat. Who struggled with everything. Somehow, seeing that damn thing made me violently angry. But it wasn't just that, free-floating as it was. It could go anywhere, take any shape, and it became the thing of my nightmares.

It would take on the most hideous forms. Skeletal, horned, dripping somehow. It didn't matter, it would form these grotesque creatures and follow me around. Or wait to scare me at any moment. I was never prepared. And began to feel crazy.

I had been to the mental ward of a hospital before, I did not want to return because of my sold-off shadow. Was it angry with me? What would it do with that anger?

Life was getting better and better. It was almost suffocating me with how well it was going, and all the new obligations and restrictions I had. I was exhausted all the time. Trying to create, trying to make meetings, and fan greets, and interviews, and spend time with the family. And then there was the time I woke up to my shadow sitting on my chest, choking me until my lips turned blue. Then sleep became impossible. I never knew when that shadow would appear or how it would torture me next. I could only steal fifteen minutes here and there. Never enough, but enough to keep me going. I went through a lot of concealer for my under eye dark circles.

Sleep was the one thing I so desperately needed but couldn't afford to get. And my time blindness returned, despite the meds. I lost track of a lot of stuff. If it wasn't for my personal assistant, I don't know what I would have done. I wouldn't be nearly as successful. Not with the product lines making constant demands on my time. And how quick they are to fire you.

My shadow was waiting for me that night when I went home. It stood very still and very obvious in my doorway. I brushed past it, hiding my shiver of repugnance and opened the door and calmly walked in. I was too tired to panic or be scared. Something was going to break tonight, or I was, and that would be the end of it all. And I was at peace with it.

Shadow me grabbed a pen and piece of paper off the kitchen table.

*You seem different tonight*

I stripped off my long coat and dumped it on the floor. "I am. I'm done with this. What do you want?"

*You are done?*

"I am done being affected by you."

*But I have only started*

"I am too tired to care. Kill me if you want. My brother has enough money now for a good life. "

*Tsk, tsk, tsk. Giving up on your dreams so fast*

"No, I've made my dreams come true. Now kill me or get out."

*You have no regrets?*

"None."

The shadow flared up like a raging flame for a moment. Then stilled in its previous form.

It paused, regarding me closely. I yawned.

*You are free now. You won't see me again until it really is time to die.*

"Thanks," was all I could muster. I turned and walked towards my bed, slumping under the covers and falling asleep. I didn't pay any attention to my shadow leaving. It was done with me now, and I could finally rest.

In the morning a chill ran through me as I remembered the last thing it said. I would see my shadow before I died. I had no idea when that would be. Perhaps that thought would haunt my life. Perhaps I would soon forget it. Either way. I had a life that needed living. No one had a better guarantee than me. So be it.

# Afraid of the Dark

## Carol Allen

Kelly turned on the light of her bedroom and saw the shadows flee to the closet and under the bed. The queen-sized bed in the middle of the room was the biggest piece of furniture in there. The dresser was against the wall, close to the door, so she was able to go in quickly and grab the pair of socks she needed for her cold feet. Usually, Kelly wouldn't pay any attention to a dark room, but she was alone now. Bobby wasn't here anymore. The car accident took him away from her. *He was the sun, and I was the moon. Now it's just darkness, and I'm afraid of the dark.*

She sighed and turned off the light, Kelly would sleep on the couch again. *The bed was too empty without him.* Kelly had tried to sleep alone in the first few weeks after his death, but she tossed and turned all night. She could not sleep beyond seven in the morning, even on the weekend. She would always rise with the sun.

Stubbornly, Kelly tried to reclaim her bed until she rolled over to her side and saw a mop of brown hair, sticking out from under the light green comforter. The nights were chilly with the changing of the leaves, she would normally love fall and sweater weather. She was always tempted to stay under the covers with Bobby. She wanted to move closer to him and put her arms around his warm body. She wanted to nuzzle his shoulder and breathe him in. Something made her pause, something wasn't right. When she couldn't remember why this was weird, she pushed forward. Kelly hugged him tight and pressed against him. He was solid and made up of bones, muscles, and skin. He was warm and here with her.

Her tears woke her up and she sat up in the bed. Her mind wouldn't let her forget that Bobby was dead. She wiped her face with her sleeve. "Dammit. That was a good dream." When she turned her head to look at Bobby's side of the bed, she only saw an empty space. The comforter was heaped up on itself and when she pulled it away, there was only a fleeting shadow. It chased the comforter and stayed under it and Bobby's pillow. She made the bed with fresh sheets and gave up trying to sleep in that bed.

Kelly lived in the living room and was always on the couch in the weeks after that night. Most mornings, she changed the channel and tried to watch a movie when it was too early to get up. She had trouble sleeping ever since that night. That was the most vivid dream she had experienced in her life, and she has not had any dreams since. *It's just darkness when I close my eyes.*

"It's been four weeks, I have to get back to work." She turned the television off and stood up. Kelly stretched and looked around her cluttered living room.

There were multiple pairs of used socks and sweat-shirts around the couch and coffee table. The coffee table was covered in dirty plates, cups, and trash. She could see her mail piled up on the kitchen countertop from where she was standing and knew there were piles of dirty dishes in the sink and dishwasher. "I have a dishwasher, I should use it." She marched into the kitchen to start cleaning there.

Then she decided to take some more small steps, and she did the laundry. She took a shower. She stayed away from the couch and the television all day. But she did not work. She was supposed to write three chapters of her new book, but she did not turn on her computer. Kelly eyed her laptop from her kitchen. "Lunch was good," she said to herself. It was just a sandwich and a pickle spear, she wasn't ready to start cooking. "Clean home, clean heart." She shuffled into the kitchen. "Is that a saying?" She grabbed a beer and shrugged. "I don't know." She used a bottle opener to take off the cap and threw it into the trash as she shuffled back into her living room. She took a big gulp and collapsed onto the couch. She turned on the television and nursed her beer through the next movie. She didn't want to drink too much, like last weekend. She just wanted to relax, and get the ideas flowing. "I should think about dinner soon. What do I want for dinner?" Kelly drank some more beer and found another movie to watch.

She woke up at three in the morning, still on the couch with the television on. The cold night air had woken her up, the blanket was in the dryer, and she was shivering. The apartment was silent now that the dryer cycle was done, but she didn't want to get up and fold the laundry. The two options were clear in her sleepy mind. Kelly could unload the dryer or freeze to death on the couch. She hugged herself and decided there was a third option. She could just go to bed.

Kelly groaned as she shuffled toward her bedroom and turned on the light. She didn't like the darkness and didn't feel safe anymore. In the bedroom, there was no television, just the harsh overhead light. She watched the shadows jump back, and she felt like a child again. They reminded her of antelope leaping away from a lion on the savannah. But she wasn't the lion in this situation. She didn't feel as graceful as an antelope either.

"Can I run and jump into bed before something could grab me? Is there something under my bed or hiding in my closet?"

She turned the light off and the darkness descended, she took a deep breath and turned it back on. She gasped, there was a shape under her comforter, on Bobby's side of the bed. She walked towards the bed and held out her hand, reaching for it. "Bobby?"

She pulled back the comforter and the black mass of shadows slid under the comforter. There was nothing in the bed. Shaking her head, she turned away from the bed. "Nope, I won't sleep here tonight." She turned the light on before leaving the room and grabbed the blanket from the dryer. Then she laid down on the couch and started to flip through the channels on the television. "There's got to be something on."

The sunshine in her apartment woke her up, and she turned off the television. Then she turned off her bedroom light when she went in there to get ready for the day. She showered and inspected her face in the mirror. There were dark circles under her eyes, and she looked ten years older. She had given up on makeup and hair dye after Bobby died. So she had a few streaks of silver at her temples mixing with her dark brown hair. Kelly stuck her tongue out at her reflection and moisturized her face. "Baby steps," she put her hair up in a bun, then went to the store. She probably looked crazy with her purchases, but she bought nightlights, lots of nightlights. One ended up in all the available plugs throughout the apartment. Some would be on all the time and the others would light up only when their sensor detected darkness. She wanted her small apartment to be lit up at all times. She drank a beer and smiled. "Today might be a good day." She grabbed a second and third beer and sat down on the couch.

When she woke up in bed, it was dark. She searched the room for the green digital glow of her alarm clock and it showed her it was 3:27 AM. "Shit, I fell asleep." She looked for the nightlight, "Why is it so dark in here? I thought I had put one in here." She saw it lying on the floor next to the wall. "Did I forget to plug it in?" She remembered drinking a few beers. "How much did I drink yesterday?"

She didn't feel hungover, but she felt a chill go down her spine. She didn't like not being able to see what was in her room or her apartment. The door was open but she could only see the blank white wall of the hallway, there was a little bit of light coming in from the nightlight in the hall. It wasn't a lot, but it helped. She reached over and covered herself with the comforter. She squeezed her eyes shut. "If I can't see the monster, it can't see me."

Kelly squeezed her eyes tight, kid logic, and rolled onto her side so her back was to the door. She remembered doing that when she was eight years old. She curled up and felt her feet move out from the protection of the comforter. She fought the desire to immediately bring them back under the covers. Kelly did not want to be a silly child again, scared of the dark, and scared for the monster to grab her toes. She started to drift off to sleep when something sharp cut her right foot. She sat up and grabbed her foot. She couldn't see anything in the dark room. Her foot was hard to see, but she felt the pain and the warm blood pouring out.

"What the heck?" She searched around the room for a figure with a knife. "Is someone there? Am I being robbed?" There was nothing in the room, and she heard nothing.

Kelly put her left foot on the bedroom floor, and then the right. She stood up gingerly and started to make her way out of the bedroom to go to the bathroom. She took two slow steps and almost slipped in the blood that was flowing from her foot. "Ouch." It hurt to put weight on it. She felt something grab her right ankle and pull her down to the hardwood floor. Her breath was taken away when she landed on her belly. So she couldn't scream as she was pulled back toward her bed.

Kelly turned to see who was pulling her and only saw a black mass that had lifted up her queen bed. It had black tentacles coming out of it to grab her other ankle and her legs to pull her towards it. She tried to stop her movement backwards by using her hands and nails. She scratched the hardwood floor until she was flipped onto her back by more tentacles. More tentacles exploded from the monster and grabbed her arms and moved her towards its center. Kelly tried to scream as she was picked up, but her mouth was covered by another black tentacle. She shook her head and tried to free herself. The tentacle was leathery when she bit it. The monster did not react to her resistance. The tentacles wrapped around her body tightened up, and she felt more cuts in her skin from its talons.

Her clothing became red from her blood. There were talons at the end of most of the tentacles and they were ripping her skin apart as she was being squeezed. She was held up in front of the dark monster and she couldn't stop looking at the black mass. She didn't know what it was and what it was doing to her. Then the center of it opened up and she fought harder to escape. Now the room was starting to brighten up, it was almost dawn.

*Maybe the sunlight will kill it? Oh, dear God, will the light be able to save me? Please, I don't want to die.*

The sunlight filtered through the blinds.

*I should have kept the blinds open. Why did I close them? I am never in this room!*

Kelly watched as the tentacle lifted her up towards the ceiling. She watched as a beam of light touched the dark creature and waited for it to sizzle or jerk away in pain. *Maybe it would turn to ash or flame up like a vampire?* But it just moved past it, the tentacle was thick enough that it did not completely disappear, like a shadow normally would. It just disappeared where the light hit it.

*I should have left the blinds open.* Kelly closed her eyes and accepted the darkness behind her eyelids. *Maybe I'll see Bobby again.*

Kelly was lifted up over the monster, her blood dripped down her body and onto the dark creature. It rotated and she was brought closer to the mass, closer to its teeth, the saliva dripping off the pointed clear teeth. First it drank her blood, then she was swallowed by the darkness.

# Hunger

**JK Allen**

*Content Warning: Violence, Gore*

It didn't take much to make Jordan cry. He was, after all, a temperamental four-year-old. So when he started crying in the middle of the night, I didn't think anything of it. I was annoyed of course. No one likes being woken up by a shrieking child at 3 AM.

He cried and said, "It was in his room, staring at him." He was mostly incoherent. Unable to say exactly what it was. Just that it "scare him." But it kept happening. Night after night until he fought about going to bed.

He wanted to sleep with me, but that was my only space that was just mine. Where I didn't have to be a mom, and I didn't have to cater to him 24/7. I couldn't let him take that from me. He would fight, and he would cry, but he would eventually fall asleep on the couch, and I would carry him to his bed.

It became a habit to wake up at three. I would lie there, staring up at the ceiling, waiting for his cries to start. They were like clockwork, and my nerves were wearing thin.

"Dammit, Jordan. You need to stop playing games," I shouted over his shrieks as I pounded down the hall to his room. I flung the door open and froze when I saw glowing yellow eyes peering at me from the foot of Jordan's bed. He scrambled off his bed and latched himself onto me. My jaw just hung open as I watched the monster stand.

It was skeletal, with dripping red skin, like boiling flesh, hanging off its frame. It lifted a clawed hand as if waving at me and a violent shudder overtook me.

"Yum, yum," it groaned, and the hairs on my arm stood on end. I clutched Jordan's arm and began backing away. "We know where you are." Its voice was unearthly, guttural and rasping. "We know where you sleep, yes."

Tears fell down my cheek as it turned to watch me stand in the doorway. I shoved Jordan behind me.

"Soon." It was a dark promise that glowed in its eyes as I shut the door with a shaky hand. I was panting, gasping for air as my chest heaved. *What the hell was going on? What was that thing?* Surely just a figment of my imagination from lack of sleep.

"Mommy?" Jordan's voice was high.

I picked him up impatiently and scurried down the stairs.

"You saw it, right, mommy?"

"Hush."

"But you saw it too!"

"I said hush," I snapped as I set him down. I wasn't sure what I'd seen. Only that I wasn't going to bed tonight. Jordan started to wail, and I ran a hand roughly through my hair.

"Enough," I said, planting him down on the couch. "No crying."

He looked at me with wide, round eyes, his lip quivering.

"Let's watch some TV. I'll even get you some ice cream if you stop crying."

"Don't leave me." The sobs rose again, and I scowled.

"We'll go get it together."

He nodded and took my hand as he followed me into the kitchen.

I gave him way too much, but I wanted him quiet and to stay up for a while. I didn't want to be alone in the house tonight. I kept seeing that hideous creature every time I closed my eyes, like some gruesome after-image. I couldn't relax. *What was I going to do?*

Around five, Jordan fell asleep, legs dangling off the arm of the couch. I flipped channels, anything to keep my mind from racing, from imagining what exactly was waiting for me in Jordan's room. It was waiting for me, not him. It had plenty of chances to get Jordan if it had wanted him. But children were too easy, weren't they? Too small? No, it wanted me.

A cry escaped me at the thought, and I clapped my hand over my mouth. Breaking out into a sweat, I peered over at the stairs, half expecting to see the creature at the top of them. Goosebumps broke out on my arms, and I turned the TV up louder. I kept my hand clasped over my mouth for ten minutes. Then I bit my nails. Working away on them till they were nothing. The hours went by like sludge. I was on edge, my mind whirring away without settling on anything. Doubt began to grow from a corner of my mind. I hadn't slept well. Trick of the mind. Monsters don't exist. Don't be insane.

"I'm not insane." I spoke the words out loud as seven o'clock greeted me, bleary eyed. And Jordan didn't need to go to preschool today. He was going to have a mommy day. Not because I didn't want to be alone in the house, because he didn't have enough sleep to function. I called him in sick.

Peter texted me. Earlier than he's usually up.

*You should come over.*

*I have Jordan.*

*Find a sitter.*

*Not today.*

This could only mean one thing anyway, and I was not in the mood.

I hadn't been seeing Peter for long. I met him at a bar one night, and we both didn't have better options. So we kept it up when I had the time away from Jordan. Peter wasn't big into kids, which was hardly a surprise. I mean, Jordan just happened. And Peter was good enough for right now, but not today.

Jordan woke me up around noon. I hadn't even realized I'd fallen asleep until he shook me awake. My heart was pounding as I sat up. My eyes shot straight to the stairs, almost not believing when I didn't see anything there. But there was nothing to see, after all. Last night was just a bad dream.

We got ready in record time, and I took Jordan for lunch. He was happy, and I was grateful for his good mood. But he didn't want to go home. I didn't have the money or the energy to stay away.

"We'll watch movies at home," I said, pulling my hair into a ponytail.

"But it will get us," he whined.

"Has it ever got you before?"

"No."

"Then keep your mouth shut."

"It has to eat. It told me." He crossed his arms.

"I said quiet."

"Once a month."

"I'm warning you." I glared daggers at him.

"It's real."

"We are going home right now."

I drug him out of the restaurant crying, trying to ignore the stares as he went limp in my arms.

"I'll ground you to your room," I shouted as I buckled him in. He screamed and kicked his legs.

"I'll lock you in all by yourself." I slammed the door shut. This was going to be a long day.

He screamed for half an hour after we got home. I put my earbuds in and put his favorite movie on and slurped down coffee in the kitchen. I was feeling more myself and not believing all this nonsense. I don't know why I didn't let him go to school today. A mistake I didn't plan on making again.

When I couldn't hear him any more, I took out my ear buds and made my way back to the living room. His face was red and his cheeks were streaked.

"Are you done yet?"

"It'll get us, mommy."

"It's not real," I enunciated, setting down my cup. "You need to start behaving." I gave him a stern look. "Now watch your movie."

The day managed to pass by relatively uneventfully. Jordan seemed to relax and forget about the monster. That is until the sun went down. Then his fear and anxiety returned tenfold. My nerves were frayed, and I wasn't coping.

"I don't want to go to my room," he wailed.

"You're not going to your room."

"I'm sleeping with you?" He looked at me hopefully.

"No, you're sleeping in the living room."

The cries started. "I can't sleep by myself."

"Well you can't sleep with me. You'll be just fine down here. You'll be safe. It's not real anyway."

"I'm scared, mommy."

"Don't be. Just go to sleep like a big boy."

I tucked him in and kissed his sweaty forehead good night. I made my way up the stairs to my room, massaging my neck as I went. What a stressful day. I just needed a good night's sleep. Was that too much to ask for? I changed quickly and climbed into bed.

I was just drifting off when something didn't feel right. My eyes snapped open and darted around the room. It felt like I was being watched. The hairs on my arms and neck rose, and I shivered, sitting up in bed. I couldn't see anything, but that feeling was unmistakable. It took me hours to fall asleep.

I woke up at 3 AM, and it was in my doorway. I sucked in air and jumped to a sitting position, raising my arms in front of me in defense.

"We know where you sleep," it rasped out and grinned at me with too much teeth.

"What do you want?" my voice shook.

"We are Hunger. We need to eat, yes."

"Why me?" Tears slipped down my cheeks.

"Why not you?"

"It can be someone else, can't it?" The tears were falling freely now, and I sobbed.

"We are listening."

"Tomorrow. Come back tomorrow, and I'll have the perfect person for you," I said in a hushed voice. Agonizing seconds ticked by as I waited for my reprieve.

"Tomorrow then. Only till then."

It slinked away back towards Jordan's room. I let out a breath I had been holding for too long. I started trembling, staring at the spot where it had stood in disbelief. I threw off the covers and ran down the stairs to the kitchen, making another pot of coffee. My hands still shook, but I couldn't stop smiling. It hadn't killed me. I was still alive.

In the morning, I took Jordan to school and called my mom. I told her he wasn't sleeping because he thought there was a monster in his room, and I couldn't take another night of no sleep, and could she just take him for one night? I would be forever grateful. She reluctantly agreed. She would pick him up and everything. I laughed out loud when I hung up. Then I called Peter. My plan was going perfectly.

I napped all day then showered and got myself all prettied up. I wanted to look good to get Peter to stay the night. He came by around nine and we watched a movie and made out. I wanted to enjoy my last night with him and it made things more passionate between us. We went up to bed and afterwards I pretended to fall asleep so he would. It worked.

I watched the clock and finally 2:45 arrived. I sat up, careful not to wake him and waited for the creature. I couldn't stop smiling. I was going to live.

I blinked right around three, and it suddenly appeared. I clutched my shirt to my chest and started panting.

"Here he is," I whispered, and Peter stirred. I didn't dare take my eyes off of the monster.

"Very nice," it wheezed, smiling at me.

"Better meal than me."

"Who are you talking to?" Peter asked, raising his head to peer at me.

"See for yourself," I answered, heart pounding.

Peter scrambled up and yelped as he caught sight of Hunger. Then Hunger pounced, a shifting blur of red and bones leaping towards Peter. I scrambled off the bed, falling hard on the floor. I scuttled to the door as the worst slurping and crunching noises filled the room along with Peter's screams. My stomach lurched and I squeezed my eyes shut.

"We take the bones with us," its voice alerted me to my situation again.

"Yes," I blurted out, opening my eyes. The remains of Peter were clumped in its arms, dripping blood onto the carpet.

"Next month you bring us another, or we take you."

"Yes."

I stood on shaking feet and slid along the wall to let it pass by me. It would take me all night to clean up the mess, but I was alive, and I would stay that way. I smiled as Hunger left.

# Just the Two of Us

**Carol Allen**

*Content Warning: Self Harm*

Georgia had a horrible hangover and groaned. "Where am I?" She slowly lifted her head and looked around the room. It looked like an interrogation room, and she was seated at a long wooden table surrounded by harsh white walls. The brightness made her close her eyes and she put her head back down onto her forearm.

"Why am I not at home?" She moved her foot and kicked her purse. So she reached down to pick it up and found a bottle of ibuprofen. Then she shook out two orange pills. "Just the two of us." She tossed them into her mouth and swallowed.

Georgia tugged at the hem of her skirt, she was chilled and hugged her bare arms. The sleeveless top was not good in the air conditioning, but it was cute and showed off her toned arms. She should have worn stockings, but didn't think she needed to at the bars. "All the dancing would have made me too hot with nylons on."

The light was bothering her blue, bloodshot eyes, so she searched her purse for her sunglasses and put on the brown plastic frames. She also found a thin scarf and wrapped the black and white dotted scarf around her neck. "Thin, but it will do." She looked at her reflection in her compact and fixed her bangs. When she put her straight brown hair up into a ponytail, she felt a pain in her wrist. "Ouch." She inspected a bandage wrapped around her left wrist. "When did I do that?" The crisp white bandage went from the crease under her hand, up her forearm, and ended inches before the bend of her arm. "Was I in the hospital?"

The grey metal door opened and a young man in a brown suit walked in with two paper coffee cups. He handed one to her. "I believe you take yours with cream and two sugars."

"Yes, thank you." She held the cup in her hands to warm up.

He sat across from her in the other brown colored plastic chair. This reminded her of being in school and sitting in class for a test. He set his cup down and grabbed the file from under his arm. He opened it and read through some of the papers. He cleared his throat. "Okay, Ms. Georgia Smith."

She nodded and blew on the coffee to cool it down. "Yes, where am I?"

"The Determination Detention Area." He shuffled the papers, then looked up at her.

"Is this like a police station?" Georgia sipped the hot coffee then set the paper cup down.

"No," he said, then asked, "Is there a reason you need the police?"

"Yes, no. I don't know." She touched the paper coffee cup again. "I think I had too much to drink last night. I don't remember what happened." She massaged her temples. "I have a horrible headache."

"The ibuprofen you took should kick in soon." He pulled out a paper. "Looks like you grew up in a single mother home."

"Why does that matter? Wait, why am I here?" She sat up straighter and felt the throbbing of her head calm down a little.

"What do you remember?" He tented his fingers over the folder. His brown eyes sparkled under his bushy brown eyebrows. His hair was styled like a detective from the old black and white movies. Solid, shiny hair that was more product than hair and parted to the side. He looked like he would be the good cop, but there was no partner here to be the bad cop. *Better mind your p's and q's," Mom would say.*

Her mother had a lot of sayings. "It's just the two of us." Her mom had said to her when she left home. Her mom's eyes always looked sad, they were always weepy, like a bloodhound's eyes.

"Geez, stop with the dramatics!" Georgia grabbed her car keys. "I'm just moving to the city. It's just an hour away." She slammed the door and stomped her feet going down the porch stairs with her luggage. In her car, she stole a glance at the house expecting to see her mom's crying face through the front door or the window. But she only saw an empty window, so she just reversed and sped down the dirt road.

What made her think of her mom? She didn't think the man wanted her to tell him about her life's story or even go back a couple years. "I went to the club with my friends." She took a sip of her coffee. "I'm sorry, why am I here?"

He sat back and straightened out his red tie. "We are trying to determine the course of action that is appropriate for the situation."

"What situation?"

"I'm sorry, I cannot tell you more." He took a breath. "I can't influence your story. You know memory is a fragile thing. But with more coffee, you may remember more." He gestured to drink the coffee.

She obliged and drank the sweetened coffee. She thought of her boss in the city, Mr. Johnny, he liked his coffee with cream and two sugars. That was when she started drinking coffee, when she worked in his office. She would take notes on his meetings, and afterwards he would say, "How's my girl?" Her stomach still fluttered thinking of him. She always said, "I'm fine Mr. B, would you like more coffee?" He would wink and say, "Only if you give me some extra sugar, Peach." It would be a couple months before she would stay late and they would go to hotel rooms during lunch.

"He says that to his wife." Her friend had said to her, when she told her about their latest dinner together. "Like really Georgia, don't you think he gives her a bracelet and tells her the same thing?" She made air quotes. "Now, there's a gem for a gem, Darling. Hell, he calls all the other girls little nicknames, like Sugar or Babe."

"You're just jealous," she pouted, "I mean really, Ruby."

"Please, everyone has screwed Mr. Johnny B," Ruby rolled her blue eyes. "I do not want him. Anyways, I would not sleep with my boss. Especially if he couldn't remember my name."

Georgia looked at the man in the brown suit. "What I remember about last night is getting dressed up." She crossed her leg. "At eight o'clock, I walked to the bar near the diner where I work. Then at the bar I ordered a beer. My friends weren't there yet. They had to work, so they wouldn't get there until closer to nine." She licked her lips. "I wanted to go to the club, but they said it was too early, so we stayed there drinking until after nine. I wasn't drinking a lot, but I was feeling buzzed. I want to be completely honest for this, right?"

The man in the suit nodded, then took a sip of his coffee. "I'm assuming someone was watching Charlie?"

"Yes, of course. He's only three years old." She clenched her hands. "Ruby, my roommate is with him. She always watches him for me. She loves him as much as I do." Saying that made her feel sad. "Where is Charlie? Is he around here, in this building?"

"He's in God's hands, don't worry." He gestured for her to continue.

She was confused, but the man did not offer any more details. He just waited for her to continue and she did continue her recollection of the night. "We went to a nightclub where we knew we could dance. We took a taxi to get there. It was crowded, but there were four of us."

*The four of us in this relationship. One too many, but he probably won't leave his wife.*

Georgia remembered the positive home pregnancy test. The second one she had done that week made it real for her. "I guess it's true. What am I going to do?" She took a picture of it on her phone. "Should I text him?" Then her phone rang in her hand, and she looked at the caller ID. "Speak of the devil." She cleared her throat, and answered. "Hello, Mr. B, I was just thinking about you."

"I like to hear that, Peach," he said. "Can you bring over the papers for the Norton job? I'll be in the office on the East side." He hung up before she could answer.

She went to the office, it would have been weird to go in on a Saturday, but she had gone in on days off. Really any day or time to see him. She didn't think he was going to leave his wife, and she wasn't blind. She saw him flirt with other women in the office, but that was his way. She was his girl. He only called her "Peach" and would spend the lunch hour with her. "Well, most lunch hours." She took a deep breath before walking to her desk.

Georgia grabbed the papers from her file cabinet then went into his office. He was smoking a cigar, and that made her smile. "Celebrating something?"

"This Norton deal." He exhaled and set the cigar down as he eyed her body. "If we can get him to sign, then we got another building that will bring us money."

She sat in his lap and kissed him. "So do you have time for me?"

"I sure do, Peach." He kissed her neck, then gently bit her earlobe. "Do you want to do the secretary thing and fuck me here or the hotel?"

"Oh, you're so romantic." She pushed him away and got off his lap.

He stood up and she sat on his desk. "It's been a while since we had office sex."

"No, we are not going to have office sex." She pulled out her phone. "I have to show you something." She texted him the picture of the pregnancy test.

"Shit, really?" He put his phone down.

She stood up and walked away from him. "Wow, contain the excitement."

"Don't you have a boyfriend?" Johnny shrugged. "Maybe he could be the father."

"No, sorry to say, it's just you." She crossed her arms and glared at him. "Not everyone cheats."

"Oh, you're so high and mighty. You're telling me this now, when we were going to fuck." He sat up straighter, and fixed his tie. "How do I know that's even your pregnancy test?"

She grabbed her purse. "I don't care what you think of me. But I do expect you to take care of your own child." Georgia left the office and got into a taxi. She was angry and texted Johnny more pictures. These were of her and Johnny in her bed, and in a hotel room. Then some other pictures of them together on their trips out of the city. Then she texted him that she wouldn't be in the office on Monday because of a doctor's appointment. She ended the text conversation by typing his wife's cell phone number. "Just try me, Mr. B."

Georgia didn't go to the doctor on Monday, instead she packed her stuff and left the city. Her roommate would be mad, but she needed to go home. She needed her mom, until she didn't need her. Mr. Johnny B started to pay his child support payments after the paternity test. Then she left for the city again, with the baby, and stayed with Ruby. Johnny's wife left him after the baby was born, but then went back to him. So Georgia's relationship with Mr. B was over.

"So you ended up at the club at about ten last night?" The man stood up and went to the opened grey door. He was handed two more paper cups of coffee. "Thanks, Bobby." The door closed and he brought the cups over to the table, setting one in front of her.

She nodded. "We got in fast. Someone was friends with the bouncer." She took off her sunglasses and dug through her purse. She needed some lip gloss and noticed her wallet was missing. "Hey, I don't see my wallet." She dumps her purse out onto the table. "I don't see my keys."

"Don't worry about that right now, okay. Keep going with your story, I think you will remember what happened."

Georgia shook her head. "What am I doing here? What exactly is this about?"

He looked at her eyes and sighed. "You grew up Catholic?"

"Yes. But I don't see what that has anything to do with talking to the police."

He held up his hand and shook his head. "I am not the police. But you can think of this as a confession of sorts." He looked at another paper, and then put it down to look at Georgia. "We have to hear your side of the story, and then we can make a determination."

"Determination for what? That's what I don't understand."

He leaned forward. "Just tell me what happened after you got into the club."

"We got more drinks and started dancing. My friends and I were just having fun dancing. I don't get to go to clubs a lot. Ever since Charlie was born, I just work nights and sleep days and try to take care of Charlie." She put her head down. "I get help with Charlie from Ruby. But sometimes you just need to go out and get away. I don't know, just be me."

"So, you're dancing. Then what happens?" The man looked at the file and flipped through some papers.

"I went to the bar to order another drink, because it wasn't that late. I mean, you're only young once. My friends were still dancing, but I wanted to do a shot." She sat up and took a drink of her coffee. "Then I met a guy."

Her headache had cleared, and she closed her eyes and pictured the bar. "There was a man with blonde hair, and he was wearing a dark grey suit. He was taller than me in my heels, and he was handsome. I don't really have a type of man that I am attracted to, but he would be everyone's type."

Last night, the man in the grey suit didn't say anything to her, he just held out his hand and she took it. He led her away from the bar and up some stairs. She saw signs that designated this level as the VIP section. He sat at a booth in the corner, and she slid in next to him. She placed her purse on the table.

"I'll have another whiskey," the man told the cocktail waitress and continued, "She'll have a vodka martini."

"Of course." The waitress smiled and walked away.

"Thanks," she said, "I'm Georgia."

He leaned in and kissed her. The rest of night was a blur of drinking and kissing. She didn't look at her phone at all. She didn't look for her friends and didn't see anyone else, just the man in the grey suit. Soon she was giggling as he rubbed her leg and whispered in her ear. He asked her why she was there.

"I told him." Georgia hugged herself. "I wanted a night away from my kid." She closed her eyes, and she could see that man's green eyes looking at her. After taking a breath, Georgia opened her eyes to look at the brown eyes of her interrogator. His eyes were kinder than the other man's. "I let him kiss me, my neck, and my shoulder. He was whispering things in my ear, some of it I heard. But some of it was hard to hear because of the music. I thought he said that it was an easy fix." She bit her lip. "I didn't know what he meant by that." She put her arms on the table and looked at her hands, then back up to the man's brown eyes. "I swear I didn't know what he meant." She put her face into her hands and started to cry.

"Here, take this." He handed her a tissue. "Do you need a moment?"

She dabbed her eyes. "I think I do."

He nodded and stood up. "I'll be back in about five minutes." He picked up the empty paper cups, then her file, and left the room.

The fog was lifting and she remembered the man in the grey suit nibbling her ear and playing with her hair. "If you had to pick, would you sacrifice yourself or your child?"

"What are you talking about?" She pushed her drink away.

He whispered into her ear. "You or your son?"

"I don't understand." She put her hands on the table.

"Freedom. I can offer you freedom." He kissed her neck. "You have to choose."

She turned to look at him. "What would happen?"

He took a sip of his drink. "What do you want to happen?"

"Nothing. I love my kid. He can be a pain, but he's a baby." She shrugged then said, "But if I could have waited to have him, I would." She drank the rest of her drink. "I guess, I can always have another kid."

The man stood up and buttoned his suit jacket, then left her sitting in the booth. Georgia waited for hours for him to return. She grabbed her purse and saw that her wallet was gone. "Did I leave it at home or did that asshole rob me?"

She walked downstairs and didn't see many people there. Her friends weren't at the bar or on the mostly empty dance floor. "They probably left hours ago." Georgia walked out the door and looked at her phone. It was almost three in the morning, and there were a lot of missed calls, but none from Ruby. "She must be asleep with the baby." Georgia saw her reflection in the screen and her smudged eyeliner. She pouted, her lipstick was long gone from all the kissing. "Even if I had money, no taxi would pick me up." She started the long walk home.

"It took me about an hour to walk home." She continued when the man in the brown suit returned. "These heels are not made for walking."

"This is after you leave the club?" He sat down and gave her a clear plastic cup of water. "Did you leave with the man or alone?"

"I was alone." She sipped the water. "I was alone. He left me at the club."

"So this is in the morning? Like around five?" He didn't look at the file, but at her blue eyes.

She shook her head. "Before that, but it was early. I didn't look at my phone after I left the club. So it could have been. I just know that I walked a long time."

"What happened when you got to the apartment?"

"It was so quiet, I thought they were sleeping." She played with her purse strap on the table. "I didn't have my keys, so I was going to call Ruby. So she could let me in without waking the baby. But then I saw that the door wasn't closed." She took a deep breath. "I pushed the door open and the apartment was in disarray. Someone had come in and ransacked the apartment." She teared up and looked at her hands clenched on the table. She relaxed her hands because her left wrist started to hurt, and the white bandage turned red.

"Oh, you must have popped a stitch." The interrogator handed her some more tissues. "Put some pressure on it. We'll have someone look at it soon."

She nodded, remembering the man in the grey suit was there, in her living room. His green eyes watched her from Ruby's couch. His suit jacket was next to him and he had been sitting there waiting for her. Georgia stumbled over the overturned highchair, and stopped in front of the man. "He had my wallet and my keys. He had them on the coffee table."

She saw the red stains on his white button up shirt and she collapsed onto the love seat. "He told me he wanted to return them." He also told her that he was sorry about her friend, she was collateral damage, but she had made her choice. "I lunged at him and tried to fight him. He was too strong. He just pushed me down onto the floor."

He held her chin and kissed her. "You have another choice." He put on his dark grey suit jacket and buttoned it closed. He pointed to the knife on the counter and Ruby's phone, then he left.

"I mean, he hurt them. Why did he do that?" She wiped her tears away, "Who was that man?"

"Temptation." The interrogator answered tersely. "We all are faced with it. Some can deny him, some can't. Here, it is in this place where we face the consequences of it." He opened the file and flipped to the last page. "So the judgement has to be made." He pulled out a red fountain pen from his inner pocket. He uncapped it and proceeded to go down the page, making check marks in the appropriate boxes.

Georgia sunk back into her plastic chair.

"Okay, I think we are done here. You can leave. Just follow my assistant." The grey metal door opened and an older woman wearing a white blouse and a red woolen skirt entered to take the file from the interrogator.

She read the last page and smiled at Georgia. "You will follow me."

Georgia nodded. "I like your lipstick, that shade of red looks nice on you."

"Thank you. I like your scarf."

Georgia followed behind the more petite woman. She kept her eyes on the lady's grey bun. The woman was wearing red heeled shoes that made clicking noises, while Georgia held her shoes in her hands. The woman headed down the hall to the elevator. The doors opened and Georgia expected to see flames come out, but it was just an ordinary elevator. "This is as far as I go." The woman smiled at her. Georgia stepped into the elevator and watched the woman push a button. Then the doors closed and the descent began.

# The Shadow in the Woods

**JK Allen**

*Content Warning: Mentions Suicide*

The shadow in the woods was something often heard about in our small town, but it was legend, not truth, and I never believed it past age ten. It was like saying "Bloody Mary" three times in the bathroom mirror. You weren't supposed to go out into the woods at the witching hour, because a shadow that shouldn't be there would haunt you. And then bad things happened. It was a known fact by everyone, but it wasn't really a fact. At least, I didn't believe it was until that fateful summer.

When is the witching hour anyway? Some say midnight, some say one, others any time until 3 AM. It's hard to know exactly when the veil thins between worlds, and we become vulnerable. But vulnerable we do become. Humans are very squishy creatures easily harmed and not as easily patched up. So it isn't that we shouldn't be careful, we just aren't.

There's something about our youth that makes us feel invincible until it is too late. Rationalizing that nothing bad can really happen to us, right? We lull ourselves into complacency by statistics and anecdotes of the ones that survive. We pray to luck and whatever gods we believe in. Or we simply don't think about it at all.

Whatever my personal logic, I imagine it may have been the probability of it all, or rather, the improbability, the improbability of the existence of monsters and things that go bump in the night. I decided that meeting Titan Brandon was far more important than any stupid scary story. After all, I'd only had a crush on him for three years, and it seemed like this year he finally knew who I was and might like what he sees.

And yes his name was Titan. At six-feet-two, he was a dream to any high school girl, with dark hair and blue eyes and a smirk that could kill. I wasn't the only one who daydreamed about him, but I was the one he asked to meet in that spot in the woods. And the woods were just a few minutes away from my house, how much harm could it do? Mom worked nights anyway, and I was just responsible enough to leave on my own. What was one night meeting a cute boy I liked going to do?

So I agreed to meet him that Friday. I wore something cute but woods appropriate, after all I wasn't dumb. I wore ripped jeans and a cropped hoodie and some sneakers. Curled my hair and did my make up. All dressed to the nines I was ready. I left a note and took my keys and phone and lipstick and made my way to Sherwood at 11 PM.

The night was balmy, one of those beautiful nights that makes you think of poetry class and bonfires. A breeze blew through the rustling leaves of the trees I passed. They were a dark green in the night, with cones of yellow street lights dotting my path. I turned the corner and saw the field that led into the woods. It was a park, with swings and other equipment off to the side. The stars twinkled above me, but a chill dotted my skin as the wind caressed my neck. It was dark after all, and I technically wasn't supposed to be here past dusk. I hurried into the edge of the treeline, making my way onto the walking path that ran through the center of the woods. It was a known spot for some teens to hang out, so it couldn't be that dangerous. But that also meant we could get busted if someone decided to check it out.

I pulled out my phone to text Titan as the dry underbrush crunched underneath my feet. A twig snapped to my right, and I jumped, heart slamming into my chest. No other sound echoed through the night, so I continued on, laughing at myself.

*Hey, I'm almost there.*

*Just waiting. See you soon.*

I turned on my phone's flashlight with a grin. It was getting dark under the canopies as they stretched to block out the moon. Most of the trees were pretty skinny, but after a good rain, the leaves filled out. I had dreamed of alone time with Titan, and now I was about to get it. My pulse quickened at the thought, and my mouth went dry in a good way. It was nerves, yes, but the thrill was there underneath like a current pulling me along.

I felt the thrill all over my body as I crossed into the forbidden zone. The sounds seemed muffled this deep into the trees. As though my ears were swaddled, or I was underwater. Bugs no longer chirped, and there were less animal movements. A stick snapped again, behind me this time, and I spun around. Seeing the shadow man for the first time.

He wore a crown, jagged edges jutting up from his large head with gaunt features. His mouth seemed to hang open and his skeletal body moved in unnatural jerks. He scampered faster towards me, and I screamed, turning and running towards where Titan was supposed to be.

But when I got to the clearing, with sticks and twigs cutting my arms and legs, it was empty. Nothing there. My phone was shaking in my hand as I looked back and saw the shadowy creature loping towards me. I screamed again and called for Titan this time. Nothing answered but the monster's footsteps ranging ever closer.

I panicked, my brain went into reptile survival mode, and I booked it to the right. I didn't know exactly where I was going, but instincts had taken over. Unfortunately, without a trail, I was getting cuts left and right from lashing branches and brambles. Blood was running down one of my legs, and I abruptly veered right again to avoid a tree. My ankle slipped and twisted painfully, but I felt enough adrenaline to keep going. I headed back to the entrance and home. I could hear something scrambling after me, but somehow, I managed to stay ahead of it. I had my phone in a death grip, white knuckling it, so I wouldn't lose my source of shaking, scattered light.

I burst through the treeline, struggling to breathe and almost fell looking back. The shadow stayed at the edge of the trees, taunting me with a farewell wave as I ran the rest of the way home.

I locked the front door and bolted to my bedroom, locking that and collapsing against the wood, breathing heavily. Tears leaked from the corners of my eyes as my brain tried to process what had just happened. I collected myself enough to call Titan to see if he was okay, but the phone rang and his voicemail picked up. I hung up and texted him to call me back and let me know where he was and if he was alright. I cried for at least fifteen minutes as I wiped sweat off my face. My heart was pounding, and I felt sick to my stomach, but everything seemed too slow. And eventually, I somehow found sleep, slumped against the door.

I woke the next morning to a phone call from an unknown number. It was Detective Jones, and I panicked again.

"Good morning, is this Selena Rivera?"

"Yes, who is this?"

"I'm Detective Stanley Jones with the Sherwood PD. Do you know a Titan Brandon?"

"Oh my God, is he okay? I was supposed to meet him last night, but he ghosted me."

"Unfortunately no, we found his body in the early morning. It appears to be a possible suicide."

I sobbed then.

"So you did not meet him last night? We had a text—"

"I texted him, yes. We were supposed to meet, but he wasn't there when I got there. He was gone. I assumed he just left. It was scary being there alone at night. I immediately got out of there myself."

"You didn't wait or look around for him at all?"

"No, I scared myself, being alone in the dark, and I ran out of the woods and back home. You can come check me for scratches from the branches hitting me. I know it sounds dumb, but the local legend, about the shadow that haunts you. I swear it was chasing me last night, and I freaked and got out of there."

"That's just an old wive's tale."

"I know. I just got spooked."

"Well, if you don't mind me stopping by to get a formal statement from you, I'd like to do that."

"My mom will be home in an hour. Will that work for you?"

"It will. I will see you in an hour."

I knew he would be there before then. Probably to see what I would admit to without adult supervision. I got up on sore wobbly legs. Legs that had seen better days. I could at least have a quick shower to wash the blood from my cuts and warm up and loosen my muscles.

The shower stung, but accomplished enough to limber me up a little. I had just gotten dressed when the doorbell rang. Sure enough, it was about half an hour before my mom would be getting home. I opened the door and let the detective inside.

"You do look like you had a rough night," he remarked, striding in with a coffee in hand.

I had put on a long sleeve shirt and cropped pants, but had a cut on my cheek and some bruises on my ankles. Plus, the bags under my eyes were enough to give away I hadn't lied about running through the woods, scared for my life.

I shrugged, but just closed the door after him. "My mom isn't home yet."

"Sorry, I was closer than I realized and just headed on over. I don't do well sitting in my car all day. Hope you don't mind."

I shrugged again. It didn't really matter if I minded. I indicated to the couch and sat down. He joined me.

"So, tell me again about last night. Are you sure these marks are from the trees? Not a fight you had with Titan, or anyone else?"

I glared at him and his obvious ploy. "The only one I was fighting was branches. I was literally running through the woods. I dunno what I saw for sure, but it wasn't Titan."

"You know I have to ask. It's suspicious. We have his phone saying you two were meeting. And you have marks on you…."

"They are obviously from branches."

"Can I take pictures?"

"You'll have to ask my mom."

He sighed, but nodded. "Well, tell me about what you saw."

"It was dark, all I had was my phone light."

"You saw enough to get spooked. Maybe Titan was attacked by what you saw?"

The thought sent a shiver down my spine. I must have had a look on my face, because he patted my arm to comfort me.

"It was like this shadowy figure. Really tall and skinny. I just thought back to all the stories we had heard as kids—the local legend—and I got so scared. It was like running towards me, but it was so unnatural looking. I screamed for Titan and ran to the clearing, but no one was there. Literally, I didn't see anyone, and he didn't answer me. So I ran to the side and back out of the woods. It chased me but stopped at the treeline. I tried to call Titan when I got home. He didn't answer, so I texted him. But I must have fallen asleep. Then you woke me up."

"We just want to know if there was foul play involved with Titan's… incident. Are you sure you saw a shadow figure? Could it have been your imagination, and it was another person?"

"I'm sure it was, but like I said, it looked like the urban legend of the Shadow Man to me. I wouldn't be able to give you much about what he really looked like if it was a he…."

"Well, here's my card, I want you to let me know if you remember anything. And don't plan on going anywhere until you are eliminated as a suspect."

"I swear I didn't even see him that night. I left right away when he wasn't there."

That's when I realized he was there, somewhere. I started sobbing.

The detective looked uncomfortable, and patted me again. "I just need to be sure before I eliminate you completely. You understand." He stood and cleared his throat, leaving his card on the seat next to me. "I'll see myself out."

I didn't notice him leaving, but after a few minutes my mom walked in and nearly screamed. I was usually in bed when she came home.

"What are you doing up, and crying? What is wrong, mija?" she asked, rushing over to me.

"My friend died last night. The detective was just here to talk to me about it. Mom, I'm scared. I did something I shouldn't have."

"What did you do? I'm sorry about your friend, but what did you do that was so bad?"

"I went to Sherwood to meet him, but he wasn't there. He was already dead, and mom, I saw something. A shadow figure."

Mom made the sign of the cross. "How did your friend die? And what were you doing in the woods after dark?"

"I know I shouldn't have gone, but I wanted to meet him. They were already dead, mom. I don't even know what I saw, but it was terrifying."

"Wear this at all times, mija. Don't even take it off to shower." Mom handed me her grandmother's crucifix.

"Mom, seriously?"

"I have never been more serious in my life. My friend in high school saw the shadow demon, and may she rest in peace, she did nothing to save herself. But this was blessed by the Pope, given to me from mi abuela, and it will protect you."

"Mom, I'm really freaked out."

She kissed my forehead. "Get some sleep. Don't leave this house."

"Mom, I have to work today."

"Call in, mija. I will call the priest to see if he can bless you. Get some sleep."

She walked away, looking more tired and defeated than I had ever seen her. Tears welled up in my eyes as I put on the crucifix. I took a deep breath in and let it out in a huff. I could call in just for today. I coughed a few times to hoarsen my throat, and made the call.

***

The priest fit me in and did his fatherly thing, so I was permitted to return to work and school. It was on my first day back in classes that I saw it again. It was lingering in the field outside, where the track team practiced. It seemed only I could see it, but it waved at me and danced and moved slowly closer throughout the day. My heart was pounding and by lunch I had hives on my neck and chest from the stress of my fear. I couldn't catch my breath, I felt on the verge of collapsing every time I stood up. It was just looming ever closer to me with each minute that passed in screaming agony. What happened when it reached me? Would I meet the same fate Titan did? My mind reeled.

I ended up leaving at lunch. It was too close to the building for comfort, so I sprinted with all I had in me to my car. Luckily, mom had let me drive and didn't make me take the bus in case I needed to get away. I sped like a demon to my house and locked all the doors and windows. I called my mom sobbing. She couldn't get out of work, but she told me to stay inside the rest of the day and don't let anyone in. "Block the windows with newspaper," she said. "Don't let it see you. It has no power over you then."

I didn't know what that meant, but I kept repeating it like a mantra as I taped old papers to the window. We never got the newspaper except on Sundays for the coupons, so I ended up plastering mail in adverts all over the windows. Soon it was dark in the house. So I turned on all the lights. I was torn. If it was dark, could a shadow survive? But if there was no light, then I couldn't see it come for me either. I decided I needed to see if it was anywhere near me and that was more important than whether the shadow could exist or not. I did not need it sneaking up on me.

I fell asleep on the couch, crashing from the adrenaline of the day, and woke up to a rattling at the door. Like someone was shaking the door, trying to release it from its frame. I screamed, before clapping my hand over my mouth. Cold sweat broke out on my hairline, dripping down my face and neck. I shuddered as I watched the front door knob turn all the way to the left, then the right. A tapping happened on the glass panes of the door, and I was thankful I remembered to cover those as well with paper. My entire body shook as I listened to those unnatural tap scratches on the glass. *Don't let it see you. It has no power then.*

I sat there frozen, shivering, for I don't know how long. Just listening to the ghastly nail on the glass before I noticed its absence. I wiped my forehead, chewing frantically on my bottom lip as I tried to unmold myself from a sculpture. If it wasn't at the front door, it was trying to get in another way. I had to make sure it didn't get behind me. So I made my way shakily to the kitchen, gulping in air awkwardly. It was like the fear had taken over my brain, and it no longer functioned properly. Just enough to propel my body forward. But not enough to formulate a plan or really defend myself. All I kept whispering was *don't let it see me.* Over and over again in my mind as my feet stumbled forward. I held my arms out like I was blind, though everywhere was well lit from inside. It was at the kitchen door now.

Trembling took on a whole new meaning as it rattled the doorknob furiously. I didn't know how old the door was or what condition it was to withstand a creature that I didn't understand. It looked like a shadow, but was clearly able to touch and move things. It did not seem to have a problem with lifting heavy objects like the bodies of cute teenage jocks. And I was even smaller than Titan was. My stomach cramped, and I doubled over to a crouch in the middle of the kitchen. Arms hanging onto the countertops for support as my butt hovered inches from the ground. I knew I looked ridiculous, but he couldn't see me. That was the point. Until it looked through the keyhole and laughed at me.

I screamed, falling to the ground as it pushed itself through the hole like a wisp of smoke. Scrambling backwards, on my elbows, I turned, clawing the floor to get to my feet before it assumed its regular shape in my doorway. I ran to my room and locked the door.

This door now had no holes at least, but there was the gap where the door met the floor. I grabbed an old shirt and stuffed it there, praying it would be enough.

Sobs overtook me then, as it clawed up and down my door, announcing its presence.

"Leave me alone!" I shouted, voice hoarse and cracking. Betraying me. Sweat stung my eyes that leaked tears constantly now. What the hell was I supposed to do in this situation? A shadow creature was stalking me. How could I fight against that? I grabbed my abuela's crucifix and said a prayer. I didn't even know what prayer to say. I asked that my ancestors would protect me. That's what I believed in, not some being that had never once intervened in my crappy life, but in the people in my family, who shared my blood, who loved me and cared about me. I prayed to them to save me from this monster, and to let me live. I prayed in my ragged, jagged hybrid of Spanish and English. Hoping they would get the intention of my words. I prayed, squeezing that crucifix between my palms until I could feel the heat of it. *Wear it like a bracelet mija*, a voice said in my ear.

I wrapped it loosely around my wrist like a rosary. It felt heavy on my arm, like a weapon.

*A weapon, yes. Use it like a gauntlet. Against the shadow demon.*

I felt power radiating from my wrist and took a deep breath. It calmed me. I felt hands on my shoulders and back, like my family was behind me. I could do this, with their help. I knew I could. I opened the door.

The creature laughed for one moment, then he saw the figures in the light behind me. It screamed in fury, and I aimed for its face with my blessed necklace wrapped around my fist. The shadow's head exploded. Fragments splintered and went flying. I laughed in relief, and kept pummeling it as it fell backwards to the ground, now mostly a mouth on a skeletal body. I aimed for its leg, and it broke off at an angle. Then the other leg. I kept punching strategically to take away its ability to escape. Then I punched it into tiny immeasurable bits to take away its life. Until my family was clapping and cheering and told me I was finished. The necklace still shone, after all the damage it hadn't incurred even a dent or a scratch.

"Gracias, mi familia," I said in a humble whisper. I was exhausted and crumbled to the floor where I fell asleep, waiting to tell my mother what our family had done.

# Lost in the Woods

**Carol Allen**

"The big house was where you want to live," the older woman said, combing the newcomer's long black hair. She would braid it to keep it out of the way, ignoring the aches in her knuckles. This young one would not have hard tasks to perform, but it was beautiful, shiny black hair. Of course she was a beautiful girl, so she would have the attention of the leader. "It's a blessing and a curse, but it is where you want to live."

"Why?" The young one turned her big brown eyes to look at the older woman's squinting ones. The older woman tugged the braid and pushed her head to face forward. "Ouch. Sorry, ma'am."

"You can call me Missus Shirley. Leave the ma'am for the leader's wife." She shook her head, "Didn't your momma teach you any sense?" She tied off the braid. "Do you know how the world works? Did she teach you about being a woman?"

The young one looked down at her hands in her lap. "I didn't know my momma. I was made a house maid when I was eleven."

*So, she has experience, that's how she got the referral here.* The older woman put the wooden bristle brush down on the vanity. "So, you got eleven years with her. That's more than most, Mika. You are lucky."

"I was sent to school before that ma'am." Mika stood up and put her hands behind her. She was almost as tall as the elder at her young age, and her slender figure was flattered by the plain blue dress uniform issued to students. The other woman wore the black dress uniform that most of the staff wore.

"Then you know the way of the world." Missus Shirley stood in front of her and tucked her loose grey hair behind her own ears. "Mind your manners, listen to those who rank higher than you, and lock your bedroom door." Shirley shook her head, "I should make your face ugly, but that wouldn't get you the good job." The older woman rubbed her achy hands together. "Then we know that an ugly scar doesn't always keep unwanted attention away."

"Ma'am?" The young Mika blushed.

"Just be a good girl and be careful." Shirley opened the door and said, "You may leave and return to your room. Your new dress uniform should be in your room."

"Thank you, ma'am." Mika bowed and left the room.

"Good night, Mika." Shirley shut the door and prayed silently for all her girls.

Mika walked down the hall to her room and remembered to lock it behind her. Her lone tan suitcase was left by her twin bed. "At least the bed is made." She touched the brown woolen blanket. "Not too scratchy." She looked at the bare room. "At least it's a warm place to rest. I'm working in the big house." The small closet was without a door, and she saw her new purple dress uniform hanging in it. The material was thicker than her school uniform, and the white apron was edged with ruffles. It would be a nice uniform to wear. "This is a nice job."

She changed into a plain pink cotton nightgown and lay down in her new bed. She wondered how the staff at her old household was doing. Mika missed her old employers, the elderly couple that let her call them Grandpa and Grandma. They let her continue her education while she lived with them. That was what helped her get this position after Grandma passed and Grandpa went to live with his children. This house was bigger, and the family grander than she was used to, but she was sure to do her best.

Her first day was uneventful, she was kept in the kitchen area and dining room. The first days were always spent learning the habits of the employers and their preferences. Rule number one was always, what the leader wants, the leader gets. She was able to progress to helping in the nursery before long. This promotion came with the added benefit of new black boots and black stockings. The white apron was replaced with a black striped one with pockets. She would be required to hold tissues and some candies to help the nanny clean or soothe the children.

The leader's wife was a beautiful woman, younger than the leader, with light brown hair and eyes. She seemed nice, but did not spend more than an hour with the children daily. The nanny would update her on the children's progress in their early education, but the older one would be going to boarding school in a few weeks. Then there would be just the younger two children to mind. The mother would then leave the nursery to either go shopping or to lunches with her friends. The leader was a tall man with the expected blonde hair and loud voice. She often heard his bombastic voice throughout the house more than she saw him.

Those first couple months were great for Mika and she said, "This is a nice job," every night before she fell asleep.

Things changed after the eldest son went to boarding school. The nanny was sent with him to help him settle into the new town and his new school. Mika and another minder were expected to continue to teach and watch the five year old daughter and the almost three year old son. Mika had the least experience and was to play with the toddler. The boy loved to go outside, be pushed in his stroller, and to play at the children's park near the big house. The swings at the playground were his favorite. But it was at the park that she got the attention of the leader's wife.

"What are you doing out here with my son?" The leader's wife swooped in and took control of the stroller. The wife's matching red coat and sweater dress was the same color as Mika's burning cheeks.

"Ma'am, I'm sorry. Young Jack likes his morning strolls." She bowed her head and kept her gaze down. Mika stared at the lady's red high heels and she slowly breathed in. "I did make him wear a hat and gloves, because it is a little chilly out."

The leader's wife didn't say anything and stared at Mika's black coat, then at her son in his stroller. He just sat in the stroller watching Mika. "Well, I couldn't see that he had his gloves on or his blanket. I was just upset because of how cold it is out here."

Mika slowly looked up at the wife's stern eyes. "Of course, you were concerned, ma'am. I think I will take him right home and make him some cocoa."

"Yes, do that." She nodded and stepped aside to let Mika take the stroller and walk back to the big house.

Mika smiled at the young boy and hummed to him. He smiled at her and looked around with his blue eyes and pointed at the trees, the birds, and the other people walking around. He tried to verbalize the names of the objects and Mika had to laugh. This was their game and she was getting better at understanding his babbles. "Yes, Young Jack, that is a tree. The tree has branches and soon will have green leaves. Spring is here, Young Jack." She was able to ignore the clicking of the wife's heels behind her. Mika didn't see the wife's eyes behind her brown sunglasses, or she would have seen a worrying glint of jealousy. She wouldn't have been surprised at the meeting that would take place with the leader.

Mika was called into the leader's office after the return of the nanny. The nanny resumed her duties of taking charge of the toddler and overseeing the activities of the daughter. Mika felt sad not being able to spend hours out of the house and her days with Young Jack. She wanted to rush to him when she heard him crying. But she knew to keep to her station and continued to clean the children's rooms. She was preparing Young Jack's room for the transition from the crib to a small bed. *He's growing up so fast,* she thought as she packed up his too small baby clothes and other clothing to make room for his new wardrobe. The other minder came into the room to take over. "You're wanted in the leader's office immediately," the minder told Mika.

"Yes." She nodded and left the minder, she took deep breaths to calm her nerves as she made her way to the main floor. The leader's office was flanked by his butler's men and one of them announced her arrival after he knocked on the dark wood door. He smirked at her and let her pass before shutting her into the large room. The walls were covered by large bookshelves or paintings of the leader's ancestors, the big house, and of the surrounding grounds. The leader stayed seated at his desk and he continued to write with his ink pen as she walked toward the desk. She stopped in front of the desk and bowed her head. "Sir?"

"Just a moment." She heard the scratching of the nib over the paper. He had not looked up from his work, and it was mesmerizing watching the flow of the black ink marking the white paper. The flourishes of cursive writing made her miss her school days. She couldn't read his upside down writing, so she looked over the leader's head and out the window. The trees that bordered the property could be seen, and then she noticed the map of the property next to the window. This was the first time that she realized the forest was behind the house, the property was at the edge of town.

If she could go east, then she could go home. The leader slammed his papers into a drawer; everything he did was explosively loud. She jumped to attention, and her eyes locked onto his until she looked to the side. "So you are the new nanny's aide?"

She held her head up. "Yes, sir."

"Since the nanny has returned, and now that there are only the two children, it has come to my attention that your position will be reassigned." He watched her expression stay neutral. "My wife requires a new attendant, and she was impressed by your referral to us."

Mika stayed quiet as it was always better to let the leader speak unopposed and uninterrupted.

"So you took care of Elder Masterson's wife?" He was looking at her file and eyeing her.

"Yes, sir. I took care of her daily requirements." She focused on the large pine trees outside the window. She missed her morning walks with Young Jack, and the trees seemed darker and larger in the moonlight. She blinked a couple times to refocus her attention to the leader. Mika tried not to make eye contact, she knew that sometimes that was threatening. Either she would be the threat or she would see the threat of wandering eyes. The schoolmaster was the worst for the leering, and that seemed worse than any hands put on the body. In her experience, with bad actions, the punishments could be doled out, but implications were harder to discipline. She focused on a spot on the leader's shoulder and fought the urge to look out the window.

"Freedom," he said.

"Sir?" She blinked and looked at his blue eyes.

"It looks like you had a lot of freedom in that household." His eyes stayed cold.

They were older, nice people and decent. Their generation was from before the changes and they were able to stay in their comfortable status in society due to their fortune. Elder Masterson wasn't political, but he rebelled when he could, like paying for a young maid's education. He told her that she had to be careful and she didn't want to get his family in trouble. She had to be careful in how she described her time with them. She definitely couldn't say she was happy there. "Because of her age, the lady of the house allowed me to do some of my errands unsupervised. I always had her permission to leave the house and had a schedule to keep, sir."

"How did you do your duties, while you were attending school?" The leader sat back in his maroon leather chair and clasped his hands together without taking his eyes off her.

"There was another servant to run the household duties, sir. They allowed me to go to school, so I may represent the lady better. She felt that if I had an education, I could help her with her correspondence, sir." Mika swallowed, trying not to look nervous. "Also, I did not board at the school and would do the housekeeping in the evenings, sir." She had practiced this many times and often in front of the schoolmaster. She wasn't entirely lying and with the practice she knew she wasn't blushing. She didn't like the scrutiny of the leader's gaze and looked out the window. The wind was picking up and it looked like the trees were beckoning to her.

"Go see Missus Shirley, and she'll give you the new uniform as my wife's attendant. You'll start tomorrow morning." He waved her away and went back to writing.

"Yes, sir." She bowed her head and rushed out of the large office. The lush decorative carpeting silenced her quick steps, and she didn't look at the butler's men as she ran down the hall. Her head was spinning, this was a promotion, but she felt that this was what she didn't want. Soon she was at Missus Shirley's open door, and she knocked on the doorframe before entering. "Missus Shirley, I am here for my new uniform."

"Come in, child." Shirley was washing some laundry in a small bucket and dried her hands with a hand towel. "What uniform do you need?"

"I am going to be the wife's attendant." Mika relaxed her hands, not realizing she had them clenched as fists the whole time she ran to this room. She cleared her throat and said, "I start tomorrow morning."

"Oh." Shirley put the towel down and turned to go to her large wardrobe. "This is a promotion for sure." She opened a couple drawers and pulled out a box of new black dress flats. Then she pulled out a navy blue apron dress and crisp white blouse. Shirley handed the hangers and the shoes to Mika. "There will be more clothing made for you. Leticia will measure you in a couple weeks. Once you have the approval of the wife." Shirley crossed her arms and told her, "You should wear your white stockings with this uniform and keep your shoes shiny. They don't like any dirt around them. You should wear your hair up in a bun during this trial.

Once you're approved then you can wear it down. They will give you more freedom when they give you a new room and clothing."

"I can't stay in my room?"

"No, you will be closer to the wife. You will be at her beck and call." Shirley put her hands on her hips. "If she wants something at midnight, she will ring for you. If she requires any item, you will have to acquire it for her. Don't worry, they will give you a credit card to use." She pointed a finger at her. "But you have to be careful about how much you spend. You cannot charge anything frivolous on it, or they will punish you." Shirley put her hand into her apron pocket and pulled out a brass key. "They won't give you a key to your room, but this will lock the door. You will have to hide this." She put the key into Mika's hands. "I used to hide it on top of the door frame in the closet." She held Mika's face in her hands. "No one will find it there." Shirley went back to her laundry. "Remember to mind your manners and do what the wife tells you to do. This is a good job for you, if you can stay out of the way of the leader."

"Yes, Missus Shirley." Mika slowly turned and walked to her room. She hung her new uniform in her closet and looked at her small room. The emptiness of the bare walls and plain bed filled her up and she fell onto her knees. "This is a good thing that is happening," she whispered. "I wanted to work here and live here." She wiped her tears. "This is a promotion." She curled up on the floor and hugged her knees, waiting for sleep to take her.

The next morning was uneventful, she followed the wife and stood behind or beside her. She had a notebook and pen to take notes of the wife's demands. It was decided that Mika would be in charge of the wife's clothing. She would lay out most of her outfits, make sure items were laundered and pressed. She would fetch shoes and other accessories to present to the wife. Then she was given the job of going into town to pick up the wife's mail. Mika was also responsible for picking up packages from the boutiques the wife frequented. After she did as she was told for a month, Mika received a closetful of new dresses. Missus Shirley said it meant that the promotion was permanent.

"This is a good thing, child," Shirley said after she tied a ribbon around Mika's braid. "I would still wear your hair up, but now you can style it as you see fit."

Mika wore a blue cloth dress with a flower print and looked at her reflection in the brass colored framed mirror. The new room reminded her of the time she had with Elder Masterson, but they allowed her more books to read. She only had a few books on her nightstand here, but she lacked time to read leisurely. Mika made her full sized bed and smoothed down the purple satin trimmed quilt. She was putting on her shoes when her bedroom door opened and she was startled by the nanny's aide. Mika hadn't locked the door that night, but she expected people to knock. "What do you want?"

"I'm sorry, but I've got a tear in my stockings. Can I borrow your black ones?" She held her hands up to her face. "I can't have Nanny yell at me one more time, I think I'll get demoted."

"Don't cry." Mika went to her dresser and got her black stockings. "You can keep them until you get yours mended."

"Thank you," the minder said as she ran out, leaving the door open.

After taking a few breaths, she turned to her dresser and pulled out the white apron with a ruffle. Her hand brushed against the black striped apron she wore when she helped the nanny. She missed being around the children. Mika tied her white apron around her waist, then went out to greet the wife. Today, she would go into town, and she needed to make sure her task list was complete. "Good morning, ma'am." She smiled at the wife who was sipping coffee at the table. The leader was sitting opposite his wife, reading the newspaper and she bowed to him. "Good morning, sir."

He just nodded and continued to read. She went to the buffet and made a plate of fruit for the wife. Mika placed the plate in front of the wife and refreshed her coffee. The leader did not drink coffee, so she poured him a glass of orange juice. The wife picked at the fresh fruit and ate a piece of kiwi while she watched Mika walk around the room. "Mika, you will go into town today and pick up my new dress from East and Main."

"Yes, ma'am. Was there anything else you needed?"

"The florist should have a bouquet ready for pick up," the wife replied.

"Yes, ma'am." Mika wrote down her notes and placed her notebook into her apron pocket. She bowed and left the room.

*It is a beautiful day to walk into town. This is a good job.*

Mika smiled and grabbed her light grey coat to wear on her walk. The big house had a long driveway, and once she was past the gate, she heard footsteps behind her on the gravel shoulder. She expected it to be a driver or a security guard, but when she turned around, she saw a boy her age. He was taller than her with a floppy tan cap on top of his curly brown hair. His blue eyes widened and he held up his empty hands. "I'm not following you. I didn't mean to scare you. I'm just going into town."

"Then you will be following me, because I am going into town."

He chuckled and said, "Well, I can walk ahead of you or next to you." He tugged his tan blazer and smoothed down his maroon tie. "My name is Timothy."

She shook his hand. "I'm Mika, and I work in the big house. Do you work there too?" They were now walking through the park and past the playground. She looked to see if Nanny was there with the children, but did not see them.

They continued down the main road. "No, I live on the grounds. My dad is a gardener for the leader, and I help out. There's a few green houses and vegetable gardens in the back, near the woods."

"Oh, I didn't know that. I haven't been here long, just a few months, and I've been very busy. Of course."

"Of course." He winked at her. His smile was easy, and she liked his freckles.

"I work as the wife's assistant." She looked at the town's buildings in front of them. "That's why I'm going into town. I am picking things up for her."

"Well, maybe I'll see you on the way back." He waved and sauntered towards the grocer's.

She crossed the street to go to the boutique and picked up two boxes. One contained the evening dress the wife was to wear for the dinner with the other leaders that evening. The other was more fabric for Leticia, the store owner told her, to make outfits for the children. Mika smiled and tucked the packages under her arm. "Thank you." She went over to the florist and he showed her the large bouquet of yellow and white magnolia blossoms with other little white blossoms and baby's breath. "I'm not sure I can carry those to the big house." Mika set her packages on the counter. "Unless I can trouble you for a bag."

The bell over the door tinkled and Timothy walked in. "Hello friends."

The florist returned the greeting. "Oh, Young Timothy, I have those seeds in the back. Just a moment, miss, and I'll get you a bag for your packages."

"Thank you, sir." Mika smiled.

"Wow, you have to carry all that back to the big house? Why didn't you have a driver accompany you?"

Mika blushed. "This stop was a surprise. I wanted a walk, but I didn't realize how big these flowers would be. I thought I would just have to carry one package."

"Well, I suppose I could be a gentleman. I will carry your packages for you, so you can carry the flowers. I only have a couple small things." He held up one plastic bag.

"I would appreciate the help." Mika smiled, and Timothy bowed with flourish.

"It would be my pleasure." He smiled.

The florist returned with a small packet of seeds for Timothy, which he rang up at the register. Then he handed Mika a large canvas tote bag and she placed her two packages into it. Timothy grabbed the bouquet and held the door open for her. "Thank you." She said to both men as she exited the florist shop with Timothy. They walked towards the big house and he told her about the small group of people that lived with him at the edge of the woods. They all worked on the gardens and the farm nearby. He or the others really didn't need to come into town, except for some material things. This group of growers also didn't have to go into the big house, but they did work for the leader. Most of the crops were sold to the town, but it was the leader's crops and land. The florist was the only person who had a greenhouse outside of the leader's property.

"The florist grows all of the decorative plants, of course. But he also grows quite a few herbs and medicinal plants." Timothy told her. "I think he's a better healer than the doctor sometimes."

They were past the park when a large black car stopped ahead of them. The driver stepped out of the car and walked up to Mika. "I presume you are the wife's assistant and returning to the big house." He held his nose up at her and sneered.

Mika didn't like his thin mustache or his attitude, but she nodded. "Yes, sir."

"Then you may follow me, the leader has allowed you to ride back in his vehicle." He held out his hand to accept her bag.

"Oh, I have these flowers too." Mika took them from Timothy. "Thank you so much for your help."

"What are friends for," he whispered and bowed his head to her.

He remained in that position as she walked away. The driver placed the packages in the trunk and opened the back door for her. He took the flowers from her to place on the passenger seat. She found herself sitting next to the leader, who was reading papers and smoking a cigar.

"Thank you, sir. Good afternoon." Mika bowed her head.

"Next time, have one of the drivers take you into town. Reginald, did you hear that? I don't want her going into town without a car."

"Yes, sir." The driver nodded.

"I don't mind the walk, sir." Mika looked forward and caught the driver's glare in the rearview mirror.

"It's not about what you mind or don't mind. It's about safety. I don't want someone robbing you when you're alone on the road." The leader exhaled a plume of smoke and inspected the cigar. He tapped the ash into an ashtray and left the rest of the cigar in it. "Also, you are not to talk to that boy again."

"Yes, sir." She nodded and bit her lip. "Of course, sir."

The leader touched her knee. "We can't be too careful. There are monsters out there."

"Yes, sir." Mika looked out of the sedan's window at the passing woods.

That night Mika picked up a book she saw on the floor of the wife's dressing room. "The children must have dropped it," she said to herself, "The girl likes to watch her mom try on her gowns." The book was about woodland creatures and tales of the woods. She flipped through it and was shocked by the scary illustrations. There was one of a wolf attacking a flock of sheep with blood splattered everywhere on the page. Mika almost dropped the book when the leader entered the room looking for his wife. "No, she is not here, sir." She held the book behind her and said, "I think she is in the dining room."

"Aw, yes. She is probably overseeing the seating arrangement." He nodded and turned to leave. "You can have the rest of the night off, Mika."

"Thank you, sir." She bowed and kept her eyes down until he left.

She counted to fifty before venturing out, using the time to breathe deeply to calm her nerves. The book was forgotten, as she hugged it to her chest and she just counted and breathed in then out. Mika left the dressing room and walked to Missus Shirley's room. She needed counselling.

Shirley was sitting in her wooden rocking chair and knitting a hat. "It's never too early to prepare for the winter," she said as Mika walked into the room.

Mika set the book on the nightstand and sat on the bench in front of the vanity.

"Do you need me to braid your hair?" Shirley looked over her glasses at her.

"I think I have to leave this place." Mika covered her face with her hands, trying not to cry.

"What happened child?" Shirley put down the knitting and squatted down in front of Mika. "Did something happen?"

Mika shook her head and wiped her eyes. "Not yet. Not really. But I think it will soon."

Shirley went to the door and looked down both ways of the hallway before closing it. She walked back to Mika and patted her on the shoulder. Mika accepted the tissue she offered, then Shirley went back to her rocking chair. "I'm too old for this." She groaned as she eased back into the chair. "So, you say nothing has happened." Mika nodded and Shirley rocked for a while in silence. "Do you have anywhere to go to, if you leave here?"

"I can go home." She wiped her eyes again. "I just have to go east."

Shirley shook her head. "East. To get to the next town, it'll take over a couple days on foot."

"I think I have to." Mika stood up and went to the window. From this upper level, she could see the edge of the gardens Timothy told her about. She looked past the fenced area and the small cottages to the forest. The tall pine trees were imposing and there were other trees mixed in with them. She thought that they looked like good climbing trees. Mika turned back to face Missus Shirley. "I think I am losing my freedom here."

"That is something." Shirley sighed. "Perhaps a walk would do you good. Then a good night's rest. See how you feel about things tomorrow." She picked up her knitting. "Sometimes it's best not to make any rash decisions. There are still the same dangers in the outside world."

Mika nodded and left Missus Shirley's room. "Good night, ma'am." Mika walked slowly down to her room and took off her shiny dress flats. They had gotten dusty from the walk into town and she cleaned them. "No wonder the wife was upset with her appearance. They do not tolerate dirt." The wife had been waiting to greet her husband when he came home and was angry to see Mika exit the leader's sedan. The wife ordered Mika to leave the bouquet with the butler and grabbed the tote bag from the driver's hand.

When she was done, she took off her dress and set it aside to be laundered, Mika tried not to think of the hushed argument between the married couple that she walked into before the dinner. Mika was bringing the wife her jewelry she requested to wear that evening. The wife was already dressed in her blue evening gown and she was pointing at her husband, accusing him of being a wolf. Her hair was still in rollers and her makeup was not done yet. Mika presented the pearl jewelry and left it on the vanity and tried to leave the room quietly. The wife pointed her finger at Mika.

"Hey you, what is your favorite animal? Do you like wolves? I thought I did, but now I think they are disgusting."

Mika looked at the wife. "Ma'am, I have always liked bears."

The leader left the room, and the wife sat down in front of her mirror. She started to moisturize her face. "Why do you like bears?"

Mika stood behind the wife and started to carefully remove some of the rollers from her hair. "I liked how the mother bear would protect her cubs." She picked up the pearl necklace, and the wife allowed her to clasp it onto her neck. "Plus, they are cute. Ma'am, was there anything else you needed?"

"No, you may leave me." the wife put on the matching pearl earrings, and Mika turned to leave the room.

"I'll come back to do my night duties in about an hour, ma'am."

"That is fine Mika. Good night." The wife applied her red lipstick and watched Mika leave in the mirror.

Only cold water flowed from her bathroom faucet, and she splashed a couple handfuls of it onto her face. She was trying to decipher those words the wife spoke to her husband.

*Why would she ask me about what animal I liked? Did the wife see something in her that was bad? I didn't do anything inappropriate. I didn't think the leader would do anything inappropriate. He was a married man with children, and his wife was beautiful. But something didn't feel right, even though nothing had happened.*

Mika washed her hands and face with soap in her bathroom, once the water warmed up. Wearing a pink terry cloth robe over her slip, she looked out her window and saw that the grounds were dark on this side of the big house. "Maybe I could go for a walk." She dressed in a plain blue dress with long sleeves and put on her grey cardigan from her school days. She put on her black boots over her white stockings, then she left her room.

Once she was outside, she took a big breath and felt better. She always felt better outside, in nature and amongst the greenery. The big house did not feel like a home, it was like the boarding school where she started her education. That was why she preferred her bare bedroom, it was more like her old dormitory. Her new bedroom made her miss her former employers who treated her like a family member. The bricked big house was starting to feel like a prison. Was she allowed to go for a walk? She would tell any staff that Missus Shirley had allowed it.

But no one stopped her from going out of the back door by the kitchen, and there was no one outside. Everyone was busy with the dinner of the leaders and wives. She walked past the sheds in the back, to avoid the garages and the drivers. Mika wasn't sure how often the security guards patrolled the grounds, but she was never told she could not walk around. Just not into town.

She was supposed to stay away from Timothy, but she found herself walking towards the gardens he told her about. She ran to them, past the stables where the horses neighed, and across the lawn. Mika didn't look back at the big house or the large windows. She didn't think anyone would notice her. Mika only focused on the green plants and stopped when she reached the fence around the vegetable garden. The sweet peas were wrapped around half of the fencing and she thought it was a shame it was so late and dark, she would have loved to see the bright purple flowers. Mika walked around the fence to guess at what the other plants were. When she walked past the green-houses, she was startled by Timothy.

"What are you doing out here?" Timothy had a rake in his hands. "You scared me. I almost hit you with this." He tossed the rake to the side. "Are you okay?" He put his hands on her shoulders and looked at her. "Do you need help?"

"I just needed a walk. Some fresh air." It had been a long time since someone had shown concern for her. "I needed to see the garden." She stepped closer to Timothy and hugged him. "I needed a friend."

He patted her back. "Come on back and meet my dad. We were just finishing up some cake. Do you like cake?"

She held his hand and let him guide her to his cottage. The cottage was cozy, and she sat by the fire between Timothy and his dad. They told her stories about the townspeople and some gossip about the staff at the big house. She smiled and laughed. The cottage wasn't exactly like her home was before the change, but it felt close. She began to miss her home that she left over ten years ago. After a few more stories, Timothy's dad said that it was getting late, and she should get back to the big house.

"Yes, thank you." She stood up.

"I think there's a curfew for the staff and they lock the doors by midnight." Timothy's dad looked at his watch. "There's still time yet to get back."

Timothy walked her out of the cottage and to the greenhouses. "This is as far as I go." He took her hands in his and pulled her close. He kissed her lips, and before she could close her eyes, he let her go. "Good night," he whispered, and then ran back to his cottage.

She slowly walked back to the big house, aware of how open the lawn was and how vulnerable she felt. There was no one around the stable or sheds behind the big house. The door was still unlocked, and the kitchen was quiet. The dinner must have ended hours ago with the clean up over. Mika quietly walked toward her bedroom. She removed her boots and cardigan and laid down on the bed. Her heart was fluttering and she placed her hand over it. "Calm down," she whispered and closed her eyes. "It was just a kiss."

The next morning she was in the dining room before the wife, and she prepared a plate of fruit for her. She also placed a plate of bread and jam by the leader's seat. Mika did not have a full schedule today, and was hoping to spend the day by herself. She was going over the task list when the leader and his wife entered the room. Mika bowed her head and greeted them. "Good morning."

They nodded at her and seated themselves. The butler gave the leader the newspaper, and he started to read it. The butler then poured the wife's coffee for her and added cream before leaving the room. Mika approached the wife and asked, "Is there anything you needed, ma'am?"

"Where were you last night?" she asked before she took a sip of her coffee.

"I was in my room, ma'am." Mika stood up straighter and looked ahead.

The wife stirred in a spoonful of sugar and tapped the edge of the white cup with the small silver spoon. "Why were you in your room?"

Mika took a breath. "I was given the night off, ma'am."

The wife placed her manicured hands in her lap. "I did not give you the night off. I called for you last night, and you could not be found." She grimaced at her assistant, and Mika felt the same meanness she did when she took Young Jack to the park.

"I apologize, ma'am." Mika swallowed and watched the wife take another sip of her coffee. "How can I help you now?"

"I want to know where you were." She set her cup down and looked at her husband reading his newspaper. "You were not in your room."

Mika wasn't sure if she should tell the wife about her walk, she didn't want to get Missus Shirley in trouble for suggesting it. She wasn't going to tell them about visiting Timothy and his father. Mika turned to the wife and bowed her head. "I apologize. I went for a walk before turning in, ma'am."

"I don't think you are responsible enough to be my assistant." The wife crossed her arms and glared at her husband. "I think you need to be reassigned."

"Dearest." The leader looked up from the newspaper and turned the page. "I gave her the night off. If you are mad at anyone, it should be me."

"Sweetie," she said through clenched teeth. "I don't tell your staff what to do. I would appreciate it if you did not interfere with my staff."

"Then dismiss your assistant so she can run your errands for you." The leader turned back to the newspaper.

The wife looked at Mika. "You are dismissed for now. But you have a demerit, I do not allow many demerits before I discharge you from my house."

"Yes, ma'am." Mika bowed her head and left the room. She almost ran to the wife's library to set out the magazines and the week's mail for the wife to peruse. Mika sat at her little desk in the corner to address the wife's correspondence. Her calligraphy was admired by Grandma and was encouraged, especially when Grandma was unable to write her own letters due to her tremors. Mika closed her eyes to calm herself and proceeded to address the first of many envelopes for the wife. She was done with her work before lunchtime and left the wife's office before the wife's scheduled office time. When she was eating her lunch with the staff, she was given a handwritten note by the nanny's aide. She read that she wasn't going to be needed for the rest of the day by the wife. Mika left the kitchen and walked to Missus Shirley's room upstairs, only to find it empty.

"She must be still at lunch," she said to herself and went to the nightstand. "There was that children's book I left here." But the book wasn't there. She frowned and left the room.

There was nothing she had been assigned to, and she didn't know what she should do. This was only the second time she had leisure time, and she wasn't sure if it was truly her time. She went to her room and shut the door. "Maybe it'll be safe to stay here, that way she can call me if she needs something." She sat on the chair next to the window and stared out of it. She could see the woods from her room, but not the cottages or the vegetable gardens. There were flower gardens on this section of the property, closest to the park, to allow the townspeople another area to stroll or sit on a bench. There weren't many fences around the property and she didn't see a fence along the woods.

*Was that a way off this land? Through the woods?*

Her phone rang and she answered it, "This is Mika." Deep breathing sounds just flooded her ear. "Yes, this is Mika." The call ended with a click, and the dial tone was welcomed. She set the phone down. "There's lots of these phones." She shrugged and told herself, "It was probably the wrong number." She thought about grabbing her secret key and locking the door, but she didn't want it known that she had a key. Mika put on her black boots and her grey cardigan over the maroon dress she had picked that morning. She paused to put some candies into the pocket of her dress and slowly opened her bedroom door. When she saw there was no one in the hallway, she walked quickly down the hallway and to one of the main staircases. She went to the wife's office and saw the wife in a pale blue blouse and suit lounging on her sofa reading a magazine.

*Looks like she doesn't need me, so I will go for a walk.*

Mika slowly walked back to the kitchen and went out the back door. There were many people bustling around, the food delivery men, garbage being taken out, and the staff coming and going. There were men cleaning a few of the black sedans used by the leader and his wife. Mika saw the horses she had heard in the stables last night. They were all large work horses, varying from white and covered with grey spots to black with a white patches on their face and legs. The men wore a uniform of grey and black. They were an extension of the security team and she heard them called The Huntsmen. She walked past them and everyone else to go to the flower gardens. She might even walk to the park.

"Hey, you." A gruff voice stopped her. "Where are you going?"

She turned her head toward the voice, unsure if the speaker was talking to her. Then she saw that the driver with the thin mustache was walking towards her.

"Are you going into town?" He stopped in front of her with his hands on his hips. "Well, are you? You are supposed to ask for a car if you are."

She shook her head. "No, I am not. I am just going to the garden."

He looked at her old grey cardigan, dusty boots, and nodded. He turned and walked back to the garage, lighting a cigarette.

Mika slowly walked towards the park, and away from the shadow of the big house. Once she got to the flower gardens and among the other people strolling around, she quickened her steps. She had to tell herself not to run, fighting the urge to just sprint away. She could keep going and going and go into town. It would be going west and towards a new start. The east was an old life and probably a dead end. She was now in the park and walked toward a trail that went into the blooming dogwoods. Mika was drawn to the falling petals and caught a blossom in her hands. Her parents were probably gone, they would not have placed her in another home if they could keep her.

*They said I was special. I could be whatever I wanted to be, and for now, I had to be a good girl.*

"I don't know what to do," she whispered.

"Don't know what to do about what?" a familiar voice asked behind her.

She turned around to see the leader standing behind her and no one else around. "I don't know what to do with my afternoon. I haven't had this much free time since I can remember." She put the blossom in her pocket and stepped to the side of the trail. "But a nice walk is something to do. If you excuse me, sir." She tried to walk past him and back to the main trail.

"I will give you another demerit if you leave the house without permission. Then another one if you talk to that boy again." The leader paused, then continued, "Or should you already have two demerits?"

"Sorry for leaving the house, sir." She bowed her head. "I should only have one demerit for my punishment, sir."

He leaned towards her ear and sighed. "If you see that boy again, I will have to think of another punishment. Do you hear me?"

She felt his hot breath on her ear and neck, and she did not move. "Yes, sir."

He inhaled and watched her for a few more moments. Mika stayed as still as she could and looked at the petals falling onto the grass in front of her. The sound of children's laughter cut through the silence and the leader stood up straighter and walked away from her.

*I should not have tried to leave before him.*

She counted to one hundred before she moved and walked forward. The dogwoods ended and there was a small pond with ducks swimming in it. Mika sat on the nearest bench and counted to sixty before opening her eyes again.

*I have to be a good girl.*

The Mallard ducks' quiet quacking sounds soothed her and she watched them floating in the water. She wished she had brought Young Jack here, he would have loved this pond.

*I can't keep thinking about the children, I won't be their nanny again. I won't be anything but the wife's assistant. I can't be the wife's assistant. I can't stay here anymore. I can't stay here.*

She stood up and walked briskly back toward the big house. Mika didn't stop until she was back at the big house. Missus Shirley was by the kitchen door and with a basket of clothing. She was going to hang the laundry outside due to the nice weather. Mika saw Missus Shirley's surprised brown eyes and saw Missus Shirley wave her off.

"Go, what are you doing here?" She stepped towards Mika. "Go on now and leave."

"What? I don't understand." Mika continued to walk towards Missus Shirley.

"You have to leave now, if you want your freedom." Shirley pushed her gently with her free hand then walked away with the laundry basket on her hip.

Mika turned and ran past the stables and back towards the vegetable garden. The openness of the lawn was broken up by the workers and staff moving near the big house, but her running drew attention to her. She wasn't going into town, but she didn't want to make it clear that she was running to the woods. "Sorry, I may put you in danger, but I need to go through the greenhouses to get to the woods," she reasoned. She could not shelter in the cottages and put them or Timothy in danger. "I don't want to put Timothy in danger." She sprinted past the greenhouses and past the cottages. She didn't stop when the voices told her to or didn't look at the shocked faces of the people watching her run.

Mika slowed only when she had to run between the trees of the forest and the rocks, brush, and fallen trees. She tripped over a large branch and caught herself by hugging the tree in front of her. She tried to slow her breathing and listened to the sounds of the woods. There was some shouting she heard, and then she heard the sounds of the horses. The Huntsmen were looking for her. "How am I going to get away?" She looked up at the leaves and pine needles above her and could see bits of the blue sky. "I have to go deeper. I have to keep going."

She started to run again and went in the direction away from the edge and towards the larger and older trees. The foliage became denser and it was darker, she was able to run again without a fear of tripping due to less vegetation on the ground. The silence was broken up by an occasional bird song and shouting. The trees buffered the shouting, and she couldn't tell if they were close to her or not. "I'm going to have to climb."

Mika found a tree and jumped up to grab a lower branch. It held her weight, and she used the trunk to walk up to sit on top of the branch. There were some other branches and knots on the tree that were good hand holds. She was able to climb halfway up the tree and use its leaves to hide her from the men. She put her hand over her thumping heart and tried to slow her breath. She tried to be quiet as she waited for the men to search this area for her.

After counting to 689, she heard the hooves of one of the large horses. The rider was silent and he was looking for her tracks. Mika covered her mouth and did not move anything but her eyes. They followed the man on his horse as they moved near her tree, almost passing under her. She held her breath until he moved past her and out of view. Then she was able to breathe again. "He will probably come back around on the way back to the big house. So I have to wait. The other riders can come through here too. I have to wait," she whispered.

She let her legs hang down once the woods got dark. The birds had gone quiet long ago and were replaced by crickets, frogs, and hoots from an owl.

*This is going to be a long night.*

Mika fought the tiredness that made her head heavy. She would fall out of the tree or miss the sound of the men looking for her, if she fell asleep. Then the cold air added to her suffering and made her shiver and her teeth chatter. She was able to bring her legs up to her and cover them with the skirt of her dress. "That's better." She hugged her legs and started to feel better.

The sky lightened up with the dawn, and she had not seen any other creature or person. "Maybe I can climb down?" She stayed on her branch and slowly stretched her legs. Her body ached from all the running and then the climbing. She stretched her arms and looked at the lower branches. "I can't fall out of this tree." The sound of a twig snapping stopped her movements and her breath. Her brown eyes flitted around trying to find the source of the sound. After a few minutes she saw the light brown fur of a doe. Mika relaxed again and waited for the doe to leave before moving again. She turned her body to face the tree trunk and stopped when she heard another noise. This was louder and she realized it was the horses. They thundered past her tree and followed the path of the doe.

The men were silent and focused on what was in front of them. Mika closed her eyes and put her forehead to the tree trunk. "I can't climb down now."

She turned her body on the branch, to get more comfortable. The day was spent stretching her legs and arms or letting her legs hang down. She listened to the silence around her and decided that it would be better to try to climb down when it was dark. She could not stay in this tree forever.

When it was dark again, she turned to face the tree trunk and waited. She counted to one hundred then started to move down to the lower branches. Mika went all the way down to the lowest branch and she rested. She had the candies in her pocket and she took one out and ate it.

*It is probably good to take a break and just listen. I don't know how much noise I made climbing down.*

"I'm probably going to make a loud noise when I fall out of this tree." She closed her eyes and focused on the sweet taste of the orange candy.

The sounds of birds made her open her eyes, she had fallen asleep against the tree trunk. Her legs were hanging down, but she had not fallen. Mika looked around and didn't see anything. She made a fist and hit her thigh. "I wasted time. I need to move." She closed her eyes, trying not to cry. "I need to find some food." Shaking her head, she took a deep breath before turning her body. "I'll have to either try to climb down the rest of the way or just jump." Mika hung from the branch by her arms and looked at the gap from her feet to the ground. "It's not too much. I just can't break any bones." She looked up at the branch, her arms were getting weaker and she would not be able to pull herself back up. After taking another deep breath, she let go and landed on the leaf covered forest floor. Her body stayed in the crouched position as she looked and listened for any movement.

There was just silence, so she stood up and looked around for a sign of where she should go. Mika was completely lost, but she knew she didn't want to be tracked and found. The horses that had run by her tree earlier left a large trail and she decided to hide her footprints in theirs. "They knew where they were going, maybe this will lead me home. They would go north or east." Her steps quickened. "No one would go north, so this has to go east."

Following the tracks was easy, she just put one foot in front of the other, and the path was easy. The hard part was the pain in her stomach, her legs, her back even ached. The urge to put her hand in her pocket and grab a candy was unbearable. There were only six candies, and she had to be careful. "That's not real food anyways." She looked at the tree trunks, there wasn't much moss growing on the bark. "Maybe too early in the season." She looked at the forest floor. "I wouldn't know a poisonous berry or mushroom from a safe one. But there isn't anything." The forest was getting dark, and she started to look for trees other than the pines. They were starting to take over, and the pine needles were starting to cover her trail. She broke off a lower branch and used it to sweep the ground when she wasn't sure where to continue. There was a group of shrubs just to the left of her trail. "I can't climb any-more." She walked toward it and used her broom to poke the closest bush. No wild animals scurred from it, so she pushed her way into the center of the cluster, and lay down on top of her broom. It wasn't long before she had fallen asleep.

The dawn and the birds woke her up, and she scrambled out of the bushes. She ate a piece of candy and looked for the horse tracks. It took her a few moments to find her bearings, but she was able to see the depressions the hooves left, even when covered by the pine needles. Mika continued her journey without the need of her broom that she had left in the bushes. It was another long day of walking before she saw a large boulder in front of her. It was bathed in sunlight, so large it forced a clearing in the middle of the towering pines. The horses' tracks went up to the rock and ended. She felt a sense of this was where she was sup-posed to be.

Mika stepped into the sunlight and looked at her hands made bright and golden. She walked up and touched the light grey rock. It was mostly smooth, but there were ridges and some bushes and small trees grew on it. It could be climbed. Mika circled around the large rock and saw no crevice to hide, unless she went up. There could be a way to see where she was and to decide where to go. "I'll have to rest before I try to climb up."

Mika circled back to where the tracks were and picked up a twig. She held it up in her palm. "Would I be able to make a sundial? Maybe I can figure out east and west, it has to be past noon." The shadow fell to her right. "That has to be east, so that is north." She looked straight at the boulder. Then she looked to her left. "That has to be west." She put the twig in her other pocket. "I have to make a decision." She leaned against the rock and looked to the east first. "Missus Shirley is the only one I told that home was in the east. Would they go there to look for me?" Mika closed her eyes to picture the map of the big house, there was nothing north of the woods. The woods just went up to the top of the paper. "Maybe that's why there weren't any fences. They didn't need any." She looked to the west. "I might be expected to go west, to the town and to civilization. But that has to be better than wandering the woods forever."

Mika looked to the east again and saw a set of glowing red eyes in the dark shadows. She stepped away from the rock and away from the creature. It moved towards the clearing but did not leave the shade of the pine trees. "The sunlight," she whispered, "it won't come into the light."

The creature laughed and the trees shook. Its deep, guttural voice chilled her, and she shivered listening to it say, "Soon." Then the red eyes were gone.

Mika looked up at the sky above her. "It'll be dark soon and nothing will be able to stop it." She looked back at the forest. "I can't go east now." The woods looked less scary going south. She had not seen any creatures in those trees, but she would not go back to the big house. "I'm going to climb up." She found the lowest ridge to climb onto, then used other ridges to climb to a small cluster of bushes. After she checked out the lay of the land, she would hide behind them to rest until she could run away tomorrow morning.

She looked around her from the top of the boulder and could not see over the treetops. She could see how dense the trees looked to the north. Their shadows were darker, the pines looked black, and there was no clear path through them. The west looked like the southern woods and there seemed to be a path from the rock into those trees. There was more undergrowth along that path, it must have been used by travelers in the old days. "I'll have to go west."

Mika sat on top of the rock until the sky changed into the pinks and purples of a sunset. She hurriedly climbed to where the bushes were and crouched behind them. She could see the eastern side of the woods, and when the sun set, the large trees shook as the creature passed by them. It was larger than anything she could imagine, and she whispered, "It would have to be to survive among these ancient trees." The red eyes stopped at the edge of the clearing, and she hoped the moonlight would stop the creature from coming out of the trees. Then she watched it put one large black paw onto the grass, the moonlight shone over its blackened claw. It growled before emerging from the darkness of the woods, into this side of shadows from the rock.

It lingered in the rock's shadow, and she heard it sniffing the ground for her. The creature stood up on its hind legs, almost towering over the top of the boulder, sniffing the air. Mika curled up and tried to make herself smaller in her shelter.

*The creature is a bear. But bears don't talk.*

The creature turned to the rock. "Human, I know you are there." Its booming voice rattled her body. "I offer a deal." It lowered its body to walk on its four legs and back to the eastern woods. "You or your village." The dark creature disappeared into the darkness of the woods, and Mika fell asleep.

She woke up with the sunshine and climbed down from her hiding spot on the boulder. She collapsed on the ground, where the horse tracks were, and she ate a piece of candy. "There's maybe three pieces left." She looked at the ground and saw the large track left by the creature, its claw was as long as her arms. "Maybe it'll be a faster death than starving." She leaned against the rock and closed her eyes. She ate another piece of orange candy and looked around. "I won't be able to run back and warn everyone. I won't be able to run away." Mika closed her eyes again and saw the red eyes of the creature in her dreams.

The monstrous bear came upon the sleeping Mika in front of the boulder. It sniffed the life in her and rested its snout near her feet. "Human, I can help you."

She could not open her eyes, but she answered, "I need food."

The creature blinked its red eyes and puffed up its cheeks, before using that breath to fill up Mika with its energy. Its spirit revitalized her. Its power changed her. Mika's body was shaking on the ground. Her muscles were tense, and she could not move. The pain made her scream and she tried to break out of this paralysis. Finally, she sat up and opened her eyes. They glowed red before dulling down to their normal shade of brown.

There was nothing in front of her and the darkened woods were quiet. "I must have fallen asleep again." She looked at the dark sky. "I need to find some food." Mika used the boulder to help her stand up, she was shaky at first and took some small steps towards the southern woods. She found a large branch and used it as a walking stick. "Maybe I can use this to kill an animal," she said and chuckled. "Which way to go?" She walked into the eastern woods. "I'm not afraid of the creature."

Mika repeated that with each step deeper into the woods. "I will meet it head on, I am not afraid of the creature. I won't let it hurt those innocent people." Mika felt stronger with each step forward. The loud thudding noise behind her did not make her run or hide. She merely turned around to face the monster.

Raising the branch above her head, she opened her mouth to yell at the creature's red eyes. She was going to tell it to go home and leave her alone, but she stopped at the sight of two Huntsmen on their large horses.

They stopped the two large black horses a few feet from Mika and looked down on her messy hair and her dirty clothes. "Well, it looks like we finally found her." The blonde one laughed.

"The leader will be happy." The dark haired one sneered at her as he dismounted. "Come here girl. You've been enough trouble."

Mika stepped back and gripped the branch tightly when the second man stepped off his horse. She was feeling herself get smaller, and she was going to lose herself. She had to fight. The creature didn't scare her, and these two men were not going to scare her. Mika stood up straighter and threw her walking stick aside.

The men stopped advancing and watched the dirty, skinny girl square her shoulders and hold up her hands. The blonde one laughed and said, "She's not even half our size. Does she think she can fight us?"

"Are you going to give us trouble?" The dark haired one took off his gloves. "We will make you comply."

The men were stopped in their tracks by Mika's glowing red eyes. She stepped forward and sniffed the air. "Why do you smell so good?"

Her dark hair loosened from her braid and flew around her as laughed. The men's horses neighed and bolted away from this strange girl. Her voice deepened as she grew bigger in size. She wouldn't get as big as the bear monster, but she was now as tall as the men. They fell onto their knees when she raised her arms and opened her mouth.

The red glow of her eyes grew brighter as she inhaled the men's spirits. Their energy made her stronger and their souls would sustain her for some time. The men were trying to cover their faces and tried to crawl away from her. The blonde one was the first to fall onto his side, his body shriveled up after his soul left. The dark haired one covered his ears, closed his eyes, and repeated, "No, no, no, no, no."

Mika inhaled again and laughed after his body fell over. "I am not half your size. I will not comply." Her red eyes dimmed down and she was restored to her smaller size. "I am not weak anymore." She stormed past the bodies and followed the scent of the horses. "It won't take me too long to get back to the southern border of these woods."

She looked up at the dawn sky and stopped in front of a beam of sunlight that filtered through the canopy. Her hand slowly moved toward the bright beam and she pushed her fingers into the light. "Nothing happened." She smiled and moved her arm into the light. "These woods are my home, but I won't be trapped by them." Mika started to sprint towards the scent of other horses and Huntsmen. There was a team of them, all searching for her or her body. They would not expect to find her running back to them, for them. Then she could go back to the big house, if she wanted.

"Freedom," she whispered, "I have freedom."

# About the Authors

## JK Allen

JK Allen received her BA in Creative Writing and English from Michigan State University. She wrote her first story when she first learned how to write and hasn't looked back since. Common writing themes that can be found in her work address identity, everyday magic, and the type of strength that can be found in ordinary people. The Angelborn series is her debut series. Angelborn, Heavenfire, and Demonkind will be re-released soon. She is currently working on her second series, the Half Blood Alliance trilogy, set in the Angelborn world but with new characters. Her reading tastes are as varied as the genres she enjoys writing, from Jane Austen to Diana Wynne Jones. When she's not writing, you can find her painting, drawing, or lost in another world between the pages of a book. Or on Tic Tok.

## Carol Allen

Carol Allen started writing as a hobby to bond with her sister, or something to do during lunch or breaks between appointments. The first story she shared with her sister, started with a scene in her head. That led to many conversations about world building, dialogue, grammar, and other tips to finish the story. Once the pen was uncapped, the stories kept flowing, and the new writer has spent the last decade trying to perfect this craft. She has written mainly for fun, including a few short stories and picture books for the children of friends. This Side of Shadows is her first published book of short stories. She is currently working on another collection of short stories of monsters, and she wants to publish a collection of stories for children. Her reading tastes include the murder mysteries of Agatha Christie to scary novels and stories of Stephen King to Neil Gaiman. Her to be read book pile is high and ever growing. Carol also enjoys watching movies and TV shows, drawing, and playing the piano.